I0738418

LEAH ERICKSON

THE GILDED LYNX

1

It was the spring that wild animals began migrating to the cities in unheard of numbers. There was a sweet dampness in the late March air. As the melted snow ran into the gutters, and patches of grass sprouted wet and green, it wasn't uncommon to see a black bear crossing traffic, or muskrats in the subways. A theory was going around that magnetic fields and cell phone signals had confused the animals' honing instincts.

At first newspapers featured photos with cute captions like 'CITY LIFE IS A ZOO!' But people began to feel uneasy about it. It seemed unnatural. Portentous. No longer cute. Some religious groups called it the end of the world. People began to board up their windows and store their water in jugs.

The promise of spring was too much for Daphne to resist. She slipped out of the side door in the corner of the empty auditorium that day. Every once in a while, she liked to escape in this way, cut her classes. Now she was free to wander dreamily through the bustling streets of the surrounding city. A tall, fourteen-year-old girl with long blonde hair in a plaid uniform jumper, walking down a sloping street past narrow Victorian row houses with curling metal gates. Past concrete office buildings and outdoor coffee houses.

Though she had no destination, she usually found herself spending her truant afternoons at the Square. That was where all the people were. Under the great awnings of luxury stores, beneath the signs for Macy's, Sak's, Dior and Gucci. These were places that Daphne had shopped in, with her mother. Airless, austere places full of glossy surfaces and eerily backlit shelves. How she hated going into them. Thankfully, her mother often waited until she was in Rome to buy Dior, where it was cheaper.

She liked to walk the wide sidewalks, down to the great concrete patio where there were street performers and vendors selling strange things from kiosks or simply spread out on blankets. As usual, there were preachers and protestors, who each held their signs, competing to drown each other out with their messages. Less usual, however, was the presence of the National Guard who had recently begun patrolling the streets to keep the peace. The sight of them made Daphne nervous, so she stepped widely around them, averting her eyes from their camo uniforms and black guns.

Also, there were homeless people. Many more of them than there used to be, it seemed. She had always been taught, if she passed by one while walking with her mother on their shopping trips, Do not look at them. But she could not look away. Some of them seemed to be about her own age, and she looked at them in frank astonishment. Often they would look right back at her, coolly neutral. Some would give her school uniform a once-over and smirk. Sometimes they would just hold up a plastic cup without looking back at her at all. But she never carried money, so she had nothing to give.

An Asian woman had a kiosk of gas masks for sale. Some were patent leather. Some were encrusted with crystals. Some were covered with high-end designer logos. Daphne had recently seen a fashion spread featuring similar masks in a teen magazine, and it had given her an unnerving jolt. PROTECT YOURSELF FROM THE SICKNESS IN STYLE! the caption had read. Daphne had snorted when she saw it; Yeah, right! They'll try to sell us anything! But the air that day felt dirty, dark with soot, and there was a smell as of singed hair, that she had never smelled before. Would one of those masks make it easier to breathe?

The saleswoman smiled gently at Daphne as she slowed down to look, but Daphne shook her head: she did not want to buy anything. She wanted only to soak it all in, the noise, the randomness, the jagged angles, the life that people were constantly keeping her away from.

She had just walked away from the gas mask-wearing woman when she heard the ruckus up ahead. Daphne looked up just in time to see what looked like a large cat-like animal running up the street. A bobcat? she wondered dimly, as her limbs instinctively went weak with fear: It was swift, low to the ground, and she caught a flash of its intelligent golden eyes as it sped right towards her. Too frightened to scream, Daphne froze in her tracks, hypnotized, as people around her retracted and scattered. There were screams. Someone pushed her to the ground, out of the animal's path, and she rolled up in a ball to keep from getting trampled.

Faster than she could process what was happening, two uniformed National Guardsmen sprung out from opposite directions, holding rifles. "Stand clear!" one of them yelled. Two gunshots cracked out, and the animal fell dead. The street was silent.

After a paused moment's catch of breath, people moved on their way again. Gunshots in public places were beginning to seem normal. One expected it when a wild animal appeared, or when the homeless were protesting again. Everyone resumed walking to wherever it was they were going, All but Daphne and a dirty man with a long white beard, wearing layers of rags. The two of them stood looking down at the dead animal.

It wasn't a bobcat. It was a real lynx! Its fur was pale brown and it had dark spotted legs. Daphne had only ever seen them in photographs, or stuffed behind glass at the museum, and she had a vague sense that they were endangered. It had long tufts of fur under its chin and above the eyes, and ears rather flat to its head. It was so beautiful. It looks like Genghis Khan, she thought. She was studying him in history class. She didn't know whether to laugh or cry.

She and the homeless man looked up at the same time, and locked eyes for a moment. Now there were a couple of people from the Earth Liberation Front shouting threats at the gunmen. There were also a couple of people from a church group passing out tracts. One carried a handmade sign that said ASK THE ANIMALS AND THEY WILL TEACH YOU JOB 12:7.

The bearded man had pale, bleached-out looking eyes. "A terrible thing," he said.

"Yes." Daphne thought, Why did it have to die?

He looked at the man with the Bible sign, who was shouting at one of the Earth activists. He shook his head.

"You know...I'm retired military," he muttered softly. "I remember the days of the one hundred yen dollar. The world was ending then, too."

She nodded. She was feeling a bit sick. The gunshots still rung in her ears.

The man, like a father, patted her on the shoulder. "Don't worry, young lady. Somehow the world always manages to right itself."

She gaped at him, feeling a little staggered. The man's gaze, warm and concerned, was so unexpected that she had to turn away. When was the last time someone had truly looked at her?

She stumbled backwards, then turned and began to run, as fast as she could, tripping over her own feet and bumping into passers-.by. All the way back to school she ran, blinded by hot tears in her eyes. When she got there at last she buzzed at the gate again and again, desperately.

Her school took up a whole city block. It was a huge white Art Moderne building, like a big ocean liner. There was no sign on it, just the logo of a stylized globe that represented The World Nation's Academy. The security guard also wore the logo on the brass tag on the front of his hat. He shook his head and led her to the principal's office without a word.

~

"Why?"

The question hung in the air between them. The room seemed to echo, though the office was thickly carpeted in white. She looked around at the glass brick walls and low-slung, graceful furniture.

Mrs. Pierce leaned forward across the dark polished teak of the desk to peer more closely at Daphne. She was a thin woman in her fifties with dark painted lips and high cheekbones. Her eyes, under the soft recessed lighting, burned with exasperation. They searched out Daphne's, but Daphne would not meet her gaze.

"I'm afraid only you can answer the question. Why? Why do you continue to break the rules in this childish manner? You are a ninth grader. A young woman! You have so much going for you! Your achievement test scores are very impressive, though your grades are lower than to be desired. And you are, artistically, very, very talented. I mean, that painting of yours in the library of the... light, the... Aurora Borealis? I mean... you do have a gift."

"Thank you," Daphne murmured automatically, though she still would not look at the principal. Her jaw was clenched painfully, her fingers dug into the armrests. Her skin flushed hotly against the white blonde of her hair, and her gray eyes, with their transparent lashes, were red rimmed.

Mrs. Pierce gazed at Daphne in silence, assessing her. A pretty girl, but something gauntly intense about the face. She had a knowing directness that was off-putting to Mrs. Pierce. But something about her stooped posture, and her fragile, narrow shoulders filled the principal with pity. Her voice softened.

"So much potential... if you can only harness it." Her eyes roamed the girls face like a searchlight. "Is your mother at home?"

Daphne glanced up, a flash of something like anger in her face. "No. Ma'am."

"I would imagine she is working? I heard she was being listed for a part. With that director. That Eastern Bloc director? The one who was in exile? Incredible work, I can't think of his name..." Mrs. Pierce's eyes had gone misty and far away. This was the effect her mother's fame always had on people. Even steely Mrs. Pierce, principal of the prestigious World of Nations Academy, could go all fawning and fatuous at the very mention of Daphne's mother. Even though she hadn't made a movie in years. Not since marrying Daphne's father.

"My mother is in Japan. She's making a commercial for diet soda." She said this with an ironic twist to her lips.

"Oh. Well. I'm sure she has a large following in that country. But. Back to the problem at hand." Her expression hardened again. "Your mother was very upset by your previous... infractions."

Daphne had been disciplined for cutting classes already, twice. And recently, she had been caught vandalizing a wall in the restroom. Another girl had caught her sprawling "INFORMATION RULES!" in black marker, with a Grim Reaper drawn underneath.

"I really hate to have to contact her again about your behavior, but what choice do I have? What if something were to happen to you? I would be held responsible. You don't know this city. You don't understand what it's become nowadays." She pulled up Daphne's record on a slim computer screen. "Who am I to contact, while your mother is away?"

"Cathy."

"Who is Cathy? Your nanny?"

"No. She's my stylist."

Mrs. Pierce glanced up at her, frowning.

"It's just that... I get along best with Cathy, so she kind of looks out for me when Mom is gone. It's easiest for everybody."

Mrs. Pierce paused for a moment, with eyes closed, as though her head hurt.

When she opened her eyes again, she said, "I worry about you because I care. Don't you know how dangerous it is for a young girl?" She leaned forward and lowered her voice to a whisper. "Don't you know that there is a sickness out there? And there is no vaccine..."

"That's a rumor. It's not really true. Now they've got all these paranoid people are all buying gas masks. It's all about the control. And money!" Now Daphne, too, was leaning forward. "I mean really, my father used to tell me that the reason people..."

"Shh!" Mrs. Pierce held a finger to her lips, then drew herself back again and looked at her icily. "Rumor or no, it is dangerous out there. There is a training camp in a warehouse down the street, for God's sake. A training camp for activists for left wing causes. The activists fight with the evangelists who fight with the Earth Liberation Front who fight the... who even knows!" She laughed, a little hysterically. "And here I have you, slipping out the door, we have no idea where you are, until you show up again, buzzing at the security door to get back in. That door is locked for a reason. That door keeps you safe from..." she gestured wildly, "from... insanity! Chaos!" She shook her head. "Do you know how many children your age would trade places with you? Do you not understand what a blessing it is to be safe? Do you?"

Her favorite place to be was the studio. It was a peaceful place, large and spare, with big windows that were open on either side of the room, letting in a breeze that stirred the pads of drawing paper propped on easels. The students here were always quiet, sketching with charcoal, heads bowed, lost in their own worlds.

Daphne had taken to coming here on her own during lunch breaks and after school. Because it was only here that she was able to clear her churning mind, by losing herself in her work.

She was working in acrylics. It was a new piece. A painting of the lynx. Majestic in profile, its eyes scanning the horizon. It had the same black tipped ear tufts and golden eyes as the one she saw killed in the Square. But this one was gloriously alive, with a halo of light around its head. She had often felt sad, wondering if she could have done something, anything, to save the animal's life. Her work gave her consolation, because it was almost like bringing him back again.

Sometimes the teacher or other students would come and watch over her shoulder as she painted, saying things like, It's beautiful, it looks so real! You're so talented!

"Thank you," she would answer. But when they asked her where she came up with the idea to paint a lynx, she did not answer. She went mute. She had told no one of her day out on the streets, of the lynx shot dead and the homeless man who had spoken to her. Every time she thought of that day she had no words, she only brimmed with emotions that she couldn't name.

Most strange of all, though, was that the same evening, the lynx had come to her in a dream. She dreamed that it was the day two years ago that her father had gone missing. The day she had locked herself in her room, angry and hating the world. In this dream, the lynx had come to her as she lay in her high soft bed swathed in lavender tulle. He had padded soundlessly across the carpet, past the gilded Regency furniture and the shelf of china dolls, right up to Daphne where he licked her hand with his rough pink tongue. Then he disappeared. And for some reason, this dream left Daphne with a feeling of great love and calmness. The feeling that everything would be okay.

LEAH ERICKSON

Cathy kept her eyes trained on the sleeve, the narrow white sleeve, on which she had spent hours sewing the beads. Her focus was intense, her expression shrewd and alert as she put a finger to her lips to tell Daphne to shush.

Daphne stood still on the low stool as Cathy walked around her, inspecting, arranging the folds of the dress that she herself had designed and sewn for the young girl to wear. It was made of ecru satin, with an overlay of silk faille. The silk faille was strategically ripped, elegantly ruined, falling about Daphne's knees in soft tatters.

"This dress looks like it was dug up from a grave," muttered Daphne. When Cathy let out a heavy sigh, she hastened to add, "but in a good way, I meant!"

Cathy put her hands on her hips and tilted her head to the side, looking at Daphne askance. "Oh, really?"

Daphne smiled. She liked to rile up Cathy. She had been Daphne's stylist since she was nine. Still in her twenties, Cathy was dark haired and big boned, from a large, close-knit Italian American family in Queens. She was an ambitious girl, with a straightforward manner and a nasal, honking New York accent. But she was also jokey. She liked to tease and be teased. She had come to the West Coast to make a name for herself in fashion. *Even if it takes dressing a movie star's brat to get noticed, I'll do what I have to!* But then she would wink, with a playful swat to the butt, making Daphne giggle.

Cathy didn't intend to stay only a stylist. She designed her own clothes, and now that Daphne was growing into a young woman, she could wear Cathy's designs. And there were red-carpet photographs and the occasional paparazzi shot. Her work would be seen. Which made the fact that she was a de facto babysitter more bearable to her.

"Hold still, let me look." The beading was arranged over the dress in shapes like jagged lightning bolts, sharp and defined near the top but then becoming sparser and unraveled looking down near the bottom. This was worn over a pair of wide-legged white silk pants. On Daphne's feet were pointed white high-heeled boots, covered with silver buckles.

"I can't walk in these shoes."

"Relax. We're only walking through the airport. There will probably be some photographers. At least I'm pretty sure someone tipped them .off. If you need help I can take your arm."

Now she turned her attention to Daphne's hair, which she had braided to one side and woven with delicate white cord strung with tiny pieces of broken shell and animal bone. She had also powdered the girl's face a chalky white, on which she had painted cheek contours in a shade of violet taupe.

"I look like a freak."

"You look like a work of genius. They better give me a credit if they run you in the tabloids or by God, I will shoot somebody."

"But what if you will become famous and leave me..."

"Oh, stop your whining. Be a big girl." But Cathy stopped for a moment, and looked at her with a beaming smile. "You really think I'll get famous?"

"Yeah. Everybody will want to dress as haute couture zombies, just like me."

"Oh, shut up, you. Always giving me a hard time..." She frowned for a moment. "The thing is? I get frustrated sometimes, I mean, I work really hard. I want to create things that are beautiful and really different, yada yada yada. But sometimes I feel like I will never get anywhere. You know, when people say they want something "unique" and "exquisite?" Usually, they don't really mean it." She paused for a beat, then turned to Daphne with a challenging look on her face, as though expecting her to argue.

Daphne felt chagrined. She'd only meant to tease. She didn't want Cathy to not believe in herself. Not knowing what else to do, she stuck her tongue out at her.

"Get over here," said Cathy with another heavy sigh. "You

brat. I've gotta pencil in your lips again. You already chewed them off."

The car that drove them to the airport was sleek and black with tinted windows. Though the soft, cushiony backseat area was luxuriously spacious, Daphne snuggled close by Cathy. Cathy had her black hair pulled tightly back and wore dark sunglasses that made her look cool and aloof, totally unlike herself. But she smelled of her usual warm and talcy scent, and Daphne rested her head on her broad soft shoulder and closed her eyes.

"Are you going to tell mom about the stuff at school?" She drew her legs up under her, spiky heels, buckles and all.

Cathy took off her sunglasses and turned to look at her, considering. "You have to promise, promise me to stop pulling this shit. I mean it. Something could happen to you. You don't look like a little girl anymore, not to most people. I don't think you understand what can happen to you."

"I promise Cathy. I already decided I didn't want to do it anymore, anyway."

Cathy put her sunglasses back on and looked out at the scenery speeding by. The interstate was full of traffic, but they couldn't hear a thing, the car was so well insulated. There was only the soft purr of the engine.

"I can't even imagine being your age these days. Even I get scared when I go out into the city. People all seem so angry, just fighting in the streets all the time... And when you see all the homeless, waiting for the motorcades to go by every day so that they can throw things at the politicians... you know something bad is going to happen. I don't like the feeling in the air. "

All the homeless. Daphne thought of her friend, the one with the white beard. Was he one of those Cathy was talking about?

"... but I think the worst thing is all the funeral pyres. At least at school, and in your big house, you can't smell them. How do the other people eat and breathe, with the smell of death everywhere? God. It is insanity."

Cathy looked so upset. Daphne gathered herself up, looked at her solemnly, and tried to take a calm, authoritative tone: "The world may seem very confusing now. It's a building up. A rising tide. The hive mind building upon itself. It's OK. Things are just changing into something else. Patterns will become apparent. Connections that you can't see now. But don't worry. You will."

Cathy stared at her for a long moment, eyebrows raised, and then shrieked with laughter. "Oh, give me a break! You're obviously quoting somebody. Where'd you read that, kiddo?"

Daphne, annoyed, moved away, crossing her arms and turning her head. "My father said that to me."

Sobering immediately, Cathy put an arm around her. "I'm sorry. I didn't know. I'm sorry I made fun of you. Hey."

Daphne still wouldn't look at her. "My father had access to information that regular people don't. And I miss him because he would actually talk to me like an adult. We would have the best conversations. I can't talk like that with anyone else. And especially not with you."

When he was home from business her father would always tuck her into bed at night. In the glow of her pink fairy lamp he looked different than he did in everyday life. His fierce blue eyes behind their rimless glasses looked kinder, his face softer, the close-cropped steely hair like the fluff of a chick.

What do you do at your job, Daddy?

Good things, Teacup. Good things. I invest in knowledge because I want to help people.

How?

Oh, all kinds of ways. I want to help science to stop diseases and pain and hurt. The government is even talking about investing in my group. They think, with the right research, we can someday stop terrorism. Can you imagine a world without terror?

She would never see him again.

At first, no one would even tell her what happened; her mother had locked herself in her bedroom, and the staff wore strained, anxious expressions. Finally, suspicious about the fact that she was being kept away from TV and the Internet, Daphne began hiding in corners to eavesdrop on the adults, picking up the phone extension to listen to their conversations. Finally, she dug a newspaper from a recycle bin and saw the headline that read BIOTECH BARON MISSING. Sitting on the kitchen floor, lightheaded and numb, she read the whole story of how her father had gone to a travel agency that catered only to the very wealthy. The agency didn't even have a name, it was so exclusive. People called it "The Black Box," and it specialized in the unattainable, adventures that even the regular well-to-do couldn't have. Her father, and a group of three other men, had requested to be dropped into the Amazon with nothing but their knives.

Weeks passed, and no one could find the men, though there were expeditions into the Rainforest to look for them. It was feared that they had been killed or kidnapped by indigenous people. The only trace left behind was her father's monogrammed Rolex, now worn by a brilliantly painted and feathered Indian man. And he would not speak.

Cathy gave Daphne's hand a squeeze, though all at once a great weariness had overcome her; she loved the girl, she cared very much for her, but at some point she had become so entrenched in this family and all of its problems, and it made her feel exhausted. She had been there for four years. It wasn't where she was meant to be. She knew in her heart, she would have to get out, soon.

At long last the car pulled up to the airport entrance. "Friends?" Cathy asked as the driver got out to open the car door for them. Daphne nodded sullenly and allowed her to take her hand to help her walk in her difficult shoes. The enormous automatic doors swooshed silently open before them.

The high domed airport was huge, but quiet, like a cathedral. Crowds of people moved briskly across the floor and up and down the tall narrow escalators. Angled screens up on the walls scrolled lists of flight information. They took a seat on the hard plastic chairs and waited for Daphne's mother to appear.

At first nothing unusual happened, but then here and there Daphne could feel eyes watching them, little flickers of interest that seemed to build bit by bit. Of course, they all knew. They had been waiting for her. If she closed her eyes, she could feel the soft clicks and flashes as they took pictures. Being photographed was so familiar to her, it was almost like stepping into a bath. And as Daphne made more appearances, the photographers were starting to recognize her more easily. When she accompanied her mother to charity parties and movie premiers, they liked to take pictures of what she was wearing.

Cathy sat, looking silent and impassive, yet behind her sunglasses, her eyes shifted around alertly, taking in where, and how many.

One of the men called to Daphne. "Hey, Peanut, want to stand up? Can you give us a smile? How bout a look at that outfit?"

Cathy looked at her with a small smile and a covert nod, but Daphne shook her head, keeping her eyes trained straight ahead. In spite of her demure, white powdered face and dark geisha lips, her expression was steely and resolute. The shells and bone woven into her pale hair tinkled softly as she turned her face down from the men with the cameras. But she peeked up at them covertly, from beneath her lowered eyelids.

She was relieved when she felt the focus of attention shift all at once up and away, to the top of the escalator in front of them. The excited buzz could only mean that her mother had at last arrived.

Amelia Andrews. Amelia Andrews is here!

And indeed, in silhouette she could see that it was her mother. She had the lithe body and straight-backed carriage of a dancer. With her pulled-back blonde hair and pale, ethereal face, she could pass for a young ballerina. She did not acknowledge or wave to the photographers, and she limped slightly. She had twisted her ankle after falling down some stairs, and the injury hadn't quite healed all the way.

But her face wore a soft expression of vulnerable hope as she looked up, and out, searching for them.

Where? Up there! You sure that's her? She hasn't worked in so long it's hard to tell. She doesn't look like herself.

Surgery.

They rose from their seats. There was a flurry of flashes as Daphne tottered forward on pinched and throbbing toes, toward her mother, who rushed forward to hug her. Her mother always smelled of tuberose and gardenia, flowers that were overripe and bruised on their petals. And underneath, another smell of something faintly metallic.

Up close, Daphne was stunned anew by her mother's face. She was in her early fifties, but was aging backward. She had been getting gene injections for the past several years. The practice wasn't legal yet in most countries, but she had connections. With her plump unlined skin and thick shining hair, she could pass for twenty-five. Except for her eyes, which somehow didn't match; Daphne sometimes had the odd feeling that a whole other creature was peering out at her, as through the holes in the eyes of a Halloween mask.

It wasn't the only risqué procedure she had had. Long ago, she had gotten an implant to stimulate electrodes in her brain, in order cure her alcoholism, and to make her a happier person. When Daphne asked where the implant was, her mother smiled shyly, eyes downcast, and said, "That's not for you to know, honey."

It was understood that no one should talk about any of the procedures. Although sometimes there were side effects that were impossible to ignore. Sometimes Amelia felt very nervous and over stimulated. Other times it made her feel fuzzy, and she had trouble remembering even the most obvious things.

She would go away to the Clinic sometimes, to have things "adjusted" when things got too out of hand.

Amelia held Daphne's face in her hands, hands that were beautifully manicured and jeweled, but also cold and dry and shaking slightly. "Teacup, you are so grown up, sometimes I can hardly recognize you!"

And indeed, for a moment, her mother's large beautiful eyes had a look of opaque blankness; they quivered in their sockets as they searched Daphne's face, as though she couldn't place just who she was.

2

There were mornings when the wind blew ash in from the east. It would settle in soft drifts and mounds around the brick wall surrounding their house. It coated the tall windows. If they ventured outside for too long that the grayness could settle into their hair, the folds of their clothes, into their very lungs.

It came from the fires. Arson was becoming rampant, and nobody knew what would be burned down next. It was said that there were flash mobs of homeless and revolutionaries, and no one knew where they would turn up, or why. Now that they had crossed the bridge and weren't just burning things in the city anymore, people were starting to be afraid.

Usually, Daphne, her mother and Cathy had no need to go out. Their home was so large that they didn't have to. Built on a cliff, the Mission Revival mansion glowed softly in hues of pastel. With its arched dormers and roof parapets, it resembled an old Spanish church, but one that was settled up in the clouds by itself, and with no parishioners. It was a self-contained world onto itself. Library, gym, movie room, bowling alley. They had everything they needed. There was an enormous rear patio from which you could see the entire bay and the city skyline.

If she ventured out shopping with her mother in town, it was only in one of the new mega complexes with aerial walkways high above the streets, so that they didn't have to come in contact with the chaos below.

Sometimes Daphne felt claustrophobic, as though she were living in a series of gerbil tubes. She would find herself trying to escape, once again, though no longer from school. She would climb the stone wall of her own house, just so she could get away undetected and feel free.

There was a little park with a lake and a gazebo down the road a bit, but it seemed spooky and haunted now that families were not going to it anymore. If people were not avoiding breathing the ash, then they were afraid of catching The Sickness. Sometimes she even saw people wearing gas masks all the way out here, just as they were doing in the city.

Daphne liked to come to this park because it had a little lake. Here, she could visit a friend. He was a swan she called Freddy. She could tell Freddy was not a real swan. Back months ago, during the period when the animals were making their city migrations, a guerilla engineer had developed some robotic swans with cameras in them. He put them into the lake to interact with the real, wild swans in order to study and understand their behavior.

Supposedly, the experiment was not successful and was scrapped. But most of the artificial swans had been left to roam as they wished. Freddy was graceful and beautiful as a real swan, but there was something a little off about him. He swam just a little bit too fast. When he came close she could hear faint whirrings and tickings coming from his body. And he did not avoid her as a real swan would. He always swam up very close, craning his neck, swiveling up his narrow face with its tiny black eyes set in their tiny black eye mask. He was taking footage of her with his hidden camera, she guessed. She didn't mind. She even smiled for him. Daphne preferred his mute, calm presence to that of most flesh and blood people. Freddy did not care about money or fame or who her family was.

She stroked his long neck, which was feathery and soft though taut with cables underneath. Then she lay back and looked at the sky, which was a dullish, heavy gray. The trees were tinged orange and the air smelled of autumn.

She daydreamed, thinking of the long vacation she had been on that summer. Her mother had taken her and Cathy to a beautiful island, where they had explored and seen crumbling stone ruins and strange twisted trees with foliage that dripped like lace. Tall spiky orchids and humongous spongy mushrooms as big as footstools. Nature's wild abundance had made her feel dwarfed, a feeling that she actually loved. It was beautiful and mysterious as another planet. A sci-fi diorama. A place where at any minute something could eat you.

Her mother had planned the trip so that she and Daphne could spend time together. She said that she had been feeling guilty about being away so much and that she wanted to make it up to her. They rented a luxury bungalow with an overwater cabana. Each bedroom was large with gleaming wooden floors and wide window seats heaped with pillows that looked out on the white-sanded lagoon.

But any time spent alone with her mother was too fraught with expectation; sunning on the deck together, her mother seemed too nerved up and anxious, her voice too tightly high pitched though she tried to sound sisterly and offhand.

"I think this is fun, don't you? I want to do this all the time. I think things are going to change for us, I really do. A fresh start. No need to look back, right?"

"Sure, Mom."

"I mean, you had kind of a rough school year, right?" Her mother was smiling, though she still looked nervous; her eyes were blinking compulsively. She dropped her voice and asked softly, "Is there anything you wanted to talk about? With me?"

Daphne didn't know what to do. Having her mother's attention was something she had always thought she wanted. And yet when it happened, she wanted to disappear.

"Well, I guess I haven't been doing that great in school. I'm going to try to do better in the fall."

Her mother took her hair down from its tie, then wrapped it up again, tighter, and said, "I guess we all should… try to do a little better." She turned her face away, toward the sea. Her face that seemed to get younger every day. In profile she could be mistaken for a girl, fresh and untested by life. "That thing on the stairs where I messed up my ankle… I just… It got me really thinking… I should just cancel everything and stay home for a while. Maybe do a detox. Maybe we could both do a detox… together?"

"Sure." She was aware that her voice was going dead.

"You know, since the thing happened with your father, I know you've suffered a lot and I really…"

"There's nothing to be said about it. I already had it out with the shrink."

"Yes, dear, I know, what I'm trying to say is that it's okay to talk about it. We've never really done that. Don't you think—"

"I'm going to go for a swim now, if that's okay."

"Of course, hon." The hurt look that rumpled her mother's features made Daphne panic with such clausterphobia that she flared up with a wild urge to hit her. But then the rush of shame at the thought made her go red in the face.

She had enjoyed herself most on the trip during the times that she was alone with Cathy, who had come with them and had a small cottage of her own. Cathy didn't seem to enjoy being around her mother very much either. It made her go quiet, whereas usually Cathy was brash and loud and fun. It was a quiet heavy with tension. Daphne seemed to know deep down that Cathy did not think very highly of her mother.

The two of them would go walking together down the overgrown trails while her mother took her long nap in the afternoon.

"I love this place. I think I must have lived here in a previous life!" she joked to Cathy.

"It could be true," Cathy huffed as they went up a steep incline. "I read somewhere that DNA can actually hold the memory of your ancestors. Like, your genetics are haunted! I mean, I'm Italian blood. Think about it. I come from the mighty Tuscan!" She pumped her fist playfully. "My genes probably remember walled cities and grand cathedrals, cobblestoned streets... not a tropical island, postcard places like this. I mean, it's beautiful, but too perfect. A banal kind of beauty."

Daphne felt slighted. "You think I have banal tastes? You think I'm boring?"

Cathy looked at her and smiled, considering. Then she said, "No, you are not boring. You are totally different from the social set you come from. You're subversive. You're witchy. You are an artist, like me! And anyway, aren't you from English stock? When I look at you I see Druids, Stonehenge. Fog on the moors..."

Daphne turned away so Cathy couldn't see how happy her words made her; it gave her such a good feeling that Cathy could look at her and see so very much that others couldn't.

She smiled even now to remember that day, as she lay alone in an abandoned park in autumn, on the edge of a black lake. Freddy the swan made the little putting noises that meant he was going to swim away. He always ran the same circuit. He drifted past the fat green Lilly pads, then opened and flapped his wings; when he did this, the afternoon light shined through. She could faintly see the metal hinges and rods beneath the feathers. It amazed her, how small and precise and graceful his movements were, how real someone had made him look. It gave her goose bumps.

The thing she missed most about being on the island was the freedom to move about outside. Here, at home, someone was always keeping her in. And it was only getting worse, now that the fires had started.

There had been one night where they could smell fire strongly in the wind, and actually see the red of a blaze in the distance, glowing like a lurid red sunset. It had made her afraid.

"They won't come here," her mother said, "Don't worry.

They won't let them get this far." Her arms were folded tightly to her body as she stood on their rear patio, watching across the water. Lately, her mother had not been looking well. Her face looked thinner, which made her eyes seem larger and slightly protruding. She slept a lot and complained of headaches. Daphne couldn't guess if it was caused by the implant, or by stopping drinking too quickly during her "detoxes."

"Yeah, I think we'll be okay," Daphne answered. "They have the national guard out. Dad always said that stuff like this happens in cycles. It'll settle down soon."

Her mother looked at her, her mouth a tense line. She looked so small and dry and brittle, as though any moment she could burst into flame and then puff away like a cinder. When she wasn't sleeping too much, she was up all night, roaming the house like a ghost in her filmy nightgown. "Sometimes... I feel like I can't think straight. I mean... part of me thinks maybe we should get out of here. We could buy a place on the island. They have an academy there I could enroll you in. You could make friends there. I think you need more friends..."

"I'm fine the way I am."

"Well. I'm just saying. It could be so nice. We wouldn't need a big place. Just a little condo. We could weave fishing nets with the village women and... and pick guavas... and... and maybe carve some of those little dolls out of roots and sell them..." She was getting excited again, giggling for no reason that Daphne could discern.

There would be other times when her mother's mood changed and she became steely and resolute; "No! We will not be leaving our home. The bastards are not going to drive us away!" And yet she would make fretful shopping trips to stock up on water and canned food. She had even looked into having coiled rope ladders installed beneath the windows in the second floor bedrooms.

One day, when her mother was at the hairdresser's, Daphne was looking for a missing pair of shoes and found a large cardboard box tucked away in her mother's bedroom closet. When she opened it, she found it contained two gas masks, one in a deep green houndstooth check, and one in a bright glossy red with white pin dots. She wondered where her mother had to go to buy something like that, since she had only seen them sold in kiosks in the street.

"I'm worried about her," Cathy said in a low voice as they played cards in the kitchen one afternoon. "I think she needs to see the doctor. She isn't acting right to me."

"I don't know. I don't think she'll want to. She's on one of those kicks where she thinks she can do everything herself. I don't think she'd listen."

"Yeah…and it's not like my opinion means very much to her. I mean, she's obviously trying to be a better person, but…" she shrugged, "I think she needs a little guidance."

"Well, what can we do?"

She cut a quick sidewise glance at Daphne. "We can only do what we can. Which probably isn't much. There's always been a lot of undue influence surrounding her. Poor woman. She's Amelia Andrews, star of her generation. Sometimes I think she never had a chance."

At the sound of the chime students flooded the hallway. Shouting, laughing, banging locker doors. When Daphne stood still, they would flow past her like river rapids.

They were talking on phones, squealing and tussling, lingering in doorways. Long haired girls in the plaid uniform jumpers, the boys in pressed khakis and polos embossed with The World Nation's Academy logo. And everywhere, the smell. The hectic smell of adolescent sweat. A smell ripe likewith sex mixed, with fear, and all kinds of invisible signals that she couldn't begin to understand.

And all of this against a stark backdrop of sober luxury. The floors were marble, the walls high with scripted molding. In the center of the hallway was a pillar in the shape of a goddess, holding a globe above her head. Her upturned face was bathed in golden sun streaming through the skylights.

When she sat at her desk watching the other teenagers, she saw them as through a great temporal distance. She felt like an old woman. And the rooms of her school had the feel of a future recollection, fuzzy around the edges. Sometimes she had to shake herself just to come to when she felt like this.

She had noticed over the past week that there were fewer students in class. Every day there were more empty desks. It gave her a nervous feeling.

Though she kept to herself, she overheard the rumors. Yeah, his parents are home schooling him because they're so freaked out. Julie's parents are staying at their place in the country until the riots are over. Did you hear, Steve isn't coming back. One of the maids caught the Sickness and now the whole family is locked away wearing gas masks!

She tried to shut it all out. She couldn't wait to get back to the studio because she was excited about an idea for a new piece.

She was planning to paint a portrait of her mother, as she had been years ago. Daphne's earliest memory was of being brought to visit her mother as she was working on a film set. It had been a period piece set in the Middle Ages. The details were fuzzy to her now, but she remembered how beautiful her mother had looked with her hair coiled on top of her head. Her elaborate dress was so heavy and strange with its brocade and jewels and high lace collar. Her mother smiled and held out her arms for a hug, but, in a sudden grip of overwhelming desperation and panic, young Daphne lunged for her mother, trying to claw through the elaborate costume, trying to get to her, the real life flesh and blood presence that she missed so much and needed like she needed air in her lungs. Mine! She remembered crewmembers pulling her off, and a whirling confusion of hot lights and cables and camera platforms as she was carried, howling, away from the set.

The film, In a Dappled Wood, failed at the box office, but won critical accolades, particularly her mother's performance as the duchess caught in a doomed secret love affair. Amelia Andrews shows such pained vulnerability, such fluctuating emotion. It is like watching a hummingbird trapped in a chimney.

Daphne stood at the easel, frustrated, trying to make the image come up from the ether of her memory and imagination. How did she look? Like this? Like this? But every time she tried to get the face right, it looked like a woman she did not know. A stranger in a costume, simpering back at her. A generic character from a stock fairy tale.

Daphne's mother decided to see a new doctor, recommended to her by her financial advisor. She got in quickly in spite of the long waiting list; he was said to be young and brilliant and up on all the latest pharmaceutical research. The doctor, she said later, was kind but excitable, patting her hand frequently, his eyes darting around the room. He spent most of the time telling her about the television talk shows he was set to speak on later that week. But after his examination, he prescribed her a new drug that he thought was just right for her needs.

The pills were small and blue, and at first gave Amelia a head rush that made her feel weak and dizzy. But later on another feeling would come over her. A sense of magnanimity and well-being. She began to smile again, though her cheeks were flushed a little too pink, and her pupils dilated, making her eyes as dark and limpid as a cartoon deer's.

"The best way I can describe it," she said, "Is as this wave that keeps washing over me. It feels just like first love. Like falling in love for the first time, over and over."

Things were easier around the house, less fraught. Cathy

found it easier to talk with Amelia, and became a sort of cheerleader. She encouraged her to expand her horizons and find a new direction for her energy. "How about charity work? It would be perfect. You have the money and the time. You could maybe set up some kind of small foundation? It would improve your image and help you make more friends. Killing two birds, right? It's what I would do, anyway. Doesn't hurt to consider it. Get on some committees, join a board or two. Maybe do a fundraising event..."

The idea gained traction, and Daphne's mother became focused and energized for the first time in a while. She met with her accountants and advisors about possibilities. In time she decided that as a first step she would host a fundraising dinner for the local animal sanctuary, which was a popular cause. At night she and Cathy would sit together, planning and brainstorming ideas in a notebook. Themes, decorations, catering.

Daphne was not used to the change in dynamics. Cathy and her mother used to be stiff and wary in each other's presence. Now they were becoming friends. They didn't only talk about practicalities. Cathy was becoming her mother's confidant. Once, Daphne lurked outside the living room doorway just to hear what the two women were talking about:

"Amelia, things will be all right. You're heading in the right direction. This will be a good way to make some friends. You'll meet new people, and that's when you'll really start to feel better."

"Well," her voice fretful, "I don't know. I used to try to fit in with...these types, when my husband was alive and involved in so many of these causes. They weren't exactly welcoming. I know they don't take me seriously. I'm not an intellectual, like they are. I mean, what am I? I'm an actress. I guess I was kind of a deep thinker when I was younger. I read a lot. I used to aspire to a life of the mind. I don't know what happened to me. I really got off track."

"I think you're being too harsh on yourself!"

"Oh, come on. They read the papers, too. I'm a washed up actress and a drunk. David married me at my peak. When everybody loved me. I had Saudi princes offer me a million dollars to sleep with them. I mean, I used to be put up on this incredible pedestal. I was worshipped just for being me. Do you know how empty that can make you feel after a while? To be applauded for no reason? A black spot started growing in me back then. No one knew it. They were so blown away by my so-called talent, how could they see it? That black spot grew and grew, until I had nothing inside me anymore..."

"Shh. The past doesn't matter. This will be the new you. You've had time away to think, obviously, and now this will be your rebirth! Look out, world!"

Daphne was watching from behind them, as they sat close together on the couch. They could pass as the same age in a photograph. But there was a subtle difference between them; Cathy was so ambitious and full of life's possibilities. And her mother so hollowed-out seeming, in spite of her beauty. One could see her struggle to believe the stories the younger woman was telling her.

And so the dinner idea became a real thing. The best party planners were brought in. The guests were invited to dress in an animal theme. Invitations were sent to local politicians and the most prominent supporters of nature conservatories. There would be forty people attending at a thousand dollars a plate. Notice was sent out to the press. Social buzz began in earnest.

Cathy disappeared into her design studio for weeks, and Daphne hardly saw her. When she did, she was electrified, glowing.

"Oh my God, I'm working around the clock. I've been so inspired, I think this is going to be it, you know what I mean? I feel that tingle."

"What am I going to wear?"

"Something totally different than the others. A little

politically incorrect for this particular occasion, sure. But. Get this: I see you as the young goddess Diana. You have that body, compact and lithe, you know? And a spritely face. I can see you very naturally with a bow and arrow. Gamine. Wispy. Fleet foot…"

She was speaking excitedly, her eyes gone glassy. When she got caught up in her creative work, sometimes her language would devolve into stream-of-consciousness: "I'm seeing brambles and heather. I'm smelling wet earth and animal fear. Imagine a diaphanous green, like the shell of a beetle. Short, sheath-like, asymmetric. Bound in leather cord…"

"But I don't get it. What am I wearing?"

"I'm feeling plumage…feathers in a headpiece. And jewelry made from animal teeth. Lots of embellished detail…" When Cathy was inspired, the feeling to her was like a dive through, a clear, bracing stream. Or like flying at super speed through a tunnel. She had to stop herself. How to convey a feeling like that to a sad, stillborn fifteen-year-old-girl who lived her life in this huge, dead mansion? "You see, all of the layers of symbols! You will be like a walking…a walking…um, uh…what's the word…"

"Palimpsest," Daphne said quietly, sarcastically.

Cathy stopped and looked at her with surprise. Sometimes the girl shocked her anew with her intellect; she didn't even know what the word meant.

"Yes. Sure. That."

The grand dining room was all set, and otherworldly looking in its beauty. Dozens of potted trees rimmed the edges, strung with sheer white drapery and tiny white lights. Each round table for ten was covered with a tablecloth made of entirely of woven lemon leaves. Towering centerpieces spilled with white florals and vines, in containers made cleverly from twigs. A woman had been hired to play the harp in one corner while the guests dined.

Daphne stood upstairs at her bedroom mirror, enthralled by the costume that Cathy had spent so much time making. It was a short tunic of bluish-green silk, roughened by pumice stones, embroidered with tiny teeth and scales. It was bound at the waist with leather cord. She also had sandals with leather cord that wrapped around her ankles. There was a frothy headpiece of green feathers and jade stones. And best of all, strapped to her back, a narrow parcel of arrows. Real arrows. And there was a tall, graceful bow that she could carry with her, or hang over her shoulder. Diana, Goddess of the Hunt! Daphne posed with her hands on her hips and smiled.

Cathy had dressed her mother as a fox. The gown itself was long and lean, of a reddish-orange velvet had a diaphanous sheen in the light. It had a long slit for her right leg, and a daringly low scooped back. There were armbands with long furry pieces attached that hung down, edged with white at the bottom. And she wore a half-mask of the same gingery velvet, with perky fox ears, two up-tilted eyeholes resembling her own pretty almond-shaped eyes, and a delicate, pink tipped nose.

"Don't you think it's kind of odd," she asked, eyeing Daphne's costume, "for one to be dressed up as a huntress at a fundraiser where we are trying to save the animals?" She laughed feebly. Her mind was elsewhere. Guests would be arriving at any time.

"Oh, I don't know," said Cathy, "I got on a tear, I guess. And it suits Daphne very much, don't you think? She was born to wear this. Our young goddess!" She gave a Daphne a wink.

The front bell rang, and Amelia hurried down the staircase. And from then on things did not slow down again. Car after car pulled up the wide gravel drive, and then the valet would it take away to park it on the grass lawn down below. The house, usually so quiet, filled with the buzz of multiple conversations. People drifted through the living room and the hallways, and out onto the patios, drinking pre-dinner cocktails, talking and laughing.

There were members of the board of the nature conservatory. There was a senator and his wife. Local philanthropists. There were people her father had known, people in biotech and people who worked in the think tanks. Most had arrived in costume. The women were dressed wildly and lavishly in animal themed eveningwear. There were long gowns of leopard spot and zebra stripe, with fascinators angled atop piled-up hairdos meant to suggest stylish animal ears. Here and there a long, beaded-and-tasseled tail dangled from a pert derriere. There was one panther in a black velvet wide-legged jumpsuit, her chest strung with large emeralds. And there were birds. Many birds wearing shorter taffeta skirts with feathered petticoats peeking from underneath, dazzling jeweled peacocks and parrots. The men, however, wore their normal tuxedos, occasionally with a half-mask of a lion or a tiger.

Daphne kept to herself, lingering in a corner behind one of the wait staff's drink stations. Here, she didn't have to say anything, only listen to the rumble of voices and the odd phrase that she could make out now and then from underneath it all. Daphne let the noise and colors and impressions wash over her in a gentle wave.

Well, if you withdraw US influence over there, you create a vacuum...

A tinkle of crystal.

I hear they want to make it over into a bed and breakfast, but the preservation society said that...

Somewhere, a woman's high, fluting laughter.

...undeserving. Anyone who would burn down their own country deserves what they get...

Thirty million. Can you imagine the taxes?

The flicker and glow of wine flushed faces.

Of course they shot it, it was a public danger! But they kept the horns and the hoofs, if you know what I mean...

She saw it all as a painting in her head, the over rich colors, the glinting of glass and jewels, the animal patterns. She imagined herself as a predator. She imagined how the sight of the zebra stripes would unleash a torrent in her brain, something primordial that would set her brain cells into motion urging her to hunt and kill. Quietly she took up the bow, pulled an arrow from the bundle on her back. Fit the arrow to the springy cord and began to pull back, just partway. She chose a victim's head to center in her mental crosshairs, a young-old woman like her own mom, this one deeply tanned and laughing loudly, zebra ears a little askew, the ruff of black fringe down the back of her blonde hair swaying to and fro, to and fro...TWANG!

But it was all just pretend, and she abandoned her game when it was time to convene in the dining room. There, speeches were given about the fundraising effort. A toast was given for Amelia. She stood with her head bowed modestly as the crowd applauded her hard work and generosity.

The first course was brought out, some sort of peppery tomato soup. Daphne had been seated to her mother's right. Also at their table, was Nelson Holmes, an old venture partner of her father's, and his wife Rosemary. The couple had been good friends of the family, back when her father was alive. They had often gone on ski vacations together in the winter. Nelson was a youthful looking man in his late sixties with thick silver hair. Rosemary was younger, in her forties, with a handsome, sharp-boned face and dark red hair cut in a fashionable, jagged-edged bob. She was dressed in a tight column of green snakeskin, with gold python-shaped bracelets wriggling up both arms. The pythons had ruby eyes.

"My, my, Daphne," Mister Holmes beamed a fatherly smile at her. "What a beauty you have grown to be. How old are you now?"

"I turned fifteen this summer, when we were down in the islands." She smiled shyly; she had forgotten how fond she had once been of Mister Holmes, how twinkly eyed and fun he had been. He had given her piggy back rides when she was little, and showed her how to do disappearing coin tricks. She hadn't realized until now that she missed having him in her life.

"Well, I can see you got your mother's good looks! You are a-dow-rable honey!" Mister Holms had what was either an accent or a minor speech impediment that made him pronounce his or's in a drawn-out, rounded way: sow-ry, bow-ring, dowr-way.

"She has David's brains, though," her mother said, "She's very complex for a young girl. She likes to ponder the nature of life, like David did."

"Well!" his smile grew larger. "We could use your brains! Maybe when you grow up you can join us at Teacup Ventures?"

"I..." Her father had named Teacup Ventures for her. It had been his nickname for her. My little Teacup. Everyone knew it. She blushed deeply and looked down.

Her mother stroked her hair. "Actually, she thinks she wants to go into the arts. Daphne is a very talented painter."

"The arts, that's great," said Mrs. Holmes, fixing Daphne in her pale green gaze. Her eye makeup was painted thick and glossy as Cleopatra's. "We are patrons of the arts. We're on the Museum Board. Maybe your work will hang there one day!"

"Your father was a brilliant CEO," Mister Holmes said low and fast into her ear, "But art was what he revered. It was the soul of an artist he really admired. What did he tell me... he was saddened by the disconnect between the art world and technology space. It made him really disheartened to see so few start-up people at the galleries. He wanted to change all that..."

"How is the Museum holding up, Rosemary? With, the, um, troubles and whatnot?" Amelia asked shyly, looking up at her through her fox mask.

"Oh, we have security in place to keep those yahoos away," Mister Holmes quickly interjected, "It should all die down soon. It's not even a unified group that's doing these things. They have no mantra, no message. It's just ragtag gangs that spring up, so I doubt they will last"

"They attacked the flagship store of Van Cleef and Arpels.

Smashed the windows, set the carpets on fire. It will take at least a year to open back up! If they come back." Mrs. Holmes spoke her words in a whisper, as though in fear she would be overheard.

"But anyhow," Mister Holmes took a sip of his wine. "You can't worry too much. Can't stop living, can you? We have to go about our days. "His skin was incredibly pink, as though his blood had all rushed to just below his skin's surface. He always seemed suffused with health and goodwill. "I miss David. I think of him every day. I'm so sow-ry about the way things turned out to be." Sow-ry. His accent, though odd, had the effect of making even the simplest statements sound foreign and intriguing. "But.I think if he were here today, he'd be proud of how the company is doing. We've had some amazing projects in development. And the overseas conflicts look to be turning the corner soon."

"Yes, the conflicts. I don't keep up with that as I should," said Amelia in a small voice. "I'm terrible."

"Well, it's a different kind of war, so that's not surprising! The new war. The war for data, for information. Not as high profile. Not as bloody. You can't be blamed for not keeping in the loop. Most people aren't."

"Well, what is going on, Nelson?" She kept her eyes on him as she signaled to a passing waiter for a flute of champagne.

He leaned forward, and spoke in a low voice, a twinkle in his eye. "I think they've got their guy, to tell you the truth. I'm privy to some of that information. They made the invasion, swift and sure as could be. Our soldiers draped the Corporate flag over that statue's face. I saw the footage. I won't lie to you, I got a little choked up..."

"Nelson is a lot more sentimental than you know," laughed Rosemary. She gave Amelia a conspirational smile. She smiled back. Then Rosemary leaned in toward Amelia, her bobbed hair swinging silkily forward. "How are you, Amelia? Really? I haven't seen you in so long."

"Oh, you know. I'm cutting back on the show biz stuff. Trying to figure out my real priorities. Not like I'm fending off the offers, anyway!" She laughed and took a small sip of champagne. Just one glass to steady her nerves.

"Well, you look gorgeous. I take it you've been seeing, what's the name...Doctor Chong?"

"Yes. He gives me the gene injections. Incredible stuff. I would only trust him, of course, because David had stakes in that company..."

"Biospan. I know!"

"So I've known Chong for a while. And I honestly think everyone will be doing it, sooner or later. Once things get past the regulations, and the, you know, activist groups. It can be dicey stuff. But once people can see..."

"Well, to be truthful, I wanted to get some contacts from you. I may be making a trip out soon, if you know what I mean. If those are the results. You look twenty-five!"

"But Rosemary, you already look so lovely and full of life just as you are!"

"Ugh. I need to upgrade. I'm forty-five. "She lowered her voice to a whisper. "And you know, Nelson can't even go up to the Lodge any more to make deals. I won't let him. The women. All these young Eastern European things in slit skirts and high boots. The women lie in wait there, and they are so aggressive. And less than half my age!"

They both seemed to remember at the same time that Daphne was there, and the topic was cut short. Though Daphne was only sitting, dazed with boredom, ripping green chunks from the woven lemon leaf tablecloth and balling them up in her fingers.

The main course was brought out, some kind of thin-cut pork folded into origami type shapes resembling blossoms, set around mounds of couscous. The noise in the room grew louder as people shouted across the tables to each other to be heard.

Nelson was conversing now with one of his associates, a

man in evening dress with a furry, full-headed bear mask that he had worn as a joke and then set on the table beside him. The eyes were hollow, but its rubber teeth were bared in a growl.

"Unless the underlying drives are so strong that a new vertical can sustain itself!" The man spoke in a mincing, mocking voice. "Pffft! Yeah, right!" The man's face was red with drink, joyfully belligerent.

"They're talking about the new Cleantech funds," Rosemary said gently to Amelia, who was taking frequent, nervous sips from her glass and sitting quietly with a stiff smile on her face, eyes darting back and forth as she watched the back and forth volleying of the business talk. Daphne wished she could wrest the champagne away from her, before things got out of hand.

"Well, I've got to convince my stakeholders to take the longer term view," said Nelson, wagging his eyebrows suggestively. "It ain't easy, believe me!"

"I'm still fighting with that son-of-a-bitch guy from the German parliament. About those regulations. The nanotech stuff."

"What a bunch of bullshit."

The evening seemed to stretch on interminably to Daphne. It felt like years had passed when eventually desert was served, scoops of exotic sorbets garnished with mint leaves. And after it was consumed and the dishes cleared away, the mood began to shift, from one of exuberance to one of rowdy drunkenness. There was loud laughing, the sound of breaking crystal. One woman, the one in the zebra get-up, was howling, "Oh Robert STOP!" as she swatted under the table at the advances of a cackling bald man in black tie.

People began to get up and wander from table to table, and then out from the dining room into the rest of the house. All sense of order and decorum had vanished, and a giddy sense of anarchy seemed to be taking over the group. Daphne's torpid boredom was replaced with slowly growing sense of alarm. It was so unnerving to see adults behave in that way. And no one seemed to be in control.

A little later, it seemed that a game had taken shape: The women in their glamorous animal costumes were being chased, hunted, by the men. They ran from room to room, shrieking and laughing. Great flanks of spots and stripe, sequin and jewels, scales and feathers streaked through the grand dining room as predators in dark suits pursued from all sides with snorts and growls and strange yodeling animal cries. The woman at the harp played on, not looking up.

Amelia, though, remained in her seat. She was watching the scene around her with her eyes wide, her lips parted. From the way she suddenly grabbed at and pulled off her fox mask, Daphne got a worried feeling.

"Mom? Are you okay?"

She looked as though she didn't know where she was or what was happening. She looked slightly frightened, but at the same time, amused.

Daphne looked down at her mother's glass. It was empty. She had had at least three glasses of champagne before Daphne lost count.

"Did you...have too much to drink?" Her mother was swaying slightly, not to the music. "Or do you think it's the implant acting up? Are you having one of those weird surges again?" That was the way her mother explained her occasional memory lapses that had lately been increasing. A surge in her electrodes, like a crashing computer, only a temporary nuisance.

Her mother looked at her, not comprehending. A shy and wide-eyed young girl.

"Come on. Maybe I should just take you..."

She was cut off by a sudden loud noise, like thunder except indoors. There was a ripple of heat, a flash of light. The noise of happy hijinks abruptly ended. There was a hiccup of stunned silence, followed by screams as the guests were quickly shocked sober in a rush of fear and adrenalin. People didn't know which direction to run in. The glass of a French door had been broken from the outside, something had been hurled through it and the heavy gold drapes were on fire. Acrid smoke was beginning to fill the room, settling in a heavy haze at the high ceiling.

Daphne pulled her mother out, away into the front foyer. Everyone was crowding out the front door. It all happened in an instant, but that instant was stretched out infinitely, it felt as if time had stopped moving. Daphne was in danger of fainting, she was so overwhelmed by the noise, the crowd, the smell of smoke and the heavy aroma of white flowers. Her vision seemed to black out in flashes, like a strobe light. She looked back into the dining room, where she could see a flicker of flame start to consume one of the fabric strung trees. A giant arrangement of greens and orchids had been knocked over, and water streamed onto the floor.

And in the midst of all the chaos, Daphne was stunned to see something else: it was the lynx. For an awestruck moment she caught just the briefest glimpse of him. She saw him between the ruined tables, in mid-flight. He was intent and graceful with his ears drawn flat to his head. Just a blurred streak of brown and black and gold eyes. As clear and real as day, though no one else seemed to notice him. Daphne stood stock still while the people ran past her, just staring after him in wonderment. But in the next instant he was gone again, as though he had never been.

3

The part of the house they now inhabited had gone back to being very quiet. Amelia was spending most of her time sedated in bed, or else sitting on the patio wrapped in a blanket, staring out into the distance as though she were in a fugue state.

The dining room had been closed off as the fire damage was being repaired. The policeman said it was caused by an improvised device. A petrol bomb, specifically. It was thought that only one person had been acting. There had been no group. They just wanted to scare you. It was just a lone kook. Copycat if you ask me. Lucky the firemen got there fast.

But Amelia had become paralyzed with fear and paranoia. Much of the evening of the party she had blacked out, except for the moment of the explosion. And that she could not stop reliving. "Why here? Why us?" she asked. "I'm not responsible for the way things are. God knows. I wasn't born rich. My father was a lowlife. My mother worked in a factory for God's sake, so I'm really not who they think I am. They are mistaken!" Amelia hadn't seen her family in years, since she ran away to New York as a young girl to model and take acting classes. Her family lived somewhere in the Midwest. Amelia sent money but never spoke to them, and Daphne knew better than to ask why.

Cathy stayed with them, but the other staff members left, the cook and the housekeepers. The same had been happening at many of the other mansions. The riots were making the staff too afraid to come to work. The National Guard couldn't handle the uprisings anymore, so soldiers had started patrolling the streets in their jeeps.

Even Cathy had become quiet and grim, not at all her usual self.

"I don't know what's going to happen," she said to Daphne when they were alone.

"What do you mean by that?"

"I...I don't know. I don't know what I mean."

"You're going to stay, aren't you? I mean, you always said it was safer in here than out there."

"Yeah. Yeah..." But she trailed off vaguely.

Since school was only open sporadically, a tutor came to work with Daphne a couple of hours a day, a young man with dark curly hair and shy eyes who spoke so low and fast that it was hard to understand him. Daphne got her work done very quickly every day. She spent much of the rest of her time sketching and painting. She was trying to paint how she remembered the flame and smoke, and it was much more challenging than she thought it would be. Much of the time her rendering came out looking too harsh or too stiff and lifeless. She tried to go to a place in her mind, beyond words and labeling. She had to be the thing. Only when she was a flame, hot and sibilant and impetuous...only then was she able to get it to come alive on the canvas. She could spend hours painting flame, and being that flame, until her mind grew bleary and her eyes fogged over.

She still liked to sneak off to places on her own, though often just down to the same little park. She wanted so badly to spend time with Freddy the swan. She would squat among the reeds and cattails, calling, "Here Freddy. Here swan! Here you beautiful roboswan!" but he did not appear. Did roboswans migrate? Or did they simply stop working if their parts wore down? She walked down a winding lane to a small pergola covered in grapevine, where she sat thinking of Freddy and his bright electronic eyes. Maybe he kept that footage of those serene afternoons inside him as a memory. Did he miss her as he flew far away, high up above bright new landscapes?. Things were so confusing now. Couldn't anything stay the same?

The other day she had found her mother in the family room, watching an old movie that she had starred in when she was younger.

In this movie she had played an English nurse during the First World War. She was wearing a long dress with an apron and a cape, and a head veil that made her look like a young lovely nun. In the scene the nurse was driving a Model-T ambulance over muddy, rutted roads in a field. Her veil was blowing back and there was dirt on her face and she looked so brave and alive that Daphne was moved to sit beside her and watch the rest.

"Never let people imagine you into something you're not."

Her mother said this in such a strange, dead voice that Daphne wheeled to look at her. Amelia was looking at the television. Daphne saw that here was no great physical difference between the woman before her and the woman on the screen. They had the same features, the same blonde hair, they even looked the same age. But the one on the screen had life behind her eyes. She was scintillating and bright, The woman seated next to Daphne, now, on the couch, looked back at her helplessly, beseechingly, as though from the depths of a great pit.

"What did you say, Mom?"

"All this," she motioned toward the screen, "I moved people back then. Truly. But it wasn't something I really did. I wasn't a good actress. I was just a vessel, and I let the characters enter me. It wasn't something I had to work at. I didn't deserve the credit. Or the awards."

"You made a lot of people happy. They enjoyed your films."

"Yes, but, honey, you shouldn't sell people something that's false." She stroked Daphne's hair. "People thought your father and I made an odd couple. But we were more alike than anyone knew. We were both dark. You know. Fatalistic. Just in our own ways."

"Dad loved you."

She smiled. "I was feeling very fragile when I met your father. I met him in Dubai. At a launch party for a new luxury resort. There were movie stars, television people, royalty. Lobster and mezze. And these fireworks so huge you could see them from space! That's what they said, anyway. It was beautiful but obscene. It made me a little depressed, to tell you the truth. I was sitting alone as they were being set off. So was your father. I remember the first time I saw him, the flashes of color reflecting off his glasses, and how sad he looked even though everyone else was bubbling and happy. I went to sit near him without saying a word. I didn't know who he was. But he knew me. He smiled to see me, like he recognized me as some kind of angel. I thought I could always make him happy, because that first time was so easy."

"And did you?"

"For a while." She glanced out a window that was shaded gray with ash. "He was kind of in awe of me because he thought I had such a great gift. He thought I was special. You see, he thought all artists were special." She laughed ruefully. "Eventually he saw me for the mortal human being I was, I guess. But, like I said, we more alike than anyone knew. Both too sensitive for this world. This house was a sort of haven when he was here. We read the Greek and Roman myths aloud to each other by the fire. We would sometimes just huddle together, like two children afraid of a storm." She looked at Daphne sidewise, biting her lip, as though this were a joke. "Well. It was more complicated than that. But I loved him. Even though I didn't feel comfortable with the environment he worked in. Sometimes I'm angry with him for going away! He brought me into this world, with these people, all the ones at the party... I don't understand them! I can't live with people like that. They have too much power. They frighten me, to be honest.

Sometimes I wonder if David wasn't killed by one of his own."

"What?"

"You know. David was so conscientious. Sometimes he spoke out. Stepped on a few toes. Sometimes I think Nelson Holmes knows more than he's telling me..."

"What are you saying, Mom?"

"I'm saying...nothing. I'm just saying I know why everyone hates the people in power. That's why the mobs are coming to burn us all to the ground."

"You don't have to hang around with those people, you know. I don't like them, either."

Her mother smiled. "What do you think we should do?"

"Go away somewhere. I think the fire was a message, telling us to change paths. We can't go back to that old life. We could live someplace else. Go back to the island, like you said." She smiled, thinking of the evenings there, so soft and warm and mild, and the sound of the waves washing to the shore, unseen in the darkness.

"Well. Listen, Teacup. You may have a point. You've always been smart. As soon as I'm feeling better, I'll make a decision. I have not been feeling myself. I keep forgetting things again."

"I know."

"It's always just for an instant. But the instances are getting longer. Sometimes I forget my entire past. Well, that's almost nice. But then the forgetting passes and it all comes back."

"It's just the thing again. Can't you just go to the Clinic and have them take it out once and for all? It doesn't even work! It doesn't even make you feel happy like it's supposed to. It's messed up."

But her mother had that vague look again, and seemed not to hear her. "The forgetting passes. And then the forgetting returns. And when it does, I embrace it, like a mother or a lover..."

"Mom, you scare me when you talk like this..."

"Forgetting begets forgetting begets...presence. In the

moment."

And now she was looking at Daphne blissfully, her eyes wide and lit up with wonder.

Daphne was feeling stir crazy, so an outing was planned. Cathy was to take Daphne out for shopping, lunch and then for an afternoon at the fine arts museum.

There was a new exhibit of American landscapes from the 1800s, with many paintings of large blue skies and infinite green prairies. Looking at the wide-open spaces made Daphne feel a corresponding largeness inside. There were fields studded with peaceful black bison. There were Indians paddling canoes on placid lakes. There were deep dark forests of bluish green shadow. She felt as though she were looking through small windows of time, to a distant past that felt impossible to contemplate.

For over an hour they had meandered through the large, white rooms of the museum, awash in light from the great wall of windows. It was nice to be in a public place, with other people, but not feeling the need to say a word.

Daphne, of course, had been carefully dressed for the day out. She was wearing an a-line dress of a very stiff, shiny silver fabric, so that it stood out in a triangle. Her hair was pulled into a knot on top of her head, with a silver chopstick stuck through it that was strung with delicate strands of clear, bubble-like beads that clacked when she moved. She tottered on black platform sandals, so she had to hold Cathy's arm as she walked.

No one took their picture in the museum, though a couple of people seemed to be looking at them pointedly.

"They know who we are," Cathy said grimly. "How could they not, with so many pictures published of the incident."

"You used to like it when people noticed us."

"Well, things are different now." Cathy muttered, her lips barely moving, like a ventriloquist.

Even after they returned home, Daphne's mind felt as though it were elsewhere. She looked out the windows at the blurred, fleeting landscape of crowded buildings and storefronts and imagined it as it was centuries ago, virgin and green and untouched.

"You know, Mom's acting pretty strange," she said later as they lay at opposite ends of one of the large tufted sofas in the library.

"How so?"

"Just saying weird things. Not acting like she's all there some days."

Cathy looked at her for a long time, considering. Then said. "She keeps complaining to me about things that only she can see."

"Like what?"

"Shadows. She says she sees a creepy shadow that keeps moving across her wall. It looks like a creature, she says, with large wraparound wings, and it shuffles along from one side of the wall to another."

"God. That's crazy. For real. Even for her."

"Well. I think she is planning to go back to Doctor Chong to talk about this stuff."

"Thank God. I can't take it anymore. He'd better fix it." Daphne flexed her feet, which were still sore from walking so much. "You know, we were talking, mom and I, about moving to the islands. You could come with us. Wouldn't it be nice?"

Cathy did not answer.

"I mean, after she goes to the doctor and gets things adjusted, she said we could start making plans." She lifted her head to look into Cathy's face. "Wouldn't you love that? I think it would be awesome."

Cathy had her eyes raised up to the ceiling and was blinking rapidly. Daphne felt a lurch as she realized Cathy was trying to keep from crying.

"What? What is it?"

"Well," she sighed, after a moment, swiping each eye one time firmly. "I don't know that I will be going with you. That is, I know I'm not going with you. I've been meaning to tell you…"

"Oh my God Cathy…"

"Just stop, okay. Don't make me feel worse about it that I already do."

"You are going back on your word?"

"I never promised you anything. So don't even go there—"

"But I just don't get it! I thought all of this crazy stuff happening out there made you want to stay here where it's safer! That's what you said!"

"Well, I'm starting to think it's not so safe to stay here anymore. I'm thinking it's more dangerous to be inside a place like this than outside."

"Well, that's stupid." She crossed her arms, her jaw stiff. She tried for nonchalance. "Where on earth would you go, anyway?"

"Back home! I do have a family, if you can believe it. I did have a life before I came to live with you! I can stay with my sister in Queens. Until I figure out what to do next."

When Cathy looked over, she forgot her anger. She saw what was only a poor little girl in a grown up costume of silver and beads. Beneath the smeared lipstick and eyeliner she was after all still a child whose chin was trembling.

"Hey. Daphne. Don't be so mad at me, huh?"

"I'm not mad," she said icily, "You can do as you wish."

"Oh, for Christ's sake!" she yelled in exasperation. "I am twenty-six years old! What am I, supposed to stay here forever? Until you're eighteen? I'm not your nanny!"

"Oh, yeah?"

"Yeah! I'm a designer. And I have my own career to think of, you know."

"Well, you won't have me to be your mannequin anymore. Who will take pictures of your ugly clothes, then?"

Cathy's face puckered into a hurt expression, and she said nothing for a moment.

"Well, it wasn't really getting me anywhere anyway. They publish the pictures, but they don't talk about the clothes. All they talk about is your screwed up mother and this screwed up life I've somehow got tethered to. People think it's just all so tragic, and they can't look away from the freak show."

"Oh, I see. That's all we ever were to you. You know what? You never knew me. You always looked at me and created some... character out of me! You dressed me as a doll and told me who I was and I liked it because no one else paid attention to me!"

"Shhhh. Shh. Honey..." Cathy started to reach for the girl, then changed her mind and pulled away, punching the arm of the sofa and stifling a sob of frustration.

Plans were made for Amelia to see Doctor Chong. She had wanted Daphne to come along with her, but she refused.

"Things are so unsettled here, Daphne. I will feel better having you there with me. We'll just drive right up, it's only an hour's drive. I'll probably be there a week. You've been to the medical center before to get your check ups, remember? But you haven't seen any of the adjoining buildings. You'd have your own place to stay..."

"I don't want to go. I want to stay here. I want to do my homework and work on my paintings and do what I want."

"Please, honey. It would give me peace of mind. After what happened here I know you must be scared. And the Clinic is a safe place, no one can get in. They have a gate and you need a special card to get through..."

"It's a creepy place! All those endless buildings with opaque windows and the parking lot full of armored cars. I don't like it there! I just want everyone to leave me alone. Why will nobody ever listen to me?"

It was agreed, reluctantly, that Daphne would stay behind under the condition that she not go anywhere outside alone.

Cathy would stay with her, and the tutor would come every day.

Amelia would be gone for ten days. Her bags were packed, and on the day that she left she kissed Daphne on the cheek. "Be good until I get back. I'll be thinking of you the whole time."

Cathy and Daphne spent all of their time in the house. It was becoming increasingly messy with no one there to do the housekeeping. The kitchen counters were sticky with grime. Dust bunnies gathered in the corners. But the two of them were too lethargic to do anything about it. They lay in the den watching television.

All of her young life Daphne had not been allowed to watch much television at all, let alone the twenty-four hour news stations. Her parents had wanted to keep her pure of spirit and untroubled. Now she gorged on the news for hours every day. It felt impossible to turn it off. She watched, stunned, as soldiers in tanks drove down the center of the streets, streets in the city that she knew. Throngs of the homeless tried to stand them off, throwing rocks and bottles at them.

"Is that really for real?" she asked Cathy, though she knew it was a stupid question. "It never used to be like that. Not that bad."

"It's for real, all right. This has been coming for a while. Ever since they had the Guard patrolling the streets, it's just been getting more and more tense." She spoke calmly and so quietly that Daphne could barely hear her.

"Do you think they can just make it stop soon?"

"I don't know. This isn't the only city where this is happening. And the army is already spread thin as it is. It's insane. Jesus. Sometimes I feel like we're past the point of no return," Cathy sat up straight, growing more animated, gesturing wildly. "You know? There are no more regulations for anything. No boundaries. And you can't fuck up one thing without it rippling out and affecting everything. Like, spray unknown chemicals in the air, you kill the honeybees. Kill the bees, fuck up pollination. Plants die. Up the food chain, yadda yadda. Before you know it, animals are migrating to the cities, looking for food, and they all get shot. Which begets animal extinction, which will fuck up the ecosystem more. And then, in the future who knows? But you know what the people in charge say. IBGYBG."

"What's that mean?"

"I'll be gone, you'll be gone."

Daphne paused for a stunned moment, wracking her brain for a response to all this. Finally, she said with studied insouciance, "Well. I know some powerful people. Like at the party. There is a guy we know who has all these connections. He knows about all about this stuff, secret stuff, about corporations and data. And he said after we win some of these overseas conflicts against the terrorists, then things would start settling down over here, too."

"Ppfff. No doubt there were some people at that party who have some stake in all that."

Daphne snorted and rolled her eyes. She wanted to be on Cathy's side again. "Yeah. A lot of those guys at the party were so gross. You should be glad you didn't have to be there listening to them. You know what? It sounds bad. But I was almost kind of glad someone tossed that firebomb. You should have seen those people scatter! It was kind of great, honestly. Karma and all."

Cathy looked at her. "Oh come on. Don't you know that you are those people?"

"No, I'm not. Really. They make me puke," Daphne said.

"Your father was a big part of all that. That's what bought this house. And your school tuition, and your island vacations. You have no idea what it is for life to be otherwise."

"Well, I've seen the streets. I like to walk the streets. I can't help it if everyone just keeps trying to shut me up in this dungeon all the time. Besides, you're in here, too, aren't you, so who are you to talk?"

"But I'm not one of you."

"I don't see the difference."

"Baby, you wouldn't." She laughed, turned away, and started speaking as though to herself. "It makes me so fucking angry. These small groups of banks and corporations run the whole globe! They all own one another, too! And they have to dominate all markets. Oil. Telecom. Big pharma. Any nation steps out of line? Then it's assassinations, coups, war. Such bullshit. Go into these little countries, take down their leaders, put their guys in, and it's austerity and people starving in the street. You mentioned terrorists earlier? Well, guess who the terrorist really is? You would be shocked, baby!" She turned back to Daphne, pointing a finger at her as though holding her to blame. "I've got two brothers in the army, recruited before they even finished high school. Fighting in those wars! Just young boys, and it's like they're already owned by these corporations..."

"Did they catch The Sickness?" It came out so fast, before Daphne could stop herself. She blushed when she saw the way Cathy glared at her. "Well...I just heard that a lot of soldiers have it. I don't know if it's a rumor or not...that it's like some kind of chemical agent, or something, and it originated over there..."

Cathy was stonily silent for a beat, and she looked so angry that Daphne's heart started to race, and her words sputtered into silence.

"Is it all just a joke to you, Daphne? Gossip you hear at school? These are people's real lives, you know." Sometimes it flew into Cathy's brain that she wanted to shake such a spoiled girl.

"So...then it is real?"

Cathy turned away from her and shrugged. "I don't hear from my one brother. The other came back with problems. My mother takes care of him now."

With shame, Daphne realized she knew next to nothing about Cathy's life. But it felt too late to begin asking questions now, and she didn't know the right way to do it.

Cathy got up and left the room.

There was the basement gym that neither of them had used much in the past. They began to go down there a lot to play racquetball, each straining and huffing as she ran back and forth to strike the ball against the wall with a resounding whack. It was nice down there. It felt quiet and cool, and most of all, insulated, like a luxurious underground burrow.

In other areas of the house, they did not talk much. And in that tense silence they could hear more and more the sounds that were starting to come from outside: the boom of far off explosions, the whooshing and puttering of the small drones that had started patrolling overhead.

And it was getting dark, so dark outside, as clouds of smoke covered the sun in the middle of the day. They tried watching movies, reading magazines and playing board games. But it was hard to get silly and giggle together as they usually did when they played Monopoly or Scrabble. Cathy looked too preoccupied, her brow constantly furrowed with worry. All the time she would stop and go to the window, looking outside at nothing. The air itself felt hot and signed in their lungs whenever they opened the veranda doors. There were sounds of unseen animals scrambling through the trees and calling out in high, strange cries.

"They're running away from the fires," said Cathy, pinching at her lower lip in a gesture Daphne had never seen her make before. Daphne thought it best if she just kept quiet from then on, though a terrible dread was gnawing at her stomach. She went back to spending time in her art studio, but when she loaded up her brush with paint, she couldn't get anything to come. Her arm and her hand seemed to have stiffened up, so that whatever she painted had to be covered up and started over, again and again.

One evening after trying to work and failing, she gave up and went to her bed so that she could just lie there and think. Thinking about when she was a young girl and everything felt so safe. Her father had still been there. Each of her parents had seemed inscrutable and mysterious, locked in their own heads. But she had felt secure in their orbit. They were just one of the forces of nature that reigned supreme and immutable in her world. Things had their normal cycles and trajectories. The sun rose and set, seasonal cycles came and went. A mourning dove cooed at her window, always at the same time every day. She loved to be outside where she could get lost for hours in watching a trail of ants, or the way the tree branches swayed in the wind.

Now that her father was gone, her mother had grown young and lost, and the world was falling into chaos. Part of her was afraid. But part of her felt oddly satisfied to watch everything come apart. It matched how she felt inside. Cathy could pace and cry all she wanted. She, too, would soon be gone, and it would be as if she had never been there at all. There had been others before her that had left. People that Daphne had loved that were now just shadows of memory. Anyway, she told herself, change was what she wanted. Any change would be better than the way things were now.

And yet, even as she thought those thoughts, she wanted so badly to cry, and throw herself into Cathy's arms and beg her forgiveness for being who and what she was, even though she couldn't help it.

She got up and made her way down the staircase, looking for Cathy. She couldn't stand feeling alone anymore. If they could only be close again, everything would be okay. They could talk things over and be friends again and everything would be better.

She searched all over the house and couldn't find her. Then, at last, she discovered her in the formal living room, standing by one of the large arched windows that looked out on the side terrace.

"Cathy! What are you—"

"Shh!" She held up one hand to shush her, but she did not turn around.

Then, in the silence, Daphne heard it, too. Distant voices. Men shouting. It sounded as though it were coming from far away. You could barely hear it at all, like a faint, staticky signal drifting in and out over a radio.

"What's that?"

Cathy wheeled her face around, scowling. But her eyes looked afraid.

"Don't worry. Mom hired those security guys to stand down at the gate."

She laughed harshly. "Um, those guys are long gone. I found their belts and badges lying in the grass yesterday..." Her voice was high pitched and strangled sounding.

"Well...what do we do? Shouldn't we be calling someone?"

Cathy looked at her incredulously. Then she abruptly turned and hurried up the stairs, to her room.

Daphne, too, went upstairs, but she went to the master bedroom and looked out the window, where she would have the best view: what she saw, coming along the long curving road up the hill, was a group of bedraggled looking men. Walking among the oak trees and the Japanese boxwood. Walking past the landscaped beds of foxgloves and hollyhocks. In the moonlight they looked ghostly and insubstantial. Like a legion of phantom soldiers. Like they could disappear if you looked at them too hard.

But they were real. And there were a lot of them. And they kept coming and coming.

She ran to Cathy's room to find her packing a large duffel bag.

"What are you doing?"

Cathy would not answer. She seemed to be in some fear-induced trance as she hurried as quickly as she could, stuffing things into the bag.

"Are you leaving?"

"Honey, don't block my way. Go on!"

"No!" She grabbed a stack of shirts from Cathy's hand and flung them to the ground.

"Stop it! This is an emergency. I'm getting out of here."

"Take me with you." She grabbed Cathy's arm and stared frantically into her eyes.

"I can't take you with me. You're not mine. I'm going home to the east coast."

In a blind rage, Daphne stalked the room. There was a dress form standing in the corner, wearing Cathy's latest creation for Daphne: a long stretchy red dress of silky jersey knit, onto which she had been sewing a design of red silk rose petals. Daphne shoved the dress form to the ground, then grabbed the mesh bag of rose petals and flung them into the air; the petals drifted and settled on the ruffled white bedclothes like bloodstains.

"Take me with you!"

"Stop it! Right now!" Cathy didn't know what to do. Daphne, since her last growth spurt, was the size of a grown woman, but she was regressing into the state of an out-of-control toddler. She had taken a tray of glass beads and tossed it in the air, so the beads were ticking and rolling everywhere. Cathy leapt across the room and gripped the raging child-woman by the shoulders. "Get a fucking hold on yourself, for God's sake! Grow up! You can't act like this!"

Daphne stared into her eyes, breathing hard, she had actually grown several inches taller than Cathy in the past months, though Cathy was still stronger and held the girl fast.

"You have to take me with you," she whimpered, crying. "You have to!"

Cathy felt sick with guilt. But at the same time she wanted to slap the girl across the face in exasperation. When Cathy had been fifteen, she had lived the life of a grownup. Taking care of her brothers. Busing tables long hours at a Chinese restaurant to help her mother pay rent.

"Listen," she said tensely. "You need to calm down. Do you have a friend whose house you can stay at?" She knew the answer, but asked anyway. Her words were automatic as a robot's as her mind churned and raced with fear.

"I don't have any friends! You're my only friend!"

Cathy pursed her lips and shut her eyes tight.

From below, there was the sound of breaking glass. And shouting.

"Let's go. Now!" She grabbed her bag, took Daphne by the hand, and they ran toward the narrow back staircase.

They ran through a small side door in the kitchen and out across the large back lawn, which was edged with woods that sloped steeply down to the ocean. "Damn these track lights!" Cathy hissed. "Keep down! And run!"

"Where do we go? We can't go out the gate!"

"We have to hide in the woods..."

"This way. I know a path down to the road." Daphne had used this path for years when she wanted to leave the grounds undetected. She knew it so well, it was like a part of herself. She had never shown it to anyone before.

It was strange to be there in the dark, with her heart hammering in fear, but she gripped Cathy's hand and led her through the brush, over fallen branches, across the little creek that ran through. And still they could hear the noise from behind. There must have been fifty people. She could smell the smoke stronger than ever, and when she looked up through the branches she could see one billowing plume against the slightly paler night sky.

"Come on!" hissed Cathy. "Show me where to go!"

They hurried down a slope and Daphne cried aloud as a

deer suddenly came crashing across their path, white tail flaring in the moonlight.

"Shut up! Do you want them to hear us?"

Before long they broke through the woods to the narrow road that wound around some distance from their gate. The bay glimmered softly in the dark, and the lights of the bridge shown in the distance.

"What do you want to do, find a door to knock on so we can get help?" Daphne whispered hoarsely. Along the road, here and there, were gates to other houses almost as impressive as hers.

"We need to get into the city. I need to get on a bus. Tonight. I'm going home."

"I'll come with you."

Cathy said nothing. She couldn't fight anymore. She could hardly even think straight with the adrenalin pumping through her body.

"What, are we walking the whole way?" Daphne sounded annoyed and sarcastic, even as she kept gripping Cathy's hand tightly. "

"We'll get a ride. Help is coming. Listen." In the distance, a fire truck's siren. Moments later the road was flooded with flashing lights as the trucks roared past them, going toward the house. They had to stand off to the side so they wouldn't be run over. In their wake followed a tarp-covered truck full of soldiers.

"Oh my God, we have to get away, as far as we can, this is crazy," Cathy's words rushed out in a reedy squeak. "They're going to be shooting in every direction. Oh my God. Oh my God, we have to get away..."

Daphne knew she should be feeling afraid. Part of her was. But another part felt taken over by a strange sort of elation. The sense of emergency was like a wave, and she was riding on it, being carried forward at breakneck speed. Her heart beating in her chest, the sirens and flashing lights. The cool evening air that smelled of burning. All of it, the irrevocable sense of it, made her feel more alive than she ever had felt in her fifteen-year-old-life.

"Don't worry, Cathy. We'll be okay."

"JUST...just don't tell me that.! You don't know anything. "

"But the soldiers are here."

"And so what? Don't you see? I guess you can't see. Of course you can't."

"I'm not stupid."

"You aren't stupid. But I don't think you understand how things have changed. Totally. Forever."

"All we have to do is stick together and stay calm. We'll go someplace else. And then we'll make arrangements..."

"Make arrangements. That's cute." Cathy looked up and down the road desperately. "I hope, at least, that the way we're dressed, no one will know that we came from this house."

They were both wearing the same jeans, sneakers and sweatshirts as they had been wearing for days.

"Why would it make a difference if they know who we are?"

Cathy did not answer. There were more military vehicles and an ambulance whizzing past them. She looked all at once very young and scared as the lights washed over her face.

"We'll tell people we're sisters," Daphne offered. "We're runaway sisters..."

"Don't tell anybody anything. You just shut up. Only I will talk."

They walked on in silence. They could still hear the shouts of the crowd, and now the sound of gunfire. But somehow it seemed unreal, like the sounds of Fourth-of-July fireworks. The sky glowed red back where their home was.

Eventually they heard the sound of a vehicle coming from behind them, and they stopped and froze. When they could see that it was an army jeep, Cathy sprung into the middle of the road to frantically flag it down.

"Please! Please!" she cried.

The jeep stopped. It was driven by two young soldiers, their faces dirty with soot. Cathy ran over to speak to them.

"We need a ride into the city. We're...we're displaced. We need help."

"I don't think you want to go into the city, ma'am."

"I just need to get to an Amtrak station. That's all. Please give us a ride."

The driver, a boy with intensely pale eyes that burned in his darkened face, nodded for them to get in the back.

They rode in silence for a while. Then one of the soldiers asked: "Is that your house burning down?"

Daphne, stunned, looked quickly at Cathy. Cathy's expression was opaque, giving no indication of what she was really thinking. Finally, she answered, "I just worked there."

The past tense made Daphne reel inside. She turned away so no one could see her face.

"Who are those people? What do they want?" Cathy asked.

"Bunch of animals," said the soldier in the passenger seat. "Some commie media guy has been stirring them up. Bussing them over by the dozens. Telling them who lives where and what have you."

Daphne huddled down and wrapped her arms around herself. She thought of her mother, only an hour north at the Clinic. What was she doing now? She pictured her lying on a table in am immaculate white doctor's office, a needle sunk into her vein, becoming lost again in that soft haze of forgetfulness as the anesthesia kicked in. Forgetfulness, like a warm cocoon keeping her safe.

Daphne's former elation was suddenly gone. Her teeth had started chattering and she was trembling all over.

"You know, you girls should really be rethinking going into the city." But as the driver said this, they were already driving over the bridge, its bright strung lights suspended over foggy darkness.

"No. Really. I...I mean, we, need to get on a train. Tonight. And that's that."

Cathy sounded imperious, but her face looked frightened.

"Ma'am, I don't even know if the trains are running right now."

"I don't care. I need to get to a station."

"Well, just to warn you," the soldier in the passenger seat turned around. He was a boy, really, with large ears and acne scars. "I don't think you should."

"Well, where on earth can we go then? Tell me that!"

"Do you have anyone who can take you in?"

"Not exactly." They had lived a self-contained life in the large house for so long, alone on a cliff. From house to chauffeured car to tunnels and walkways, no contact with anything unscreened or unfiltered. It was no wonder they had no one to count on.

The jeep drove by an overpass. There were many cardboard boxes and what looked like large wooden crates beneath it, all full of people.

"We should go to the airport," Daphne whispered to Cathy. "Mom can make arrangements if we could just..."

"For God's sake, I can't get your mom!" Cathy yelled. "She doesn't answer her phone! I'm never able to reach her when she's away."

"How much money do we have?"

"Shh! Stop bugging me. I'm trying to think."

"We'll take you to the station by the mall. It's probably the safest one," said the driver.

The other soldier snorted. "Right."

Daphne evidently had phased everything out for a while, because the next thing she knew the jeep had slowed down and was inching down the city streets. She recognized the area, but it looked different. The streets were packed full of people as though they were waiting for a parade. But it was the middle of the night. The soldier who was driving revved his engine and blew on the horn, trying to get people out of the way.

Most just looked back with no expression. But some, mostly the young men, seemed to be incited by this. They yelled and jeered at the army jeep and started to crowd around. Someone threw an empty bottle that broke on the jeep's side. Someone else began to throw rocks.

"Get BACK!" Yelled the soldier in the passenger seat. When the crowd ignored him, he reached for the handgun at his hip and fired into the air.

There were screams in the street as people moved back and ran for cover; Daphne gaped in utter shock. Cathy was bent over with her hands over her head as though bracing herself. "Oh my God, oh my God," she said, "somebody is going to get killed. I can't watch, I can't watch..."

The jeep was able to move on. But by the time they pulled up in front of the train terminal, it seemed there were more people pressing in around them than ever.

Cathy was staring fixedly ahead. It took her a moment to recover herself enough to grab her duffel bag. The soldier with the gun helped them out of the back seat.

"There you are," he said. "You'd better just get in there, fast. Get BACK, you people!"

Again, the shouts and jeering. He got back into the jeep, kneeling on the passenger seat with gun drawn as the jeep rolled away slowly with its horn blaring.

They looked around them. Now the crowd's attention fell upon the two young women who had just received an armed escort, and were now standing helplessly on the sidewalk. For a moment, everything grew quiet. There were mostly men, some women, and a few children. Most looked almost ordinary, except for the raggedness of their clothes. Except for the hunger and keen-eyed desperation that showed in their faces. There was a garbage can aflame in the middle of the sidewalk where people had been keeping warm in the damp cool of the night. For a moment it seemed the only sound was the roar and cackle of the flame.

Daphne felt frozen to the spot with fear of all the eyes that were trained on them. Cathy grabbed her arm tightly and they tried to walk down the set of steps that led down to the entrance to the train platforms. But before they could make it, some of the group blocked them off.

"Who are you?" one of the men asked, a tall scarecrow-looking man with a balding head and deeply hollowed eyes that burned with righteousness. His beard and hair were long and dark. He was like a Biblical prophet in a pair of rotted-away running sneakers. "Why are you so important that they were about to shoot us?"

A young woman, squat and muscular looking, came right up into their faces. "You're one of those rats they drove out from the big houses, right?" She was so close that Daphne could smell her ripe sweaty odor. Her features were soft and cherubic looking, but they twisted into a cruel expression. "You people are shit. And you don't even know it. But you'll learn." She laughed. "You'll learn!"

"Your time has come!" someone yelled out in a yodeling falsetto.

"I'm not one of them!" yelled Cathy. "I just worked for them! It's not the same. And she's just a kid. We aren't who you think we are!" She looked around wildly, appealing to any of the faces around her for sympathy. Finding none, she tried again to go forward down the steps. But people crowded around them, and suddenly it was like a crashing surf of waves threatening to pull them down.

"You are the problem!" She could see the scarecrow guy yelling into Cathy's face. Then she lost sight of them altogether because she was getting swallowed by bodies. Her brain began to reel. Someone shoved her and yelled, "You rich twat! I saw you in the papers! Don't think I don't know who you are!"

"CATHY!" she tried to call out, but in her terror it came out as a strangled whisper. She had lost sight of her, and now it was all she could do to struggle to stay upright; if they knocked her down she would get trampled and crushed. The noise was so loud that she couldn't think. People were pressing in from all directions, not just coming for her but pushing and shoving each other. Daphne was becoming so overwhelmed by panic, she feared she would black out. There was no room to breath anymore. She tried to look straight up, but all she could see were angry faces; they seemed to spin and blur together as a surge of dizziness overcame her.

But at that instant, she felt strong hands gripping her from behind, bracing under her armpits. Cathy? But the voice, a female voice, was one she did not know. It said low but urgently into her ear, "It's okay. Come on. You're coming with me. I'll get you out of here." The voice sounded muffled and strange as though it were coming through the helmet of a space suit. Not knowing what else to do, Daphne sank back into the arms, letting them hoist her up. And once on her feet, she felt herself pulled along. The person had her hand, though she was still too confused to make out who it was in the press of bodies. She could only helplessly follow. Where they were going she could not say, and she did not care. There were no other options. All she could do was trust.

4

It was a girl in a gas mask who had taken hold of her hand and was now running with her down the street. She was wearing a vintage-looking dress, navy with white dots, and a quaint rounded collar. Over it she wore a long shawl-collared sweater. The gas mask was a leather one with metal studs; the mouthpiece was brass and narrow looking. The eyepieces were large and placed far apart like goat's eyes. That was the impression she gave off; she looked like a friendly goat, a cartoon fawn.

Daphne had an acute sense of unreality. Surely she had to be hallucinating this.

But it was real. The girl was guiding her away from all the noise. They were twisting and turning down streets. Eventually they arrived at an area full of warehouses and loading docks and garage entrances. Metal fences and metal doors and dumpsters. They ducked into a narrow alley between two tall buildings. There was a flimsy wooden door, splintered with paint peeling off of it. The girl opened this door and lead Daphne down a flight of cement steps into a basement room. There, they caught their breath, and after a few moments Daphne was able to focus her eyes and look around her. It looked like they were in the industrial room of the crumbling building. It was large, with a damp concrete floor. She could see the boiler in one corner, and candles flickered on a battered Formica table in another corner. She had the odd feeling that she had just stepped into a sacred space, like a church, and that she needed to be reverently quiet.

There were mattresses pushed against the sides of the wall, some that seemed to have people laying on them beneath rumpled bedclothes.

The girl pulled off her mask. Her hair tumbled out, reddish-blonde and shoulder length. She was snub nosed, with pale eyebrows and lashes. Her face was flushed red and she had to catch her breath. She dropped the gas mask to the floor, then smoothed her hair, sighed, and gave a small, sheepish smile.

"I thought you were going to get hurt. It's a good thing I was passing by. "

Now that her mask was off, she looked closely at the young girl she had rescued from the crowd; the girl was unassuming enough, wearing jeans and a faded sweatshirt. But something about her, something that Paige couldn't put her finger on, seemed to indicate that she was upper class. Maybe it was the well-tended look of her long, pale blonde hair with its subtly painted lowlights. Maybe it was the way she carried herself; her posture was erect and straight, almost regal. But her wide, scared eyes seemed to indicate a childlike naiveté. All over, she had that certain look of softness of someone insulated by wealth.

"What's your name?"

But the girl was not listening. She had pulled a phone from her pocket and instant dialed someone. She held the phone to her ear, her eyes distant as she listened to it ring.

"My name is Paige."

But she still didn't answer, and the girl's face slowly became clouded with sadness as whoever she was dialing did not pick up. She put the phone back in her pocket. She looked around her but seemed to be seeing nothing, her eyes quivering and darting. She was like a trapped animal.

"Listen, I don't know what your situation is, but you have to at least talk to me!"

Paige was tired. When she had happened to spot the girl in the crowd she had already been out walking the streets for hours, trying to hand out pamphlets that no one wanted to take. Earlier in the day, when she had tried to get into the office at the college just to print out a few things and drink some coffee, she had found that they'd changed the locks. She had been using that office for months, even though she was no longer officially a student in the English department. So she had been feeling defeated and depressed all day, and by evening only wanted only to go home and lie on her mattress and not think anymore. But then, she had heard the ruckus up ahead and seen the girl. She had looked so young and so helpless. Something inside Paige compelled her to throw herself into the middle of the melee and intervene, before she could even reason with herself that it wasn't the safest idea.

Now, the girl appeared to be both deaf and mute. Was she traumatized? Or did she think that she was so superior that she need not even acknowledge who had saved her?

"Do you have anywhere else to go or not?" Paige asked, a bit impatiently.

The girl answered by bursting into tears. Paige awkwardly put her arms around her, and then led her over to one of the mattresses.

"How old are you? Fourteen?"

"Fifteen," the girl hiccupped miserably. Across the room, one of the slumbering figures stirred. A tall, lanky boy with dark mussed hair and heavy eyebrows. "God, shut the fuck up," he moaned and turned over to face the wall.

"Oh, you shut up Ian. Can't you see she's upset?" Paige patted her on the back. "Do you want to stay here tonight?"

The girl snuffled and nodded yes, frantically.

"Then you have to tell me your name first."

"Daphne."

"Your name is Daphne. You're fifteen. Why were those people giving you trouble, Daphne?" Paige was becoming energized with righteousness, crossing her arms high over her chest. Though her voice was high and girlish, it rang with purpose and authority.

Daphne did not answer, but seemed to retreat into a fugue state again, rocking back and forth.

"Wasn't there someone with you that I saw? A woman?"

"Yes. I have to find her. I have to go back to the station…"

"Not tonight. You can find her again tomorrow."

"Tomorrow she might be gone. She was taking the train, if I can catch her in time…"

"Why don't you just relax? She has a phone, right?"

"Yes…"

"She can call you, right? So don't worry about it right now. I'm too tired to even deal at the moment anyway."

Daphne woke on her mattress at what seemed to be late morning. She had slept deeply, but had a frightening dream. In it, she had seen Cathy walking a block ahead of her on a crowded sidewalk. She had tried to catch up, had shouted to her and tried to make her way through. And then in the way of dreams, the crowded street turned into the white-sanded beach on the island last summer, except that it was dark and stormy. Cathy started to swim far off into the waves, which were choppy and slate-colored. Black storm clouds were on the horizon. A wave in the distance was growing larger and larger, it was enormous, coming in faster and faster…she cried out to Cathy to look out, but the wave was coming, now a powerful wall of water as high as a skyscraper, and just as it was about to break over her Daphne came awake with a start, her heart pounding.

The others were awake already. Dirty light was coming in through several small windows high up on the wall, through which she could see feet walking by outside. The cinderblock wall was splashed with graffiti. Profanities, band names. In blazing letters, arched like a mantra above their heads, was written, WHOOP THAT TRICK!

Paige and a slightly younger looking black boy with short dreadlocks were sitting at the Formica table. They were eating from a box of cookies, saying nothing, the boy reading a tattered copy of The Tibetan Book of the Dead as Paige folded some papers. The guy that had told them to shut up the night before was sitting up on his mattress, watching something on a laptop. Something with music, a woman's voice singing in a digitized whine over a drum machine. On another mattress, a very short girl with her head hidden inside an enormous black hoodie was asleep on her back, limbs sprawled out, softly snoring.

Everyone there seemed to be teenaged, which made Daphne feel vaguely threatened. Even though she was a teenager herself, she never fit in well with people her own age. And these teens looked unlike any she had ever gone to school with; there was something unkempt, wild about them, and it made her instinctively shy away. She could even, faintly, smell them. The smell of unclean bodies.

She turned over so that she faced the wall, overcome with a hollow ache deep in her stomach. A despairing wave of homesickness. She longed for anything familiar to make her feel moored again.

"Hey," It was Paige, looking over at her. "I know you're awake over there. Why don't you have something to eat?"

Daphne shook her head. She felt as though a great weight was pressing down on her, and she couldn't move.

"Suit yourself. But if you stay here all day, I'd rather you lay low for now. No coming in and out. I've got some things myself, so..."

Daphne rolled back toward her and said weakly, "I'm not staying here. I have to go to the train station."

"To look for your friend, you mean? Was she your friend, sister or what? Where was she going?"

She didn't know how much to answer. After all, it might not be safe to let these people know who she was, where she had lived. They might hate her, too. They might be angry and turn her out on the street. And then what would she do? She was completely alone.

After a long moment, Daphne answered, "She was going to New York."

"Were you going with her?"

Tears welled in her eyes. "I...don't know."

"Was she family?"

Instinctively, she knew she couldn't say, she was my stylist. So she said, "She...helped out my mom. We just knew each other a long time."

Paige looked at her, frowning. "You're a rich girl, right? It's okay. We aren't going to knife you or anything. That woman was like, your nanny, right?"

Daphne looked at her helplessly.

"Listen, we don't care. We're a civilized bunch."

"We are so above it all," droned the dark haired boy, not looking up.

"Well, we're a damn sight better off here, in a group, then all of us on our own in the fucking cesspool."

"Yes. I like to soak in our own little inlet. Where the bacteria is known."

"Excuse Ian. He's a bully."

"I'm not a bully. I'm sarcastic."

"Sarcasm is bullying, Ian! Nerds can be bullies, too!" Paige shook her head, as though to clear away her agitation. "Anyway. I was the one who found Daphne yesterday. She was in a spot of trouble. She let an army jeep drop her off right in the middle of a crowd."

"Out here, they don't care much for soldiers. I'm Calvin, by the way." Calvin spoke in a smooth, low monotone. He locked eyes with her for a long moment, with a look of serene curiosity, before abruptly turning back to his book. His air of insular calm made the rest of the room seem even more ringing and amplified by comparison.

"Are you all friends or something?" Daphne asked.

"Well, Ian and I knew each other from the university. He plays in bands and works at a punk club. Among other things," she looked at him significantly. "Wendy and Calvin are sixteen so they quit school and are just hanging. This is a safe place to squat. People like us just kind of took it over. People come and go, word of mouth. It works out okay, I guess."

"How did you get yourself into this mess?" Ian smiled at her ironically. "You seem like a real babe in the woods."

She drummed her fingers, bit her lip. What was there to say, except the truth? "They burned my house down."

"Who?"

"A mob of people. I don't know. I got out of there. A soldier gave us a ride. And then...I don't know. I don't even know what happened."

"Well, as Calvin said, there are some hard feelings toward the army presence, as it were..."

"Random people are shooting at the soldiers, it's insane," Paige's eyes grew huge. "It was bad enough when the Guard started patrolling, but now all boundaries are falling apart..." While Paige was talking, she was busy folding pamphlets. A stack of paper was on the table beside her. She was folding faster and faster as she spoke, slapping the paper down.

"So, you must have lived in one of the mansions." Ian asked.

"I...I guess you could call it that."

"Private school?"

"Yeah." She felt an instinct, now, to get it all out in the open. "My mom is an actress? Amelia Andrews? My dad was..."

"Oh my God, yeah, so...right. Then your dad was that biotech capitalist. Huh. Wild." He smiled at her now, though he still drawled in an offhand, ironic way. Though his eyebrows still arched a tad sardonically. "That's intense, man."

Paige was looking at her, lips parted, saying nothing.

"So, that means there must be people looking for you, right?" Ian's expression changed. Suddenly he looked angry. "I mean, are armed guards going to be storming this place any minute now?" He looked over at Paige. "What is this? Why'd you have to—"

"What was I supposed to do? I couldn't just walk away!"

"But what are we going to do if..."

"Don't worry!" Daphne cried out over their arguing. "No one is looking for me!"

"Oh, come on. I don't believe that. You're their princess. They will be coming." Paige had stopped folding and was looking at Daphne closely.

"My mom doesn't know yet, she's away. She's so out of it anyway, it doesn't even matter, but she has really has no idea."

"And your nanny? Or maid, whatever, staff?"

"She didn't want me with her, anyway," tears welled up in her eyes as she confronted what was the truth. "She wanted to go home and get away from my crazy family."

"Do you want to try to call your mother?" asked Paige, her voice softening.

Mother. The word stirred up so many conflicting feelings in Daphne that she could hardly tell them apart. But most keenly she felt the sting of thwarted longing as she turned her eyes down and shook her head no.

And so Daphne came to occupy the second mattress from the right.

Life in the industrial room had its own rhythms, its own everyday ordinariness. Ian, who was nineteen, slept from six AM until noon, and always spent his evenings elsewhere.

Calvin's short frizzy dreads were like a jagged crown on the top of his head. When he spoke, one had to lean forward to hear his low monotone. He had a solemn formality about him that often made Daphne feel shy and foolish. And yet, she noticed, he seemed to have a strange tic; every so often his face would pucker into anxiety, and he would reach up and touch his own face, right below his right eye socket. It was a secret, fleeting gesture that she had seen him make many times, and it made her feel a rush of protectiveness towards him. He worked a lot in the stockroom of a grocery store, unloading pallets and breaking down boxes. He didn't make much money, but he was able to bring home bruised fruit and day old pastries, his wordless contribution to the communal food stock.

Wendy, who had a pierced nose with a silver chain that connected to an ear cuff, kept more or less normal hours. She washed dishes at a restaurant. Usually she always wore the same thing, a faded promotional malt liquor T-shirt and black fetish pants, with the enormous hoodie on top. Her hair was a maroon bowl cut and she had big, black painted eyes like a panda's. She was petite, cute, almost child-sized. But she had the unnerving gaze of a feral cat when she watched Daphne from the shadows. Wendy tended to vacillate between charged, nerved up silence and sudden, reckless laughter that seemed to tear uncontrollably from her chest. Daphne had no idea where she stood with her, so kept a wary distance.

And Paige. At twenty years old, she was the oldest. She did not have a job, and yet she stayed busier than any of the rest of them. A lively and theatrical girl, she tended to make the room feel more buoyant every time she was there. She was passionate about her ideas and causes, and never seemed to run out of energy. Even at rest, her wide eyes seemed always to be scanning the room, a faint eager smile always on her lips. She couldn't be still. Paige walked the streets for hours each day, wearing her gas mask, handing out pamphlets about The Sickness.

Daphne was helping Paige to fold these pamphlets. They were nicely done, very professional looking. Paige and her group had done them up at the office of their campus literary magazine.

On the front, in large red letters, the pamphlet read:

UNTIL THERE IS A VACCINE, ANY OF US CAN BE THE NEXT VICTIM.

Inside, it continued, It is the most insidious weapon ever used against us in a time of war. It could happen to you, me, or someone you love.

Daphne, who had nothing better to do, was idly looking at the color photos. A lot of these were of people in ragged clothes, the "victims," eyes either wild with despair or flat-lined and blank. There was another page of photos were from the war zone. Soldiers in combat, fighting the enemy, the supposed source of the Sickness, supposedly a type of man-made virus. These photos all looked slightly odd to her, subtly retouched and digitalized. Daphne leaned in until her nose almost touched the slick paper; maybe if she looked close enough she could actually see the pixels. Or the world broken down into ones and zeros.

She remembered Cathy, telling her about the brother who had come home from the war with his "problems." She considered all she had never known about Cathy and now never would. A wave of self-loathing and despair threatened to drag her down.

On the back of the pamphlet it said, Love yourself. Be strong. Wear a mask. There is HOPE for a vaccine-soon. And there was a picture of two gas masks, adult and child-sized, inside the pink outline of a heart.

"Do you?" asked Paige, who had been watching her keenly.

"Do I what?"

"Wear a mask? I mean, do you have one?"

"No..." She didn't know what to say. Ian was nearby listening. Ian, who said that it was all a government conspiracy to sell drugs, and mocked Paige loudly whenever the subject of The Sickness, her advocacy group, or the pamphlets ever came up. While Daphne liked Paige and did not want to hurt her feelings, neither did she want Ian to see her as a fool.

Saying nothing more, Daphne's fingers were drawn again

to the nape of her own neck. She could not stop touching the new bristly bareness. They had all convinced her it would be a good idea to cut off her hair so that she would not be easily recognized. Wendy had done it with a pair of dull kitchen scissors. It had made her feel queasy to see the long locks of pale blonde fall to the floor, one by one. She had always had long hair. It was startling to have a piece of herself cut off that way, and so quickly. Wendy had seemed to relish the task, though, walking around her, taking snips and then standing back to take in the effect, snipping a little more. "No more prissy princess," she said, smiling devilishly, "That life is gone now. I did a good job. You should see how it brings out your eyes. I mean, you are, like, practically all eyes now, you should see yourself! "She gathered up the blond locks on the floor and shook them at Daphne, laughing. "I'm keeping this. I can use it for some kind of, like, dark magic ceremony. Scalp of a rich girl. I've always wanted one."

But Daphne couldn't see herself. There were no mirrors. All her life, it seemed she had been surrounded by mirrors at every turn. Now she had no idea how she looked. And she had the feeling, from the way Wendy had laughed delightedly, that she did not look good.

Sometimes she walked with Paige on her rounds, to hand out the pamphlets and collect donations. She declined to wear a mask. She did not believe in the cause, frankly didn't know what to think of it at all. But she did want to start venturing outside into sunlight again. She had lain on her mattress for too many days, crying and staring at the wall.

With her new chopped hair, and wearing an Army surplus trench coat (there were piles of communal clothing laying in heaps on the floor of the room) she knew she looked like a whole other person. As they passed by light-dazzled windows she was able to catch glimpses of this new self. She did not look male or female. There were long, uneven bangs that sloped into her face, obscuring her expression. Sometimes the shock of seeing herself looking so foreign was enough to rouse her from her sadness. But just for a moment.

Though Daphne refused the offer of a mask, Paige always wore hers. Paige liked to dress with great care in items chosen from her meticulously maintained thrift store wardrobe. That day she was wearing a fitted blazer and a long, blue crushed velvet skirt, narrowly cut and with a slit for walking. With her tall lace-up leather boots she looked vaguely Victorian. The whole ensemble suited perfectly the brass-and-leather mask that covered her face.

Most people on the streets ignored them or brushed them away when Paige approached them. It was amazing, the sheer number of people that crowded the streets. The older ones tended to look dazed, as though they were walking through a dream world from which they couldn't will themselves awake. Always there was the smell of burning in the air. Younger people ran around in excited packs, yelping like dogs. They liked to break windows for fun. They also, according Paige, liked to beat up other random homeless people. "Don't try to talk to them. If we leave them alone, they'll leave us alone."

They walked far to knock on the doors of some of the pretty, bright-painted houses in the nicer part of town. Paige would give her spiel about the symptoms of The Sickness, would show the photos and speak to each person emotionally, but succinctly, like the bright high-achieving college girl that she had once been. She knew all of her facts and statistics.

Sometimes the people would donate a couple of dollars to make them go away. One woman, a handsome older woman with a large ring on her gnarled finger of pale green stone, said, "I'm sorry, dears. But there is no Sickness. There is no Other. The Sickness is all in ourselves. It's in us, do you understand?" She said this softly, like a lullaby, then smiled at them sadly as she closed the door in their faces, a classical music station murmuring from the room behind her.

They used the few dollars they got to buy lunch, noodle soup from a Thai place. Paige tried to stay focused and positive in front of the younger girl, but she was tired. "You do reach people. Really. Not everyone. But you can make a difference." She wasn't sure she believed it herself anymore. But the cause was all she had. She had put so much time into it already, along with her handful of friends from the University. She couldn't let them down. And it was the only thing that could make her feel focused anymore.

"How did you get started with all this, anyway?" Daphne asked, watching the passers-by through the grimy window of the tiny storefront restaurant.

"At school. I was involved in a lot of stuff. This. Amnesty International. Even Earth Liberation, for a while. To make the world a better place, you can't just talk about it. You have to fight, you know?" But there were deep shadows under her eyes, and she would not meet Daphne's gaze. The gas mask rested on the narrow counter between them, like a third presence watching silently.

"Where is your family?"

"Oh, I don't know. Around. They're sort of hippies. My parents never liked to settle in one place very long. Last I heard they were staying with some friends in Seattle. "

"Do you see them?"

"Not really. Lately, I had been putting myself through school. Then I lost my grant money. One thing led to another and here I am!"

"It's not so bad. Living where we are, I mean. It's almost kind of...romantic, isn't it?"

Paige looked at her with a disbelieving smile and shook her head.

"I don't think I would call it romantic."

"You guys all get along there, right? Basically?"

"Well, actually, there can be a lot of tension. Someone is always mad at someone else. There are power struggles. Sometimes I feel like we were all shipwrecked together, and that cannibalism will set in any time. I myself want to get out of there as soon as I can."

Daphne tipped her soup bowl to her lips, savoring the last of the broth. When she was done she wiped her lips with a satisfied sigh. She was almost overcome with the coziness of the lunch counter, and the pleasure of having a friend to talk to. "You know? Wendy still seems to hate me. What's her deal? What did I do?"

"Wendy is just wary of change, that's what I think. She has trust issues. Fucked up family. She's basically just a scared little girl."

"And Calvin doesn't really talk to me, either."

"Calvin doesn't much talk to anyone. He lives in his own head. He thinks the world isn't real. He thinks we're all illusions." Paige raised her fingers in quote marks. "But if you ever really pay attention, you'll see he's not even really reading. He stays on the same page all day. Hiding behind the book. Poor kid."

"And Ian?"

"What about Ian?" She gave Daphne a sly sidelong smile.

"Well...nothing." She had gotten the vague sense that Paige and Ian had been involved at some time in the past. Their bantering had just a little too much edge to it. There was a quiet intensity of something not quite buried.

And anyway, Daphne felt too flustered to talk about him without color rising to her cheeks. She found herself studying him sometimes while he slept; his face was lean and fine boned, with a faint pink scar at the top of his cheekbone where he had once been hit with a bottle onstage. His bottom lip was so full and lush, almost like a girl's. But she mostly liked to look at his hands, which were large and calloused from playing guitar. There was an ornate, curlicue image of a tiny dagger inked onto the underside of one of his wrists. It made her shiver to think of the sharp artist's needles and how they would burn away at that most vulnerable place.

~

She had been dreaming that she was in her old bedroom at home. Her father was sitting on her bed, telling her a story like he did when she was little. But this time, it was a story she didn't understand:

The young girl's evil stepfather was a magician. He performed his tricks before hundred gathered in the town square. He could levitate. He could make a packet of cards leap from his hands and dance in patterns in the air. He held everyone spellbound. Absolutely transfixed. But his greatest trick of all was planting false memories. One day he planted in their minds a false memory of a broken clock. And time stopped. The world stopped. Until the townspeople figured out the trick and they stormed the stage and tore him apart limb from limb.

In the dream her father stopped and looked deeply and profoundly into her eyes after telling the story. And the room behind him, the soft lavender drapes and swaths of tulle, burst into flame, smoldering and filling the room with obscuring smoke...

She woke with a start, not knowing where she was at first. Then she remembered, she was on a soiled bare mattress, on the concrete floor of the industrial room. By herself, surrounded by the sleeping forms of strangers. Somewhere outside on the streets, people were yelling and arguing. There was a sound of a gunshot, screams, and then silence again.

She lay staring at the ceiling, with a tingling in her fingers and toes. The tingling spread up her extremities. The sensation frightened her, and her heart began to beat faster and faster. Fear flooded her synapses, gripping her like a seizure. The darkness made her feel as though she were being buried alive under heavy earth, and if she didn't scramble and claw at that heaviness then she would die. She couldn't breath, there was no air left.

She rolled onto the floor, writhing and whimpering, her face pressed against the cool, damp concrete that smelled faintly of gasoline, letting the tremors pass through her body.

There was nothing left to do but let the fear take her over, like a thundering train overtaking her on the tracks. Just when it seemed like it was killing her for sure, it began to ebb, just a little at a time, until at last she could breath again, every muscle in her body quivering and sore.

I've caught it, she thought, all alone in the early morning hour, more alone than she had ever felt in her whole life. I have it. I have The Sickness.

A rainy afternoon. Wendy and Calvin were sitting at the Formica table, passing a joint back and forth. They did not offer it to Daphne.

"You look so sad, laying there all the time," Calvin called over to her after a while.

"She's slumming," said Wendy, exhaling sweet smoke toward the ceiling. "She's the only one of us who has the option to leave, but doesn't" She turned to Daphne. "Why don't you just call your damn mother if you're so sad?"

Daphne glared back but didn't answer.

"You need to go find a job so you can contribute for once!"

"I have contributed," she answered faintly. She had gotten cash from pawning the bracelet she had been wearing when she left home. A delicate bracelet of woven fine gold chains, mesh-like, strung with tiny sparkling diamonds. It had been a gift from her mother for her birthday in the islands. She remembered opening the tiny package wrapped in silver tissue. She remembered the elegant, understated blue of the Tiffany's box. It was the color that the ocean was, which was so clear and pure, such a lovely view from the cabana. And the sand had been so white.

"Aw, back off, Wendy. Daphne's doing the best she can." He called over to her again, "What was it like, in private school? I have always wanted to know." Calvin had a habit of speaking louder and more slowly to her than to other people, as though she couldn't hear or understand.

"I don't know," she mumbled. "I liked art class, where I could just do my own work. Other than that, it wasn't that great."

"So, the experience is overrated, in your opinion." His large round eyes were inscrutable. She did not know whether he was mocking her or not.

"Well, I wasn't happy there."

"Were you happy anywhere?"

"I don't know. Maybe. Sometimes I was happy if I could get far away from everything." She had been happy on the island. There, she had walked along the shore by herself, gone down into the village. A native woman had sold her a little doll, a human figure carved out of a large root. She couldn't tell if the doll was male or female. When she put it to her nose it smelled wild and pungent like all things that grow underground. All things that are real.

He nodded, sagely, four or five times, then shrugged. "Wendy and I went to the same school. But it was a nowhere kind of school in the wrong part of town. Most kids are poor and black, and if they're white, they're usually goth." He gestured toward Wendy, who wasn't looking at them. She was tearing the empty paper sleeve of a straw into tiny little pieces, and then blowing them across the table like snow. Her magenta hair had faded lately to a dull mauve, and her dark roots were growing in. "You know what our art class was like? Nothing but cutting up magazine pictures and pasting them onto things, like a bunch of retarded kindergartners."

Wendy, who had been dead-eyed before, started laughing uncontrollably, her face gone scarlet, bent over double. Calvin remained calm and poker faced as ever. "What did you make in private school art class?"

"Well, everyone thought I was good at painting and drawing. Maybe I was good. I don't know. I guess it doesn't matter. It's just something I did a lot."

He nodded again. "I hope you don't mind me asking you questions?"

"Nooooo, I guess I don't mind. I don't really care. All of that stuff is over for me now, so I feel like I'm talking about someone else."

"I'm just analyzing, see. I'm like a sociologist."

"Oh, my God," moaned Wendy, "Give me a break."

"What kind of teachers did you have?" He cocked his head to the side and peered at her keenly.

"I don't know. I guess most of them had master's degrees. The classes were really small, like ten people. So they were always in your business. It was kind of annoying. If you didn't seem like you were doing well enough, they'd send you to the faculty shrink. They'd put a lot of kids on meds. I think they got a kickback from the pharmaceutical company. That was the rumor. It was creepy."

There was a silence. And then Wendy chuckled. "You really don't show an interest, do you?"

"What do you mean?"

"Aren't you even going to ask about our teachers? Aren't you curious about how the other half lives?"

"I am interested. You don't have to be so nasty."

"Oh, am I being nasty? It just seems like you think you have an awful lot of problems. That you have it pretty bad. It's really pretty amusing. Considering."

"Considering what?"

But Wendy just sighed.

Calvin cleared his throat. "Okay. No cat fighting. Don't need that. We don't need any more conflict, this place is bad enough as it is." He turned to Daphne, leaned forward in his chair, with his hands folded in his lap. If it weren't for the spiky braids and chunky silver rings on his fingers, he would have looked like a CEO at a board meeting, bridging a deal.

"Here's the thing. People might give you a little trouble because...well. We may have had a bit of a different life experience. You may have been sheltered from a lot. And it's not your fault. Not your fault at all. No one can help what they're born into. But people might resent you, you see?"

"Especially when you act ignorant as hell. You need to get wise. Get your head out of your own ass." Wendy hissed.

"But I do care. I am interested! What was your school like?"

"Well," Calvin looked up into the air, considering. "First of all, we had no teachers. At least not in the physical sense."

"Ha!"

"Shut up, Wendy, I'm explaining. We had these, like, telecams bolted high up on the walls? They would beam the teachers in." Calvin paused and stared into space, remembering it all. Remembering his math teacher, who had been transmitted from India. The way his face slowly took shape on the screen from blackness, like he was rising up to the surface of dark water. Every time he emerged onto the screen like that, his eyes would widen for just a second or two, as though he had actually been transported, and was surprised to find himself in America, face to face with about fifty bored and surly American teenagers. His skin was a nice burnt orange, his lids heavy and relaxed looking once he started the lesson. He was Calvin's favorite program. He always wondered if the teacher was a Buddhist, as Calvin himself was.

"Those shit things were always breaking down," said Wendy cheerfully. "Then we'd have no class at all. If they weren't already breaking down, some kid would try and make sure it did! One time this meth head kid busted the telecam all to shit with a piece of metal pipe. It was awesome."

"Wendy, it's not a good thing. I felt bad for those people just trying to teach..."

"They get paid, like, six dollars and hour? That's what I heard."

"Wow," said Daphne, not knowing how else to respond. "What else?"

"What else? What do you mean?" Wendy was smiling at her now, but her eyes looked hard and mean.

"I don't know…just what else?"

"It wasn't the most morale boosting place," Calvin said thoughtfully. "They don't even have a graduation ceremony there. When you graduate, they announce your name on the intercom, and put a Polaroid of you on the office wall."

At this, Wendy started laughing again, clutching her stomach. "That place…they were always dragging me down to the office. The secretary was this little Chinese woman who wore plastic gloves. Sitting at that desk with those Polaroids on the wall behind her head. That place was so sad, man! And that cheesy framed poster that had the tank in silhouette with the sunset behind it that said, COALITION OF THE WILLING…"

"Aw, yeah, and there was a fist hole in the wall right beside it!"

They both broke up over this. Daphne sat quietly, remembering the last time she was in her own principal's office, with its soft recessed lighting, the glass brick walls and the low, minimalist furniture. It had had a Deco feel to it, like the setting of an MGM musical. It seemed she could never really see that room, really see the woman sitting in it, until the moment was long passed. That long ago day, when the lynx was shot. Mrs. Pierce with her whippet thin body like an aging ballerina, and the way she elegantly held a teacup level between the fingers of her manicured hands. How frail and girlish Mrs. Pierce seemed now, as Daphne sat remembering her in the dank shadows of the industrial room…

But she could not bring up all of that. So she asked, "Why did you both stop going to school?"

Wendy rolled her eyes. "Haven't you been listening? What's the point? Nobody's learning anything. They just herd you up there so that they can manage you better. So they can keep all the teenagers in a big warehouse with armed cops patrolling. I'm way better off on my own."

"What about your parents?"

"Fuck my parents."

"But where are they?"

Wendy sighed. "Hell if I know. My mom is living with a violent, controlling asshole. I told her it was him or me. I refused to put up with him anymore. And, well. All I can say is here I am. And I wouldn't change a thing. I'll never go back to that madhouse."

Her dark eyes burned with so much concentrated anger that Daphne quickly looked away. She and Calvin exchanged a wary glance as Wendy smashed a cockroach with one of her scruffy black boots. "Fucker," she muttered.

They sat for some moments. Wendy's anger seemed to ring in the air like the ping of a struck crystal glass. Then Calvin said quietly, "I've been living on my own for a while. So. None of this is much different to me."

Wendy was sunk into her chair with her arms crossed, staring at nothing. Her eyes, usually so shrewd and assessing, had lost their hardness. At that moment she looked like a little girl, bewildered and hurt by whatever she was remembering. Daphne felt as though Wendy's vulnerability was something she shouldn't see. So she averted her eyes and turned quickly back to Calvin.

"Where is your family?" she asked gently.

"My mother is gone." As he said that, his face puckered for a fraction of a second, almost a twitch, and his finger again went to that spot on his cheekbone. Just a small, involuntary gesture. A touchstone that enabled him to go on with his story.. Then. he gathered himself back again, and spoke matter-of-factly:

"I remember the day they had come to take my mother away. She had been in a bad state of mind. She had been a social worker for twenty years, working for the state. But when the economy went bad, she was laid off. There were no other jobs. She couldn't pay the bills, and there wasn't enough to eat. She couldn't sleep. It seemed like being in crisis mode for so long had started messing with her mind. She'd stay up all night, sitting at the kitchen table in the dark, rocking back and forth, wailing and whimpering until I led her to bed.

"When we got the eviction notice, she threw it away. This can't happen, she said, This is not supposed to happen. Not to me.

"She just got worse. She retreated into another world, a dream world where I couldn't get to her anymore. She began wandering the streets, singing hymns, bobbing and weaving. I didn't know what to do.

"Then there came a day when she decided to spray paint the trees. She told me that she could find no beauty in her life anymore, and it was making her so sad that she couldn't think straight. So she got out these paint cans that were out in the garage, and just started painting the trees. Purple, orange... and she was so intense about the whole thing that I knew I couldn't coax her in, so I gave up and just sat in the living room. I just started reading a book and pretended like none of it was happening. And that's when they took her away."

Daphne's eyes grew huge hearing Calvin's story. He described the how an unmarked government van pulled up to his house. Two men came out wearing jumpsuits covered in patches. They looked like racecar drivers, only the patches had names of prescription drugs on them. Things like Zovirax, Nimotop, and Cyclogyl.

Theirs was a rundown neighborhood at the edge of a commercial boulevard. The house was a dingy little bungalow with a wire fence, next to a Pizza Hut. Startled white faces were looking out the window as the men in jumpsuits escorted his mother into the van.

"And the thing is, she didn't even fight them!" Calvin said, shaking his head. He described the moment the spray can clattered to the ground, and how she actually looked relieved as each man took an arm. The shaky desperation that had been showing in her eyes for months just slipped away. And they took his mother, a little woman with long beautiful braids, a high round forehead, and such tired eyes. She didn't even look back.

A third jumpsuit guy, the one who was driving, came over to where Calvin stood, stunned on the front porch. His blonde hair was buzz cut under his Noctec baseball cap. He looked not much older than Calvin. He was carrying a clipboard.

He gave Calvin some paperwork and explained how his mother had been "sponsored" by a pharmaceutical group based out of Texas. Then he gave Calvin some literature about the greatness of biotechnology. They featured cartoons of an anthropomorphic pill named Pete. It was the story of how Pete was developed, and later patented. Pete, round and notched like a baby aspirin, grinned winningly and gave a thumbs up.

After the spiel, Calvin signed the paperwork. He didn't know what else to do. Then he and the young man were both quiet for a minute. They looked at the van, but the windows were blankly tinted. An empty liquor bottle started blowing down the street, clinkety clink, as the clouds came in.

"Hey, listen," the boy said. "Your mother is what we call a dysfunctional person. But with her help we can come a long way in drug development. We can tailor a medicine just for her. And you'll have her back again, better than new. Because we understand genetics better than ever."

Calvin wondered how such a nice seeming guy could work for people like that. People who were frightening to him. Genetics. The word made him think not of chains and blueprints, but something alive and capricious, zipping through his blood like tiny neon fish.

After they had gone, Calvin went back into the house and tried to read again, but the heavy silence was too much for him. He felt numb, and mostly looked out the window. It was about to rain. The wind had rattled the chain fence at the used car lot across the street, and the bunches of balloons they had tied everywhere were trembling, burning bright against the stormy sky. His house was empty now. And there was nothing for him to do because this is what happened, this was just the way it was.

"So I had to leave. I heard about this place from some kids

at school. And here I am.”

Daphne didn’t know what to say. It was a terrible story. And an unpleasant thought was forming in the back of her mind. *Those are my people that are behind all that. People like my father behind all that...* But she chased the thought quickly away.

Now Wendy was smirking to herself. She lifted the plastic straw to her lips and blew a spitball across the room toward Daphne.

“Stop it,” Daphne whispered quietly.

“What’s that, princess?”

At that moment Daphne felt something fray and break inside of her head, and her body seemed to be working independently of her thoughts. She observed herself getting up from the mattress and crossing the room. She gripped Wendy’s wrists and glared into Wendy’s face, their noses inches away.

“You. Don’t. Know. Me!” she hissed. “You do not know me. So leave me ALONE.”

Wendy had never looked into this girl’s face before, not really. Her pale lashed eyes burned with such intensity that Wendy wanted to look away. But she willed herself not to.

“Let go of me.”

“You will leave me alone. Say it!” She squeezed harder, her heart racing

“Ow! Are you crazy?” She was growing a bit frightened. Daphne did indeed look like a girl gone mad. The expression in her eyes was of a concentrated will power that even Wendy feared she could not match. Like looking into the sun, it hurt; she had to turn away first.

“Okay, okay. I’ll leave you alone. Jesus! I didn’t realize that you were insane!” But her tone lacked conviction.

“God, will you people just stop it?” Calvin was leaning forward, with his face in his hands.

Daphne returned to her dirty mattress and lay down, facing the wall.

“Crazy bitch,” muttered Wendy under her breath.

"I'm not what anybody thinks I am," said Daphne quietly, to herself, feeling drained now that such flaring anger had released itself.

"Don't be pissed at me, "Wendy said to Calvin. "You saw her attack me. She's the psycho. Paige will just let any damn person into this place. Thought she was bringing home a wounded puppy. Hah!"

But Calvin had retracted into himself, eyes shut, breathing deeply, as though the room around him no longer existed.

Daphne had started wandering the streets during the day. She knew soon she would have to get some kind of work. She needed the money. Plus, she wanted to occupy herself. The more time she was able to stay away from the industrial room, the better.

Ian had gone away somewhere, had been gone for a week. He had not told anyone where he was going or if he would be coming back. (Daphne had worked up the will one evening to ask where he was off to, and he had snapped None of your business! It still stung.) Things were much more boring when he wasn't there teasing Paige or having philosophical arguments with Calvin or telling stories about being on the road with his band. She wondered if that's how it was going to be. If people really came and went so quickly. She hoped Wendy would leave. Though she had stopped her ridicule, she had been giving her long, dark looks from across the room that seemed to promise vengeance.

She tipped her face to the weak winter sun. At least, she had to admit, there was something nice about being totally free. She felt amorphous. She had no name, no identity anymore. She could go anywhere and do anything. No one was there to tell her not to. She could die on these streets and no one would know what would become of her. That thought gave her a small chill, of both fright and exhilaration.

The people she passed by on the sidewalk had a grayish hue to them. Everyone looked somehow antique, no matter what their age. Men, women, children. They looked shadowy and tragic, like the denizens of Pompeii. And yet they were ineffably alive, as alive and real as she was.

As she passed an alleyway she noticed movement. Quick animal movement, down back behind some trash bins. She caught a quick flash of an orangey, mangy tail with a white tip. A fox! It seemed to feel her glance, and it froze. They stood there looking at each other, human and animal, in a moment of mute wonder.

And then he darted away. Before she could even think about what she was doing, Daphne dashed down the alley, trying to follow it. There weren't as many animals in the city anymore since they were getting killed off, and some said, eaten, by the homeless. And the fox was so beautiful. She wanted to remember it so that later she could paint it. She wanted to paint this gray blurred landscape, and the way the fox looked against it, a streak of burnt orange. She would paint it, someday. Though she did not know how she could get paint, or canvas, or the space to do the work. As it was, she had to find the money just to pull her weight and buy some food every once in a while. She had never known hunger in her life, until now. Never known what it was like to feel light headed and too weak to think straight.

And the lynx had not appeared to her at all since she left home. She missed him, almost mourned his absence. Maybe he had just given up on her.

All of these things were on her mind as she rushed around the corner and down the sidewalk, looking this way and that for the fox. She had been so lost in her own world that it took her some time to become aware that she was being followed. There were footsteps close behind her as she wound this way and that, looking into the shadows and corners.

She wheeled around to see a man, frozen in his tracks, looking at her with great interest. He was not one of the usual crowd. He had graying longish hair, small, round, wire-rimmed glasses, and a long face with a wide, thin-lipped mouth. He was tall and slope-shouldered, not exactly the threatening type, but his eyes had the alert look of a bird of prey, trained right on her.

He came no closer. The smile that spread over his face was fond, and his voice soft and almost dreamy-sounding when he said, "Hello, Daphne."

The voice seemed to trigger something in her mind, some submerged memory. A half forgotten dream, one that was not good. A chill went through her.

When she turned and ran away, he did not follow.

5

Paige had been born twenty years before, underwater, on a commune full of artists and scientists. "And I can remember it, too," she said to Daphne as they walked along the brick laid walkway of the university campus. "I remember the tiled birthing pool, and the way the water threw these flickering reflections on the ceiling. And the way that the midwife spoke, in a kind of singsong, soothing voice. Just random shit like that."

"That's amazing," said Daphne. She actually found it pretty hard to believe. But she liked Paige's stories. They drew her in, and made her share in Paige's vision of the world being full of magical and uncanny things.

"Yeah. It was kind of a crazy upbringing. A lot of drama. But I have lots of really happy memories, too, like..." But Paige stopped herself mid-sentence, deciding to keep the rest to herself. She was thinking of being three years old and playing in a field of pumpkins with the other commune children. There was an old man living there, a political activist on the run from the law. He liked to fold origami. He had folded Paige a tiny prancing monkey, held it aloft, and said, It's the science of the practical, my dear.

But she didn't want to share too much with Daphne. The girl had been with them for two weeks, and was still looking a bit fragile. Talk of family might put her back in a bad state of mind. Even though Paige rarely talked to her parents anymore, and nothing had turned out the way anyone had hoped, she still was proud of her unconventional upbringing. It made her feel special. But this girl looked so pale and stunted, in spite of her privileged background. Like she had been deprived of something vital as oxygen. Paige looked at her, wondering how to go on.

Finally, she asked her, gently, "What is your first memory?"

Daphne was quiet a few moments, and then said, "I remember playing by myself, while we were staying at our villa in Italy. I was playing in the topiary."

Paige nodded. She did not want to ever give the impression of being surprised.

"There was a big chink in one of the brick walls. I liked to peek out through it. One day, when I looked through, I saw someone looking back. It was a little boy, about the same age as me. We would just look at each other and make faces, make nonsense sounds. Until my nanny saw what I was doing and took me away. But I remember him still. He was kind of dirty looking. And too young to be by himself."

"Maybe he was a gardener's kid or something?"

"I don't know. My nanny was weird about it, almost angry. Part of me asks, did it really happen? Or was I so bored and lonely that I hallucinated him?" It was certainly possible. The grimy little boy on the other side of the wall certainly had the mien of a specter. She could swear he had been wearing ragged short pants and high black shoes. But she did not want to tell Paige this detail. Paige would make too much out of it.

At last they made it to their destination: on a corner beside a lamppost covered with ragged show fliers and for sale notices, they met the person who was to give them Daphne's new fake ID. Paige exchanged a few quiet words with a skinny, chinless boy with darting eyes. He gave her a yellow envelope and they parted.

They sat down on a bench and Paige tore open the envelope.

"Looks perfect. There you go! The new you!"

Daphne was shocked to look at it. It was a driver's license, authentic looking, saying that her name was Angela Harris and that she was seventeen years old. It was the photo that surprised her most of all. She had posed for it one night in someone's squalid apartment. She did not look either male or female. She looked hunched and furtive; she looked almost, she thought, ugly.

She didn't even know why she needed this new ID. But Paige was so excited about it that she didn't want to bring her down.

"I told you I have great connections!"

They made their way through the campus streets. It felt so different there, from the rest of the city. For one thing, it was safer. The university hired its own security to patrol the perimeters twenty-four hours a day. Paige had quickly flashed her ID and told them that Daphne was her visiting sister.

The people that they passed by were all young, all healthy and clean looking. Mostly white. Their clothes, like Paige's, were a mishmash of different eras. Nineteen-forties dresses. Color block sweaters from the seventies. Rubber bracelets and ripped stockings from the eighties. They looked like children in costume flooding the streets at Halloween.

Quite a few of the young people still wore gas masks, though the trend appeared to be dying out. Daphne was glad she had never worn one; it embarrassed her that she had even thought she had caught The Sickness. She had fallen prey to the same paranoia as everyone else. She would never let it happen again.

Paige had quietly stopped wearing hers one day, but she said nothing about her decision, and no one brought it up. Some days Daphne was used to seeing them on other people, but other times she was taken aback by them all over again. Against these walkways and stately brick buildings, these friendly signs with arrows everywhere...the gas masks just didn't look right. The scene looked like a surrealist, altered photograph. The masks were in all colors, like perverse spring flowers. Acid green, heather blue, tulip pink.

They reached a modern-looking concrete building that above the door was labeled Humanities, and Paige let them in with her new key. ("They can't keep me out, they have to try harder than that!) She had gotten a job under the table working for her old department. It was menial work, lifting boxes, making copies, and organizing files.

"But at least it's something, you know? I don't like being cut off from university life, to be honest. It makes me scared. To think that out there is all that there is. Depressing."

Daphne came with her to help out a little bit, but mostly to keep her company. And she had to be honest: Paige was the only friend that she had. She was lucky that Paige not only tolerated her constant presence, but seemed to enjoy the role of mentor. She made Daphne feel brisk and purposeful, and able to see the world in brighter colors.

She watched Paige, the way her strawberry blonde hair fell into her face. She was wearing an odd outfit that day, some kind of a stiff polyester sailor dress with a chunky sweater thrown over it. This room, tucked behind the main office, was dingy and cluttered with boxes and papers, but at least it was clean and warm and well lit, and there was coffee. Daphne sank into the worn chenille sofa and sighed.

"You know," she ventured, "I think someone was following me the other day."

"Who?"

"Some guy. Kind of old. There was something about him. He was kind of like...academic looking. I don't know. He was looking right at me. I ran like hell."

"Maybe he wanted to proposition you. You do look kind of like a little boy with that haircut..."

"I don't think so. I thought I heard him say my name, but I may have imagined it. And I feel almost like I've seen him before. Almost like in a dream or something. So now I'm pretty sure my mom has people looking for me."

Paige nodded. "Well, yeah. I know you don't want people bringing up your mother, but ..."

"Why do you think I don't want you to bring up my mother?" She asked this more sharply than she had intended to.

"I don't know, I just... had this instinct that it was best to just not go there. I don't know exactly what your situation is, because you clam up about it."

Daphne looked down into her lap. All at once, she felt a swooning urge to throw herself into Paige's arms and have a good cry. But she fought back the feeling and kept her face as still as possible. She looked at Paige, who had been good to her, who had saved her from an angry mob and given her shelter. Paige, who was brave and spirited and strong in her ideals, even if they were misguided. It was Paige's caring and sympathetic face that almost made her open up and tell everything. But even as she yearned to, she felt something in her chest close tightly, like a fist.

"I guess I don't want to talk about where I came from because I'm just trying to forget about it." Because she didn't want to think of things like the night she threw the beads and rose petals, screaming like an enraged child, begging her stylist to not leave her behind as they came to burn her house down. It was absurd, it was painful, it was humiliating. And no one would understand.

Instead, she decided to change the subject. "So when is Ian coming back?"

"Who knows," Paige muttered, looking down at the desk.

"Have you two known each other a long time?"

"I don't know. It depends on what you mean by 'know each other'." She looked up through lowered eyelids at Daphne.

"Did you ever used to, like...date or anything?"

Paige shrugged, with a little laugh that sounded painful. "I first met him when I was still in school here. When I was living in the dorms. He was a friend of some friends. He had no place to stay. He had been living out of his van since he was sixteen, but then he had to sell the van. And so he was sleeping on people's floors. Sort of living the on campus illegally. I inherited him, I guess. He started staying in my room. He kind of stayed there a long time, if you know what I mean."

"What is he like?"

"Well. I'll say this, he is very interesting. I was just kind of intrigued by him. He was so smart, he could talk about anything. You know. Very quick, and street smart, too. He has a lot of potential, but he can't settle. He doesn't want to be tied down to anything. Or anyone."

"And so did you..."

"Yeah. We kind of dated, for a while. I mean, my friends noticed we were falling in love before I even knew it. I just got sucked in. For a while, he was working construction jobs, just until he had enough money to quit and go traveling."

"So what happened?"

"I traveled with him, for a while. We actually lived on nothing. Hitchhiking, staying at campsites. It was so exhilarating at first, you don't even know! But then we started fighting a lot. He's kind of a slut. He claims to have two children by different mothers in other states, but I don't know if he's lying."

"Do you still love him?"

She rolled her eyes and sighed. "I don't know anymore, it's all so screwed up. I used to get free tuition when my dad taught here, but he got in some trouble and bailed, so that was that. I got some scholarship money, but it didn't last long, and soon I had nowhere to go. Ian knew a place to squat. And here we are. I can't say I love him because I really don't know him anymore. I get this feeling he's involved with some strange people. There's something that he's keeping secret. But you can't say anything to him. He gets obsessed with whatever he's doing at the moment. Until he is not obsessed anymore. That's when he just walks away."

She gave a small, trembling smile, then quickly looked in the other direction.

~

The days were short and dark. The holidays came and went unobserved in the industrial room. And one bleak and dreary Thursday, Ian came back.

He had returned at some point in the early morning, and Daphne was surprised to find him there when she woke up. He was sleeping deeply, fully dressed and wearing his high black boots, stomach down, arms and legs sprawled out.

She was the only one awake, so there was no one to observe her. She came closer, close enough so that she could smell the scent of him that wafted from the grimy blankets. It was a yeasty kind of smell, a little like baking bread. She had never noticed his smell until he went away. Sometimes, if she was alone, she would lie on his mattress to catch the faintest whiff that was left behind.

He was snoring softly. She watched his face in profile against the filthy pillow. His lips were parted. They were dry, cracked and bleeding. She imagined lying down beside him, touching her lips to his. She had never experienced sensations like this in her body before. Her skin was flushed, her nerve endings suffused with endorphins. She felt as though she could either faint or go running circles around the block.

But she didn't do either. Instead, she felt a new bright clarity emerging in her mind. All the overwhelming feelings she had been having, feelings of rawness and ugliness, were turning into something different. A crystalline sense of resolve. Instead of feeling overwhelmed by despair, she concentrated on this feeling of something hard and diamond-sharp deep inside her. Knowing she had nothing to lose made her feel a wild kind of joy. There was no reason at all anymore not to go after what she wanted.

~

They were just little things. A pair of latex gloves filled with gravel and dirt, knotted and left in the pockets of her army coat. A muddy shoeprint on her pillowcase, placed carefully in the center. And one evening, chills ran through her body as she pulled back the covers to discover a bundle of her own flaxen hair, tied up in black ribbon and left on her mattress. For some reason this unnerved her more than anything. She lifted it with the ends of her fingers like some dead animal.

She confronted Wendy with it later the next day, tossing it onto her lap. "What are you, trying to catch some witchy spell on me? Grow up."

Wendy just smiled and looked up at her with mock innocence. "Why do you assume it's me?"

Daphne would not answer, but gave her a cold stare. "You won't get rid of me."

"Why don't you go back to your nanny and your private school you baby..."

"I'm not going back."

"Why? Do you really get such a cheap thrill from slumming with people like us? I really don't understand why you stay here. Not that I care either way. But, really, why?"

Daphne walked away. She would never tell Wendy why she wanted to stay.

"Well, fine. Don't answer me like the rude bitch that you are!"

Wendy lay back on her mattress and kicked her foot against the wall in frustration as Daphne put on her coat and stalked out the door. What she did not want to admit to herself was that she did care. She had spent a whole afternoon at the library on a public computer, looking up paparazzi shots of Daphne with her beautiful, freakishly young-looking, movie star mother. Even though she hated herself for it, she could not stop looking at clips of Amelia Andrew's films. The wonder and jealousy she felt looking at these images was like a scab she could not stop touching.

She had actually seen one of these movies once, when she was a little girl. She and her mother, a hotel maid, had been kicked out of the house by her mother's raging drunk boyfriend. They had gone to the movies to have a place to stay, buying tickets to one show and then sneaking into all the others through the afternoon, dozing when they could, eating food snuck into her mother's purse.

This particular movie they didn't even know the name of. They had walked into it mid-story. On the screen was a beautiful blond woman in a long satin evening gown. She seemed to be running out of an opera house into the dark evening. When she got far enough away, she touched one of her huge emerald earrings, setting off a bomb, and the opera house exploded. She took off her heels and ran barefoot through the city streets, laughing aloud in villainous joy.

Though Wendy was young and exhausted and overfull of too much movie viewing, and her mother was crying softly in the dark beside her, she had smiled at the scene for some reason. It was so beautiful to her in a way she couldn't name.

To steady herself, Daphne would stare at the club's high ceiling with its grimy air vents that were furred with dirt. That way, she wasn't as bothered by the crowd of people that pressed around her; the hiss and din of what felt like thousands of young voices could be the blood in her own ears. The rushing of water, a current she was able to tread. Anything can happen here.

Daphne had begged for Ian to bring her to this place, so she couldn't very well show that she didn't like it. She had tried to remain cool and aloof looking as they approached this warehouse space, which even from a block away had throbbed with raucous, crunching guitar chords. Daphne did not look up at all at the teenagers in baggy clothes, drinking alcohol in the parking lot. She did not raise her eyes to the large, shaven-headed man who sat on a stool at the door, checking for membership cards. When he saw it was Ian he nodded and waved them through with a "W'sup, man."

The smell was horrendous, the sweat of many human bodies, and more faintly, urine. Because it was an all ages club there were many people there who looked about her own age. Some even younger. Some had brightly dyed hair and wore tight, shiny clothes with lots of metal and buckles, sort of like Wendy did. But most were wearing a similar style of dark, raggedy clothes that were three sizes too big; they looked like grown adults who at the wave of a wand had been suddenly shrunk, so that their pant legs puddle and their sleeves fell past their knuckles.

The club, which didn't have a name at all but went by its street number, was run all by volunteers. Ian would be working at the mixing board at the concert that night. A band called Bleach was slated to play.

Ian guided her around the place, leaning close to her ear in order to be heard, and explained that she would be working at the snack bar selling soda and chips and candy. "Cool," she said flatly, though she felt a mild panic when she saw the plywood kiosk where she would be working. It was so small and so pressed in by bodies; it made her claustrophobic to look at it. But she would not back down, not now. She did not feel like her usual self. There was recklessness inside her that was foreign and thrilling. She would jump off a building if he asked her to.

Everyone was so loud, all of them just young kids showing off, so obviously excited to be there. Here and there teenagers were already passed out cold, though it was early in the evening. Someone had brought a little dog. She couldn't see it in the crowd, but she could hear it, its high shrill yips echoing off the grimed brick walls.

Ian walked her around some more, showing her the battered door to the bathroom, from which came the sounds of retching. He brought her over to see the panels and knobs he would be using, and he even explained a little about how to work the mixing board.

"So you think you'll be all right?" he asked her.

"Sure," she answered. He was really being quite nice, which made her beam with warmth inside. He had not seemed to want to bring her at all, but she was determined. She would not leave him alone about it. She needed something to do, she said. She couldn't find a job. She couldn't just lie on her mattress all day. She would do anything. All she asked was for one night, just to see what the place was like. At last he relented. It seemed like he didn't want anyone in the industrial room to know where he went or what he did. It gave her pleasure to be the only one to know.

There was no cash register. She kept the cash in a burlap apron tied around her waist. She grabbed the snacks and soda cans from cardboard crates on a shelf behind her. The work itself wasn't hard, she was always able to add and subtract quickly in her head and made change easily.

Throughout the evening, she became less overwhelmed by the crowd and the noise. During slow times she would just watch, fascinated. Such a raw, feral energy lifted from this packed roomful. It was nothing like being in the hallway of her school where everyone was so bland and detached and ironic all the time. This was a whole different feel. The boys and girls were wild-eyed and exultant in their own being. They chattered, they shouted, they slammed into one another, laughing even as they became bloody and bruised. Laughing even as they swooned or vomited. The point was, they were here, they were part of this now, where they were young together and anything could happen. The feeling spread to Daphne like a virus. She felt a heightened awareness. Everything seemed significant. But at the same time, nothing really mattered. And it was an intoxicating feeling. The music was full of screeching guitars and boys wailing and screaming. It was so loud that it rattled the inside of her skull and made her heart feel like it was beating at a lopsided gallop. But she could still hear bits and pieces of the hundreds of conversations buzzing around the room.

"...got to get cigarettes from the twins before we..."

"...like a political campaign. You know, from the bottom, up..."

"...so he shows up in this tweaked-out, puke yellow sports car with Locomotion written on the side and we were like..."

"I AM NOT A LID OR A POT!"

"It was the ultimate beat down! He whooped that trick!"

"...and then her dad saw the scorch mark on the wall and he said..."

"I AM NOT A NUMBER! I AM MANY NUMBERS!"

The voices began to blur and echo in her head. It was starting to seem like one long, continuing conversation. Even though it made no sense, she could in a way follow it if she didn't think too hard about it all.

A boy with rows of braided blond hair and shaved eyebrows jumped behind the counter and gave her a bear hug. "Where on earth have you been?" he shouted, staring straight into her eyes with great urgency.

Daphne was too stunned to answer.

"I am my sister's keeper!" he said, apropos of nothing. When Daphne looked confused, he pointed out into the crowd. "That's my sister, over there, for real," he said, leaning in to speak in a low and confidential manner.

The girl in the crowd that he gestured to was stout and broad-shouldered, her brown hair straight and lank to her shoulders.

"When they took her away, she was skinny and crazy. When they brought her back, she was fat and sane."

The girl, who had noticed them looking at her, gave Daphne a small, stone-cold smile, but her eyes were flat and lifeless. Daphne, unsettled, looked away.

"You are skinny," he said, poking at her ribs. "Are you also crazy?"

"No."

"Well, that's good. Because my sister? Is like a ghost haunting her own life. Never let it happen to you, because when you come back it's all different. Cause it's like—" But suddenly he stopped in mid-sentence and rushed away as abruptly as he had appeared. Daphne looked again at the big-shouldered girl, who wasn't smiling at her anymore but looking cool and impassive as a statue. Then, surprisingly, she gave Daphne a wink. She felt herself blush hotly with confusion.

Throughout the evening, she would look over to see if she could find Ian. Sometimes she thought she caught a glimpse of his profile, but it could have been any of the rangy young men yelling and laughing in the dark.

After the show was over, she couldn't find him at all. She handed her money over to one of the bouncers, then went to go lie down on a battered plaid loveseat. She leaned her head against the armrest and closed her eyes. She must have fallen asleep because the next thing she knew Ian was shaking her awake.

"You ready to go?"

"Yeah," she said sleepily. The place was as packed as ever, though it was slightly quieter. There was no music playing, but people were gathered, watching something on the stage. It was some kind of performance art. A woman in a fishnet body stocking was reciting poetry, her snarled words dropping to the ground like cigarette butts. She had a round, very young-looking face. In her hand was a small knife, which she would periodically use to slash a small cut on her arm. When she did this, the kids would cheer.

Daphne stared at this dully as they made their way out. Everything had a dreamlike, hallucinatory feel to it. None of it seemed real.

The night air felt bracing and fresh after being inside the club for so long. The moon was bright and all the streetlights were on, throwing huge stretched shadows on the ground as they made their way home.

Daphne began to feel revived again. "That place is really cool," she murmured in a small voice.

"Yeah, I've been going there since I was fourteen. It's never changed. It's an okay place," he said distractedly.

Daphne had to scurry to keep up with him, he always walked so quickly. She tried to think of something, anything, to grab his attention. Then said in a rush:

"I've never had the chance to do any stuff like that. I always had people watching me. I used to get in trouble for even going outside on my own. My mom, you know. She only ever wanted me to go to shit like movie premieres and fashion shows. She, you know, always took me to the Paris shows, even when I was just a little kid. The runway models scared me so bad, in their platform heels and all their war paint. I cried! It was a fucked up way to live when you think about it..."

She looked at him sidewise. She did not usually like to discuss any of these things. But she found now whenever she dropped details it piqued Ian's interest. And now, as they walked together with their feet echoing on the night pavement, she was starting to take a perverse pleasure in trying to shock him.

"I mean, when I was a four-year-old I wore couture and tiny high heels and lipstick. I walked in these tiny steps like a geisha. I had no idea how to act like a little kid. I didn't even have friends. I thought the paparazzi were my friends! I thought they were these friendly robots with flashing eyes, and that they loved me and I loved them back. I thought it was all normal."

Success. He was now looking at her with a disbelieving smile, one eyebrow cocked.

"So you wouldn't go back to it?" he asked. "Ever?"

"No. Never. I'm glad that I got out. And I hope they burned that house to the ground. "

"Why do you feel that way?" His voice was teasing, flirtatious. She was stymied for a moment, and could feel the heat rising to her face even in the cool darkness.

"I think people like that deserve it."

"People like what?"

"People who shut themselves away in that world. They think they're special. They really do. They think they were chosen by God or something."

"Do you believe in God?"

She shrugged, mind racing. "It's like, I guess, they don't know the value of life. You know?"

"How old are you?"

"Fifteen."

"What do you know about the value of life?"

She paused for a long time, looking down at the ground. "I know enough that human beings should treat each other with respect. Not as a means to an end."

"Did someone treat you as a means to an end?"

She would not answer that. "Well, those people take advantage. They want to keep all the knowledge and power to themselves. They...these people...they make all this money from data. Information. They go to war with other countries over information. It's incredible. Biotech and genetics and stuff..." Stop while you're ahead, she told herself. So many times before she had gotten herself in trouble by acting as though she understood more than she did.

Ian was looking straight ahead, with a faint sneer on his face. She told herself that he was sneering at the world she was describing, not her. At last he snapped out of it and turned once again to Daphne. "So, you renounce it all?" he asked with an ironic lilt to his voice.

"I spit on it. The evil and the shallowness can kill you. You should see my mom. All chip implants and altered genes and I don't know what. Trying to be young again. But it's even more than that. Trying to be alive again is what it really is."

"Well. Can't blame her for trying, I guess." They walked along a few moments in silence, then Ian said, "Actually, I know a thing or two about them myself."

"Them?"

"Your people. I've met some of them. That is, I'm acquainted with them." He smiled at her and wagged his eyebrows as though he had a secret.

"Who?" Her heart started beating wildly with alarm.

"I'll tell you sometime. But let's just say I deal with those high rollers. And they are a lot more human than they would want anyone to know." Now he was chuckling to himself and Daphne was feeling very nervous. But he changed his face to a more serious expression and asked, "Aren't they trying to find you?"

"Yes. I'm pretty sure they are. This guy in the street was watching me. He knew my name. He even tried to chase me but I got away from him. I ran through some alleys and lost him, so it was cool." In fact, he had not chased her, just given her that curious look of a scientist looking at his specimen. Which was more unsettling than anything, but did not make a good story.

"You shouldn't have pawned that bracelet," he said, smirking. "They can track you down that way. That's probably what happened."

"How did you know about that?" She was stunned that he even paid attention. It had been Paige's idea, going to the pawn shop. Daphne had never even heard of a pawn shop before. Yes, he was probably right.

"I guess I was kind of stupid."

"Naw. You're not stupid. I don't think you're stupid at all. I think you're a lot smarter than you give yourself credit for."

"Really? I don't feel very smart. Not right now. I honestly don't have a clue what I'm doing..." She had probably said too much. She didn't want him to think that she was pathetic.

"You're just young. You'll figure it out. You have potential. Your antenna is up. You have great sensibilities."

She did not know what he meant by this, so she said nothing.

"Hey. I'll tell you what." He looked at her now with great seriousness. "I think that maybe it'd be a good thing to take you with me next time.”

“Take me with you? Where?”

“I’ll show you what I do to make money. I’m sort of in the service industry.”

“What. Am I going to be helping you?”

“Well, for right now you can just watch. I think you’d appreciate it. It gives you a whole different insight into human nature and whatnot.”

Her heart was racing, but she asked, “When?”

“Tomorrow night. I’ll come get you.”

He was looking right at her, a half smile on his face that she didn’t know how to read. His eyes were so blank and expressionless, like a shark’s. It scared her, but at the same time made her feel thrilled and reckless. She would do anything with him. He was all she thought about anymore. She covered her mouth with her hand in a pretend yawn, to hide the fact that she was smiling. She tried to look nonchalant. But inside, her heart was galloping, her blood teeming through her veins. She felt ecstatic.

She slept deeply, slept until late in the morning. When she woke up there was no one in the room except for Paige, who was sitting at the table with a takeout coffee, her chin in her hand, staring into space.

“So, how was it last night?” she asked Daphne softly, absently, not looking in her direction.

“Oh, it was cool, I guess. Really loud. Really dirty. Kids passed out everywhere, it was kind of gross.”

“Ian lives at that place,” she sighed, stretching. “I used to go there sometimes, back in the day. But then I grew out of that phase. I’m too old for it now, I guess.” She was trying in vain to catch Daphne’s eye and hold it. Daphne just glanced at her, a little annoyed. Sometimes she felt that Paige needed too much attention, and right now she wasn't in the mood. She was still tired, with a small headache throbbing behind her eyes.

"It's not all performance space. They have artists's studios, too. Did Ian tell you about that?"

"No."

"Well. I know you love to draw and paint. I think it would do you good to get back into it. Don't you think?"

"Maybe."

"Hey. Are you okay?"

"Yeah. I'm fine. Why?"

"You just seem a little...I don't know. Off. He didn't try to mess with you at all, did he?"

"No!" She said it louder than she had meant to.

"Okay! Okay! Calm down. I was just asking. Because I know him a little better than you do. I'm just making sure he's not taking advantage of... you know. A young girl far from home."

"I'm not a child, for Christ's sake."

"No offense! I swear. I know you're not a child. But you have to admit, you're a little inexperienced. That's different."

"I don't have to admit anything."

"What I'm saying is that you don't have a lot of experience with boys. I mean, you've never had a boyfriend. You told me that already. "

Daphne did not answer, and did not even look up.

"And Ian is a lot older than you. He's nineteen. And he's mixed up in a lot of strange things and knows a lot of strange people, and you need to be aware of that. If anyone...suggests anything that you are not comfortable with, you don't have to do it."

"Well, I don't know what you are imagining. No one has tried to coerce me into anything. I went to the place with him. I worked at the snack bar. I didn't even see Ian all night. I fell asleep, he woke me up, and we walked home. Okay?" She pulled on her jacket roughly. "I'm going out."

Paige sat gaping at her silently, with a wounded look in her eye. "That's fine! You didn't have to say it like that."

"I'm sorry. I'm just going out. I need some air." Daphne was feeling so uncomfortable even discussing the issue that she was flushing red.

"Listen, I didn't mean to get all big sister on you. Maybe it's not my place. But I do feel kind of like someone should be looking out for you." Her body seemed to collapse a little, and she hunched over the table. Occasionally, in repose, Paige just looked tired.

"Yeah. It's okay. Really. I'm not mad. I'm just... I'll be back soon."

By the time she got out, the sun was high in the sky, reflecting off the windows and the asphalt, hurting her eyes. If only she could find a place to be alone! It seemed like up until now, her whole life she had been alone. Now she never was, and she craved solitude. It felt as essential as oxygen. There was always someone else in that dank, depressing room that she lived in. And that someone would either be staring daggers and plotting against her, like Wendy, or reading philosophy and ignoring her, like Calvin. The only person who was not there nearly enough was Ian. Even this morning, he was already gone who knows where. Probably tired of being around all of the losers.

Self pity, once started, knew no bounds. There was nowhere she could go to clear her head. The streets were full of so many people, and they were always so loud. Fighting with each other. Jeering at the soldiers until they fired their guns into the air, which only caused more screaming and more chaos.

And in the midst of the crowds, sometimes she thought that she caught a flash of the man. The man with the round glasses and the frog lips, who knew her name. She couldn't say for sure, but a couple of times she thought she'd seen him, like an image in a book when you speedily flipped the pages. An impression, a blip on her consciousness. But unsettling nonetheless.

She bought a sandwich at a kiosk. This was the last of the pawn shop money. She had to do something. But she did not know what. Jobs were hard to come by. You had to have friends and connections. She had neither.

The only quiet place she could find was a little area behind a liquor store where some plastic crates were stacked next to the dumpsters. She sat down on one of them, willing herself to think and feel nothing. There were constellations of cigarette butts on the ground around her feet. One of them still let forth a thin tendril of smoke. Suddenly she heard a shuffling noise coming from the dumpster, a thumping and thrashing that made her hair stand on end. Overturning the plastic crate, she quickly moved away.

There was nowhere that she could be alone. And yet she was as lonely as she had ever been in her life.

Earlier that night she had gone to bed convinced that Ian would not come for her, that he never intended to take her anywhere. So she was very startled to feel herself being shaken awake, as a voice whispered:

"Daphne. Come on. You said you wanted to come."

Instantly she sat up, as though she had not been asleep at all but merely lying back and resting her eyes. "I know. I am coming," she answered in a normal, daytime type of voice, even though she was groggy and disoriented. And also thrilled to have been wrong about Ian.

The room was dark and quiet as they made their way out the door. They did not say a word to each other as they ran up the steps to the sidewalk. Then he led her to a minivan that sat idling at the curb. It was navy blue, conservative looking, the type a housewife would drive her children to school in. But this one was old and faded looking, with scratches and a dent on one side. Ian slid the door open and motioned her into the backseat. With a slight tremor in her hands, she obeyed. The van was filthy with empty cigarette packs and fast food wrappers.

Ian came around and got into the front seat beside the driver, a young man with shaggy blonde hair and a sharp, hatchet-like profile. His hair must have been dyed blonde because his eyebrows were dark and met in the middle, giving an inpatient expression to his face.

"Daphne. Jonathon," Ian said by way of introduction. The young man nodded at her through the rear view mirror.

"I think this is a really stupid idea," he murmured to Ian.

"Hey, she really wanted to come. I mean, she's looks like a baby. But she's a subversive. Wants to know how the world works."

Ian himself was not even sure what exactly had compelled him to bring the girl, to shake her awake in the middle of the night. It probably was a bad idea. But something about talking with Daphne the other night had made him see her differently. Though he thought of himself as worldly, he had never met someone like this before. It was like meeting a young being from another planet, or a princess from a fairy tale dropped from the sky. It all seemed like some kind of test for him alone. Of what, he didn't know.

The thought of the privileged world she had come from filled him with anger and contempt. But also, it somehow aroused him. And the thing was, she wanted his help. She wanted him to mold her, he could see it in the way she looked at him. It made him feel, for the first time in his nineteen years, almost noble. He couldn't stop stealing glances at this pale, strange girl in the dark back of the van. What did this all look like to her, through her eyes?

The van vibrated with a strong judder as it made its way down the city streets and then out, onto the freeway. Daphne had a vague notion that they were heading south. But she was too nervous, and excited, to make much note of where they were going.

Eventually they took an exit that led to an area of wide, bucolic, tree lined streets, and then they were driving through a type of residential area that she was very familiar with. There were large estates that were so far back from the road, behind walls and gates and trees, that they couldn't be seen at all.

The van slowed down as they approached a tall iron gate with the house number written out fully in cursive script on a large oval medallion. There was a button and speaker set into a concrete column; Jonathon pressed the button, and a faint staticky voice, a man's, asked who he was and what business he had.

"RealLife. We're here for his regular appointment. We're in the book. Same time, every Sunday night." There must have been a security camera, because Jonathon held up some sort of laminated ID card with his photo on it. Daphne was able to read it quickly as he fit it back into his wallet. She saw that it said Jonathon Presley, RealLife Reenactments: Let Your Innerlife Come Alive!

There was a pause, a beep, and then the metal gate slid open admitting them.

The private road twisted and turned several times. The grounds of the estate were impressive, with lots of gentle sloping hills that seemed to be a velvety green even in that dead time of late winter. There was a large stone fountain with a spot lit spout of water burbling into the air.

"Look at all this bullshit," murmured Jonathon. "It floors me every time."

The mansion was now coming into view; it looked recently built, in a spare, modern, flat-roofed style, reminiscent of Frank Lloyd Wright.It was very long and laid out with many different decks and levels, shuffled gracefully like a spread stack of playing cards. Some of the walls were made of large cement blocks of random sizes masoned together. Some were all of one piece with shapes cut out in the center, oval and rectangular. And still other walls were all glass, and seemed to be made of sliding panels. Inside, you could see one living area illuminated in the night. A large room with a couple of long, low couches and a long, low coffee table. There was a huge painting on the wall of what looked like a gigantic red square. Standing in the middle of this room was a gray haired man, arms folded, looking out into the night. It was like the set stage of a play. Daphne watched with her eyes riveted. When the man saw the van approach, he dropped his arms and slumped a little. He clasped his hands in front of him like a penitent.

They pulled up to the front entrance, a graceful structure with wide, glassed double doors and an overhang of concrete that looked heavy, but nothing seemed to be holding it up. The whole house seemed to be a trick of optical illusions. Beautiful, but trying to play a trick on you.

The guys both got out. "You wait here," Ian said. "We'll be back."

They opened the front door without ringing the bell. Shortly, Daphne saw them enter the large living room where the gray haired man stood. He did not acknowledge them, but stood slumped over, facing away, resigned to his fate.

She was astounded to see Ian slip a long piece of black cloth from his coat pocket and wrap it around the man's eyes, looping around his eyes again and again and then tying it in a knot. Then he took another strip of black and bound his wrists together in the front. The whole time, the old man did nothing to fight back. He was utterly passive. Daphne's heart pounded in fear, her mind reeling. What was going on? What was she witnessing? Could they all go to jail? But...but the guard had let them in, and seemed to know who they were! The whole thing couldn't be dangerous then, could it?

And then they were leading the old man out the front door. They brought him out to the van and slid open the door. Then, shielding the top of his head, they helped him into the backseat next to Daphne.

As they got into the front and started up the engine, Daphne stared, dumbfounded, at the man beside her. Since he was blindfolded, he couldn't look back at her. More than anything else, this was what filled her with pity. It made him seem so vulnerable, the fact that he could be seen but not see back. And he was so hunched over, shell backed in his posture. He was working his jaw, doing something with his jaw, almost like he was chewing or grinding something with his teeth. But there was nothing in his mouth. It seemed like some kind of nervous tic. Or he was trying to set his mouth still, to keep his chin from quivering.

They drove back out to the gate, pushed the button and it slid open to let them out. No one said a word. She could not take her eyes off the doomed looking man. He was wearing a soft cashmere sweater over a button down shirt, and his pants had a knife crease down each leg. On his feet were and expensive looking pair of driving moccasins. His hands, bound together helplessly in his lap, were pink and very clean looking, the nails had a soft gloss to them, as though they had been buffed. His face was also very pink and clean and baby-soft. He smelled of a good sandalwood aftershave.

As she had been taking this all in, she hadn't noticed where they were driving. Now she saw that they had left the lovely leafy area and had headed back on the freeway in the direction from which they had come. Soon they were taking another exit that led into a commercial area of restaurants and gas stations and run down strip malls. They drove for a bit along the boulevard before suddenly pulling into the parking lot of a storage center where people could rent little garage-type spaces with corrugated metal doors that slid up and down. No other cars were there. They pulled up to one of the structures at the furthest end of the parking lot, far from the tiny front office.

Ian and Jonathon helped the prisoner get out. Daphne followed behind since no one had told her to stay where she was. They walked up to one of the metal doors, and Ian unlocked a padlock with a key and slid the door up with a rusty sounding screech.

This storage space was a large one, the size of a two-car

garage. But there was nothing at all in it. With the flick of a switch, a strip of fluorescent tubing above their heads came on. The ceiling was low, the cement floor was echoing and damp. The light fixture was buzzing like a fly and blinking rapidly, giving a little of a strobe light effect. Daphne felt all at once, very suddenly, dizzy and nauseous. She wanted to run out into the parking lot in case she threw up, but Ian had pulled the metal door down again.

He must have seen the stricken look on her face, because he asked, "You okay?"

"Yeah. I'm fine."

He leaned in a little closer to her. "Don't worry. I know how it looks. But he pays us to do this." Ian's whisper was perfectly audible to all in that little room. But the old man's face betrayed nothing. He continued to bend his bound face toward the ground, pink jaw creaking back and forth. Ian chuckled. "It's fucked up, isn't it? But just remember this is what the guy wants. It isn't cruel if it's what he wants, right?"

Now he was looking at her with a merry look in his eye, trying to coax her to smile. But she could not.

Jonathon led the man to the far wall, where he stood as though before a firing squad. He removed the cloth that bound his hands and yelled, "Sit down!"

The old man slowly slid down the wall and sat down, leaning against it, cross-legged. He started to remove the blindfold, but then Ian barked at him, "Leave it on, motherfucker! Did we say you could take it off?"

"No," said the old man quietly. "I-I'm sow-ry." Daphne's eyes went huge. I'm sow-ry. That accent. So familiar. She recognized it before the rest of her brain could catch up...

"You are pathetic," growled Jonathon. "You are to do only what we say, when we tell you."

"I-I'm sow-ry, I can assure you..."

"You can assure me? You pretentious piece of shit!"

"Who do you think you are?" Ian taunted. He came over to

the man and shoved him with his foot, and he went slumping over to the side. "Who do you think you are? Tell me!"

"Nobody!" He held an arm over his face as though afraid of being struck.

Ian did have his leg drawn back, as though he were going to kick him in the face. Instead, he shoved the man on the shoulder.

"Damn right, you're nobody. Say it again!"

"I'm nobody."

"Again! Louder!"

"I...I'm NOBODY!"

Daphne, in spite of herself, cried out, "Stop it!" But her chest was so constricted, her throat so tight, that it only came out as a hissing whisper.

"Huh?" Jonathon asked, tonelessly.

"You have to stop it!" Daphne answered, voice quivering.

The old man's face turned upwards, suddenly alert. "Who else is here?" he asked. "There's someone else here?"

"Shut up!" Both the guys yelled at once, and the old man cringed.

Ian went over and grabbed him by the collar, shaking him. "How dare you speak without permission? You worm!" The old man's head was flopping around like a flower on a drooping stalk. "You want to see? You want to see what's going on?"

Roughly he grabbed at the black cloth, untying it and pulling it off with a great jerk.

The old man blinked at the bright light, wondrous as a newborn. And then Daphne caught her breath as she realized who he was: Nelson Holmes. Her father's venture partner who he had worked with for decades. A member of her family, practically. Until her father died, and then he never came to visit anymore. She saw an image in her mind of him at her mother's fundraiser, ruddy cheeked in the candlelight, smiling in his tuxedo, his beautiful wife beside him dressed in golden snakeskin.

It was hard to reconcile that image with this one. Mister Holmes looked haggard and elderly under the sickly flickering fluorescent tube, leaning against a cinderblock wall. His eyes were still adjusting to the room. It took a few moments until he seemed to place exactly where he was. And then he scanned his eyes from Ian, to Jonathon...and then, further back, to Daphne.

His eyes grew large when he saw her. His mouth gaped open for a few moments, his ruddy face gone white. His expression was sickened and dazed. His lips were moving as though he were trying to form words, but nothing came out at first.

But at last he was able to whisper, "Daphne?" He tried again to draw his breath, and was able to stutter, "I-is that you, Teacup?"

She couldn't answer him. She was too shocked. He had been her father's closest associate...their two families had gone to Aspen together when she was little...he had always been so jolly, so smooth and self-assured! When her father had died, it had been Mister Holmes and his wife Rosemary who had practically moved in. They had helped her mother handle the press and arrange the finances. True, they had seen very little of the Holmes' since that time. They have abandoned us, just like everyone else, her mother had said during one of her low times when she didn't leave her bedroom. Those people are like a sect. We have been excommunicated! But Daphne had never held it against them. Not exactly. The Holmes' were like a lot of people that they didn't talk to anymore: not cruel people. Just powerful, which made them different. And Mister Holmes was one of those people with the most power. He was an insider who not only knew how the world worked, but how to manipulate it. He was one of the first to know the events that would shape tomorrow. He knew all about the war and the invasions before anyone else did. Our solders draped the corporate flag over the statue's face...I saw the footage. It choked me up. He was larger than life. He was a man full of secrets. Like her father.

And now here he was, trembling on the cold concrete rent-a-space floor, and he could not even look at her. Instead, he put his face in his hands and wailed, "Oh my God, Oh my God," as he rocked back and forth like someone having a fit.

Jonathon gave her an evil look. "Goddamn it," he hissed, "What the hell is all this?"

Ian came close to her and whispered, "You know him? Oh shit."

Daphne was at a loss. She didn't want to make Ian angry. She didn't want to tell him anything at all. She didn't know what to do except look away and shrug.

"Well, you must know him. He sure knows you! Why didn't you tell me that you knew him?"

"His face was all covered up! How could I tell?"

"Well, this isn't good! Our clients don't want anyone in their lives to know their business! This is an anonymous service! And now look at him!" Ian had ceased whispering; Mister Holmes was in such a state that he seemed to notice nothing around him.

"Yeah, right, and he was doing so well before, when you were roughing him up and yelling at him—."

"That was different. That was completely different."

"How?"

"That was...something he was paying for. That was role playing. But this?"

He gestured toward Mister Holmes, whose Oh my gods had disintegrated into a primal wail. He had made two fists and was pummeling himself on the head.

"Well, it wasn't my idea to come. You wanted me to come. And you didn't warn me about anything you were going to do. I guess you wanted to just shock me so badly, didn't you!"

"Well, now what are we going to do? We could lose our jobs! We make good money doing this. Or don't you understand the importance of that kind of thing?" Ian was feeling embarrassed by his own words, which made him more stammering and angry.

"Shh! Stop yelling at me! Why don't you let me talk to him

and try to handle it?”

“Okay, then handle it.” He opened the metal door back up and he and Jonathon stepped out, closing it behind them again.

Reluctantly, Daphne turned to face the crumpled man on the ground.

“It’s okay, “she said to him softly. “Really, it’s okay Mister Holmes.” She sat down beside him on the ground.

He peeked at her through his fingers. Then he slowly moved his hands down and sighed.

“Where have you been?” he asked wearily. “Your mother is frantic.” But this was said without urgency, as though he were just making a statement of fact.

She shrugged. “I’ve just been around. No particular place.”

“I should...bring you back with me. Shouldn’t I?”

“No! I’m not going back. Nobody can make me go back. So just don’t worry about it.”

He sighed, and nodded. He honestly looked relieved. They sat there for a few more moments, nobody saying anything.

Mister Holmes chuckled ruefully. “I’m so embarrassed that you have seen any of this. I’ve known you since you were a baby. No young girl should have to see...this.”

“What is this?”

“It’s...I don’t know. You’re too young and innocent to understand. Hah, I don’t even really get it myself, except to know that this is the one thing that keeps me grounded in my skin. It helps me sleep at night. Really, it does. It has become an essential. Lots of people I know do it.”

“But it’s so weird. I don’t get it? Why do you hire two kids to kidnap you and treat you like shit?”

“Because this has become the only thing that makes me feel like I’m real!” He was looking up at the ceiling as he spoke this sentence in a panicked rush, his eyes rolled up so far that she could see the whites underneath. He looked like a statue she had seen in the museum of Christ being crucified.

His lower lip was trembling and tears were rolling out of

his eyes again. "I shouldn't be burdening you with this. You wouldn't understand. And you shouldn't. Just a young girl. Just a girl. You shouldn't know the ugliness of adulthood. Not yet."

He was beginning to wear on her nerves a little bit; she sighed wearily. "Listen, you won't tell anyone that you saw me, will you? I don't want to go back to my mother."

He sniffled, wiping at his nose with the back of his hand. "I suppose not. Who am I to question you? I don't know what your life has been. Or what it is now. Besides," he laughed, "what could I tell them about the circumstances of having found you?" He gestured around the ugly little room. "You wouldn't tell anyone that you saw me, would you?" The way he was looking at her, she could see real fear in his eyes.

"No. Of course not. After this we'll just go our separate ways. No one will be the wiser."

Instead of making him feel better, he started to rock and sway again, chanting, "It's all so hopeless. Hopeless. Hopeless."

"It's not hopeless."

"Well, it is certainly tragic and ridiculous, then, isn't it?"

"The way it is...just is." She stood up and dusted off her palms. "Well. Goodbye Mister Holmes. Don't worry. This never happened."

Mister Holmes stilled himself, and looked at her with great intensity.

"I remember when you were just a little thing. Oh, yes. Yes! I can remember when you turned five years old, and the wonderful party that your parents had for you, with the circus animals and the beautiful three tiered cake with the sugared violets..."

"Yeah, well..."

"And you. You were such a little thing in your high-heeled shoes and your long dress, and the violets pinned in your hair to match the cake. Your face was painted, I believe. You were like a little Victorian doll. A child empress. A little Dauphine at her Versailles. Little Mousseline!"

He had a rapt look on his face, his eyes glassy and non-seeing.

"It made me sigh to look at you. You reminded me of so many things. There was so much history in your face. Too much. And it has crushed you, I can see it has. You were sad then. And you are sad now. I suppose I don't blame you for running away."

"I was suffocating. I had no choice."

He was openly crying now. "That was exactly what your father said. He had to get away, too. You are David's daughter, no doubt. Some would call him wrong for doing the things that he did. I think he always tried to do the best thing, by everyone. The noble thing."

"What do you mean? "

Nelson did not answer, but looked at her with a strange, coquettish expression. He was not crying anymore.

"You're a very special girl."

"Thanks, I guess."

"And he did what was best for you, to make you the best that you could be, even though others may have condemned it."

"Condemned what?"

His mouth puckered up, small, like a startled infant's. For a moment she worried he would start crying again, so she said, "Never mind..."

"I should never have brought it up, I don't know if you can understand..."

"Well, forget it then. Why don't we just get going?"

"He did the honorable thing He was never at peace, your father. He always wanted things to be better than they were. That kind of idealism is sometimes a burden, you see. And sometimes he found himself tangled into things he felt conflicted about." He was now looking into Daphne's face with a bright, feverish look.

"What? Like stuff in the war?" She was beginning to go numb all over, and there was a hissing sound in her ears, the whisper of her own blood in her veins. "Or other things? Things that are not good?" She was remembering the story of Calvin's mother and how they took her away in the government van. Those are my people who did that...

"I won't go into it all. He was a complex man. I considered him a close friend. And I just..." Something in Daphne's face made him stop and come forward, and he tried to gently touch her head. But she shrank away from him. "You know, of course he loved you very much..." He was at a loss. He started to pummel himself on the forehead with his own balled up fists again. "How could I be such an idiot? I should never have started talking about such things. Idiot!"

Daphne had turned her back to him and was fumbling with the metal door to lift it, but he said, "Wait!"

He began to fumble in his pocket for his wallet.

"I don't need your money Mister Holmes!"

"No. It's not that. I wanted to give you something that your father once gave to me."

He held it out before him and Daphne took it. It appeared to be a hundred dollar bill. But it had been painted over with what smelled like oil paint. On one side, over Independence Hall, was painted an intricate forest scene with a tiny grazing doe, furtive owls in the trees, foxes with their tiny pointed red ears and white tipped tails... It looked like the illustration from a children's book. Each animal had such a whimsical expression on its miniature face. The scale was so small, it must have taken a magnifying glass and a brush as thin as a whisker and much, much painstaking time to make it. She was charmed by it. And puzzled.

On the other side, Benjamin Franklin's face had been whited out, and another portrait painted over it. It was a portrait of a beautiful young girl with plaited white blonde hair entwined with blood red roses. Her cheeks had circles of pink high up under the eyes. The lips were painted in a tiny geisha bow. Though she was lovely, the girl had no life to her. It looked commemorative of someone no longer alive. It looked like the painted face of a sarcophagus.

Indeed, the area surrounding the girl was painted with intricate twining flowers, adding to the funereal feel of the portrait.

For some reason, looking at this made Daphne feel incredibly sad. Tears even prickled at her eyes, but she forced them back and tried to make her mind blank and bright as an empty sky.

"There there, dear. It was a secret, that your father tried to make art in his spare time. He didn't show a lot of people. It's okay. I carry that around with me. I don't know why. It's like my good luck amulet. I want you to have it."

"Why do you think I want it?" she asked coolly.

"You were looking at it so long. I thought—."

"How do I know he even painted it?"

"He did. He did paint. But he thought he had no talent, and it pained him. It was the one thing her felt he didn't have that he could not obtain. But I thought he was pretty good. And say, doesn't that that portrait bore an incredible likeness to…"

"I DON'T WANT TO HEAR ANYMORE! YOU'RE CRAZY! I CAN'T TAKE LISTENING TO YOU ANYMORE!"

She was shocked when Mister Holmes seemed to take no offense but smiled at her, fondly, with his head tilted.

"Goddamn it!" She wheeled around and started searching for the latch at the bottom of the door. She was overwhelmed by the need to get out of the storage space, but couldn't think straight enough to figure out how to slide the corrugated metal door up.

"Oh Teacup, don't be that way. I'm sow-ry…"

"I'm through with all this. And my name isn't Teacup. I hate that name."

"Honey. Darling. It's your Uncle Nelson. I wouldn't hurt you for the world." He was in deadly earnest, coming toward her, gripping her shoulders in his hands and trying to pull her towards him.

"You were Uncle Nelson. Now you're a pathetic, broken-down old man paying strangers to humiliate you. It's perverted."

"I'm so, so sow-ry..."

She finally lifted up the rumbling metal door, and walked out of the storage space with long resolute strides, folding up the painted bill neatly and slipping it into her inside pocket, leaving the man's abject wailing behind. Please! Please! So sow-ry. I knew you when you were but a glimmer in your mother's beautiful movie-star eye! The sound grew fainter and fainter in the background as she crossed the parking lot to where the two men stood smoking behind a dumpster, to get out of the wind.

It was early morning now. A pink glow rimmed the horizon, but the utility lights were still on in the parking lot, beaming down on her like a trained spotlight. Her long, stretched shadow swung crazily around her as she came toward the two figures. But her eyes were only on the one.

Ian pretended not to notice her until she was there, right in front of him, gazing steadily into his eyes, as steadily as she could will herself to.

"So what's the deal in there? Have you calmed him down? You know, I can't believe you let this happen. Certain boundaries are not supposed to be crossed. I can't believe you never said a word until it was too late."

"It's not too late."

"Pffft. As far as this whole operation's concerned..."

But he stopped. Something in the way she was looking at him made him lose his train of thought. Her eyes, slightly red rimmed, were burning with an intensity he had never seen in any person before. She was so focused on his face it made him feel stammering and embarrassed. (But she was just a young girl!)

She put her hands on his shoulders and pulled herself onto her tiptoes to give him a kiss. Her first kiss. It was clumsy and inexperienced, and yet Ian found himself responding to the very force of it: his body had gone limp. She slipped her small tongue into his mouth, probing, like a small antenna. And when she pulled back again, they were both breathless. She was staring him down, as she looked up at him, this little girl with wrists as thin and delicate as twigs. This girl who still sometimes cried at night when she thought no one could hear her. She was actually making him feel slightly afraid, and slightly awed.

But he quickly collected himself, and turned his head for another drag on his cigarette. He shut one eye against the smoke, looking back at her through the open one. Her gaze was fierce, slightly accusatory, though her cheeks burned and her lips were trembling.

She took the cigarette from his hand and took a drag from it, another first for her that night. She swallowed too much of the acrid smoke and started coughing.

He smiled, looked away. "So. Well. All right."

"Yeah. All right." She turned away from him with a shrug. "You can bring him out now if you want. He's ready. He's gotten everything he deserves. You should have heard the bastard cry,"

5

It was spring again. The sun rose earlier every morning, and there was the bright sound of birdsong. Daphne liked to keep the large windows open to let the cool, damp air blow in during the night. And she always liked, in the mornings, to stand at the windows with her eyes closed, and feel the morning sun slowly fill up this space, this brand new space, that she now shared with Ian.

They were small rooms, but they had high ceilings. Way up in the beams there was a sparrow's nest, which sometimes shuffled and stirred with life. They were up on the third floor. The apartment was so airy and free that it felt like living in a tree house.

Standing in these windows, wrapped in a sheet, she would often stretch onto her tiptoes, arching up like a plant hungry for light. It felt as though it had been so long since she had seen the sun at all, and now she craved it. When it warmed her skin, it felt as though it were permeating through her cells, feeding her, making her grow. Actually, she had grown several inches in the past year. She would be sixteen come summer. Not only had she grown taller, but she had filled out. Her shoulders were a little broader, her breasts heavier. Her hair was growing back and she tied it into rows of little braids, close to her head. It was Paige who had shown her how to do her hair that way, before Daphne had moved out. Before Paige had found out about her and Ian. She did not like to think about that day very much. Part of her had not wanted to hurt her friend; Paige had been good to her and never deserved it. But for some reason, it now gave her a certain thrill to think about the way Paige had looked at her, disbelieving, the tears not there yet but coming, hot and heavy and stormy. Even though it was a terrible thing and it made her ashamed, it also gave her a heady sense of strength and power. The mix of contrasting feelings was strange and intoxicating. She was no longer a child to be coddled and rescued and lectured to. She was a woman now, an equal, someone to be considered, even feared. Someone who could take away the man Paige thought she loved. Though she did not know him at all.

Well. She had not exactly taken him. It was more like they had kind of wordlessly drifted together. There had been an understanding between them, that night with Mister Holmes in the storage space. She had slept with Ian for the first time that night, after they had gotten rid of Jonathon. It had been in the back of that filthy van. She had wanted to, surely, and it was her idea. But strangely, she had felt nothing. There was an adrenalin pumping through her veins that was propelling her forward, forward, forward. But it had also made her numb.

But the other times, since, it had not been bad. In fact, she was starting to enjoy it, maybe even to be good at it. She wanted to be good at it. It was a mystery she wanted to solve. It was also the main thing she and Ian had in common, other than work.

For she had started working with him now. In spite of the first disastrous session, it was noted that Daphne had a talent for the job. Clients spoke favorably of her, and so she was now officially working for RealLife. In the day they slept. At night she would go out with him in the RealLife van. Sometimes they worked with Jonathon. Sometimes it was just the two of them. This was another thing she was unexpectedly good at, and she was beginning to receive special requests. Nearly all of the clients were older men, very rich. They liked to be abused by this young, slight girl with the blond braids and the piercing eyes. When she yelled at them, it was with a virulence that she never knew she had inside her. She never knew that she could be so cruel. You filthy creep! You worthless money-grubbing pig! You veneer toothed, pink cheeked Fauntleroy, suck on this! And yet she reminded herself, it was what they wanted, for whatever reason. And the money was good. They had enough money to have their own place, this place. And it made her so happy.

It was funny, how quickly reality could change. For so many years it had remained the same, static. Back when she was a girl. Those days now seemed impossibly far away so that she could hardly remember them.

Now she felt certain fluidity in her person. She had the same name, but she didn't know who she was anymore. And at some point, this had stopped bothering her.

Though it had shocked her, as she had been packing up her few belongings and moving herself out of the industrial room, when Wendy had muttered from her dark corner, "You really are a slut, aren't you?"

Something about that word, the hissing sibilance of the consonants, made her freeze, speechless, not knowing what to do. It was as though a serpent had slithered up and sunk its fangs into a tender part of herself. The sting of it shocked her.

Helplessly, she looked over at Calvin to see his reaction. He was as inscrutable as ever, watching both of the girls, the one standing, stunned and shocked, with an armload of plastic bags dangling from her arm, and the other, hidden within her blankets, looking out through slitted eyes at her target. He looked from one to the other, and she expected him to say something, but he didn't. He met her eyes once, and then he looked away. It made her sad. Wouldn't he even defend her?

So she willed herself to straighten up and face Wendy: "What the hell did you just call me?"

"Slut! Which you are. You're moving in with Ian, right?"

"So what?"

"You knew Paige wanted him."

"But they weren't together. They were never going to be."

"But she still loved him, we all knew it. It was a shitty thing to do. You're just using him to take care of you like the princess you are,"

"You don't know anything, so shut up."

"I know Paige was your friend. I know she's the one who rescued your sorry punk ass and brought you here."

"She is my friend."

"I'm the one who had to calm her down after you broke the news and left. She screamed. I couldn't stop her screaming! You think things weren't already bad enough for her? She's not strong, you know."

"I can't help it if she's that way."

"Yes, you can! You didn't have to do that to her."

Had Paige really screamed? She had been coolly silent the times Daphne had run into her, which she tried to avoid doing as much as possible.

She tried, now, to grasp for words, any words, with which to defend herself. But there were none. Maybe she was a slut,

She tried to resign herself to the idea, but it just made her feel sick and worthless.

None of this stopped her now, however, from enjoying the sight of him in her bed, the sheer physical fact of him in these rooms they called home. The smell of him, that sweetish yeasty smell that was all over the sheets, and all over her, too. She had never had a boyfriend before, had hardly even touched a boy until now. Now his body consumed her at all times, making her feel intoxicated and giddy and gloriously alive. And she was glad of this, because her lust allowed her to blot out those other, less pleasant thoughts.

She could hear him behind her, stirring and waking in their bed, which, as in the industrial room, was nothing but a mattress on the floor. They had no other furniture, save for a table and chair and a futon mattress folded and propped against one wall, which they used as a couch. Clothes were strewn all over the bedroom, books stacked in unsteady piles. She could hear him rummaging on the floor near him for a pack of cigarettes. Then there was the click and hiss of the lighter; she could feel him coming up behind her.

He reached around to put the cigarette to her lips and she took a drag. She never wanted her own, just a puff of his here and there. It still stung her throat and made her a bit woozy, but she was getting used to it. When she blew out the stream she liked to watch the smoke drift into ribbons and tendrils up, up, toward the ceiling. The nicotine made her feel steady and focused after the head rush left her.

His arms came around her, his hands gently moving over her cheeks, her lips, her trembling eyelids. It was as though he were molding a sculpture by hand, with little strokes and gentle pats. It felt good. She took another drag and settled back, luxuriating in the feeling. The sun was warm and radiant, glowing red through her closed eyes.

"I got you something yesterday," he murmured.

So dreamy did she feel, she had not even realized that she neglected to answer until he asked, "Don't you want to know what it is?"

"Yes. Of course I do. What is it?" Reluctantly she opened her eyes and saw sunspots flaring in her vision.

"Over there against the wall. The white paper bag."

Wrapping the sheet tighter around herself, she went to where he indicated and picked up the bag. Inside was a large, stiff backed artist's pad and a set of charcoal pencils.

"Wow. Thanks!" She was genuinely happy and touched, fingering these items. "I haven't worked in like forever. At least it feels like forever."

In fact, it couldn't have been more than four or five months since she had worked in her studio at home. Home. That house was so monstrously huge...how had she ever lived in such a space? A whole city block worth of space, all for a young girl and her wasted away mother and Cathy, who only ever really wanted to get out. At least she could now admit that to herself. Three people in that yawning abyss of space, no wonder they had been so alien to each other. To think of it! Her own lavender tufted bedroom was twice as big as this whole apartment. It was only a season ago, but now it felt as though she were a grown woman looking back decades.

Ian shrugged. "Well. About time you got back to work. Don't you think?"

"Sure." There was a tingle, an itch in her fingers to trace line and shade on that clean white paper.

"I mean, you don't want to waste your time just screwing around with me when you can be using your talent."

"Yes. That's true." Though such talk made her nervous. It made her remember other, earlier discussions of her talent and untapped potential. Mrs. Pierce and her art deco room, the white furniture and the tank with the angelfish. She felt herself tighten, just perceptibly.

"You're seeing the world now for what it really is. You're coming alive and sentient for the first time."

"Well, I may have been a fool, but I've always been sentient for God's sake..."

"No. You weren't. Not really." He ran his hands down the sides of her body, over her hips. "But you are now. I just find it really exciting, to try to see things through your eyes."

"I don't know what that means."

"Well, never mind all that then. Why don't you just draw something?"

"Okay. But you can't watch. It's hard for me to draw when other people are watching me."

"Okay, I won't watch."

She sat down in a corner of the room, against the wall, and took the pad of paper onto her knees. It was him that she would draw, what else was there? She studied the lines of him, the way his bare torso looked as he lay on his side on the bed, reading a book someone had given him, something about modern surveillance. It had a creepy eyeball on the cover. Ian's chest was narrow and smooth, and he was wiry. It almost hurt to lay her head against him at night. There was no give to him. The muscles were hard and compact and unyielding, still an adolescent's body. She could not stop running her hands over it, even now in her mind, As she sketched it all in dark lines of charcoal, it felt as though she were caressing him.

In short strokes, she brought out his full and impudent lower lip. The spiked dark hair. His eyes, with that scary, thrilling blankness that sometimes came over them when he wasn't looking at her. What was he thinking?

Those eyes were now raised to hers. "Hey!"

She giggled. "Hold still. I'm not done yet!"

But it was too late. Now there was a studied self-awareness in the way that he held himself, and it wasn't the same. He kept glancing up at her. The cigarette he held in one hand was burning down to the filter. Ash fell into the sheets. She worried that he would burn them all down, and they would have no place to go.

"Where did you learn to draw?"

"Mother sent me to classes at the Met one summer. And I took classes in Paris one time when we were there for a while. But I mostly taught myself."

She looked down at what she had done. It had started off well enough, but then she had lost the thread of what she had been doing. The boy in the picture resembled Ian, but it was not him. His eyes looked too hard and mean, he looked like a police sketch of a serial killer. She tore it out and handed it to him anyway.

Ian gazed at it for some moments, lips parted, brow furrowed. "Is this really what I look like?"

"Not really. I'm out of practice."

She could not read his face, could not tell if he liked it or not, but she was too shy to ask.

"How did you like it?" he asked her in a faint, dreamy voice.

"I don't. I didn't get the eyes right. I..."

"I mean Paris. How did you like Paris?"

"It was okay, I guess. We summered there sometimes." She started to doodle idly, just lines and swirls. "I like old places. Old cities. There's a lot you can do on foot there. The bread is to die for. I liked watching the people on the street. Everyone smokes there. You'd probably like it. I kind of liked the countryside better, though. We got a place in the south of France. Sort of a rustic cottage. But nice. It had running water and everything, but it was almost like living in the past. I could, like, lose myself for hours, walking in the fields. A neighbor let me feed and water their chickens. I really loved those funny chickens..."

"Are you sure you don't prefer your old life?"

"Yes, I'm sure! Why do you keep asking me?"

"I don't know. You might have to go back. Someone might find you. Someone might turn you in. It could happen any time. And you're a minor. All I'm saying is, be prepared, because anything can happen. Especially when we're working. That makes me nervous. I mean, my God, when that guy recognized you that first day..."

"Well, he isn't going to talk. I can assure you of that."

"He cancelled our services. I guess seeing you freaked him out so bad. You never even told me who he was or what you talked about that night."

It was true. She hadn't wanted to tell him. She didn't even want to think about it all. It was all too confusing to process. Thinking about that night with Mister Holmes made her flush with a shame that she didn't understand.

"It was all...nothing really. He knew my father. He was really embarrassed to see me. Which is pretty natural, I guess, given the circumstances."

"Did he say something to upset you?"

"Not really. Why do you ask?"

"No reason. You just tense up whenever you talk about it."

"I don't think that I do." She concentrated fiercely on what she was drawing so that she wouldn't have to look at him.

"He was like, your father's best friend, right?"

"They were partners, that's all." Ever since that night she kept the painted bill in her pocket, sometimes took it out and held it to the light. It made her feel a little sting of betrayal. She never even knew that her father made art. What else did she not know?

Ian had a far off look on his face. "I've seen a lot of his type. Repressive personality. Probably in love with your father or something. I wonder what he knows? I mean, I know your father was involved in all sorts of far reaching shit. Not just biotech, either. I heard that their company got some huge grant from the US Army Research Office. Do you know anything about it?"

"No! I have no idea!" Had he been doing research? She felt thrown off and confused by the sudden turn of the conversation.

"Sorry—"

"I was just a kid. How would I know?"

"I wasn't accusing anyone. I would just like to know more about Teacup Ventures. And maybe so should you. Teacup."

Her face flushed. "Don't call me that. I don't know anything. All I know is that my father just wanted to make the world a better place." She felt under siege and betrayed; she no longer knew if she could trust Ian or not. Her pencil dug into the paper. Without even really thinking about it, she had been drawing another picture of the lynx. Her lynx. In profile he looked so calm and stately. Impervious.

After a while, Ian asked, "What are you drawing?" sounding cautious and conciliatory.

"Nothing. I just like to draw animals. I'm drawing a lynx." She held it up for a split second, not looking at him.

"Hmm. That's good. It looks pretty lifelike."

Daphne looked down at it, considering. "I guess it's all right. I used to see a lynx in my dreams. I thought I saw it in real life, too. Sort of in visions."

"Sort of like a spirit animal."

"Yeah. I don't see it anymore, though." She had not seen it since the night of her mother's fundraiser. It made her feel sad, like she had lost a friend. I should have saved the real lynx when I had the chance. But still she hoped he would come back in her dreams. Of course, she was no longer pure. Visions only came to the innocent, and now that she was no longer that... But there was no going back now, no use thinking about it.

Feeling all at once despondent, she put the pad of paper down and lay down on the floor with one arm draped over her eyes. "I wish you would stop accusing me of wanting to go back. I know what you're really trying to say."

"What?"

"That I'm weak."

"That's not what I meant."

"Well, it's how you make me feel. Anyway, how do I know that you won't leave? Why are you even here with me?"

"Because I want to be here."

"Why were you even living in that place, when you were making money enough to live someplace nice? Everyone else there would have killed to get out. That room was miserable."

"They don't hate it as much as that, or they wouldn't be there, believe me. And like I told you before, I was saving up my money. That's what I've always done. I work until I have enough money to travel. Then I quit and move on to the next place. "

"Where were you planning to go next?"

"The North Pole."

She laughed.

"It's no joke. I'm going."

"When?"

"Someday."

"That doesn't answer my question. What are you doing here now with me?"

He thought for a long while, exhaling smoke to the ceiling. Then he answered, "I don't know how to answer. Something about you had a pull on me."

"So you are here against your own will and common sense?" she asked teasingly.

He did not take this well, and looked at her with fierce solemnity. "I live a life of full intent. Always. I don't do anything that I don't want to do. I am never with anyone that I don't want to be with."

"Take it easy. It was just a joke."

He did not laugh, but looked at her coldly. "I think you could do to live your life with a little intent."

"What is that supposed to mean?"

"I think you should figure out what you want to do. Be uncompromising about it. You don't like what you came from? Then you should take it down in any way you can. You think you're an artist? Then you should live that way. Walk the walk. Sometimes I actually think you are still a teenaged hedge fund princess. In your mind. You can't lay in your bedroom drawing cute animal pictures all your life."

"That's not fair!"

"Life's not fair," he said with a shrug.

"Fuck OFF!" She flung herself up and stalked out of the room, sheet trailing behind her.

"I've made you angry. Finally. Good!" He called out to her behind the bathroom door, where she was hurriedly dressing in some random clothes she picked up off the floor. "I want you to be angry. I want you to really feel things. You don't have to keep everything inside. You're way too civilized. You need to throw things more. Break stuff. Be loud! I'll love you all the more for it."

This caught her off guard for a moment. She did not know what had confused her more, that he had made her angry on purpose or that he had used that word: love. She looked up into the spotty bathroom mirror, meeting her own eyes. She and her reflection stared at each other, bewildered, for a few moments. The overhead light made her look pale and haggard with dark circles under her eyes. She looked, she had to admit, hard. She would soon be sixteen. And she had no idea who she was.

It was the music that took her away now. At least once, usually twice a week she spent her evening at the club, at first with Ian but sometimes by herself. It was not the kind of music she had ever listened to before. No one had ever played music in her house, it had always been so quiet, though a couple of times she had gone with her mother to concerts given by the New York Philharmonic.

This was something different. Amped up guitars and feedback that began quiet and then built up in its pain and tension. It didn't even really feel like music at all, really, but am aural storm that came over her like a dark heavy cloud. First, it peaked her senses, as though she could feel an electrical charge in the air and a whiff of ozone. As she became more light-headed, the notes started to rain down on her, a pattering turned to a downpour. And before she knew it she was jumping and thrashing in the crowd, caught up in a whirlwind of her own spirit. She forgot who she was, forgot about everything. Forgot about sad crazy mothers on IV drips. Forgot the sight of silk rosebuds scattered around a room like drops of blood as blue smoke drifted up from the first floor. Forgot about army jeeps. Forgot about kind, goat-faced girls in gas masks that were there to help you, thinking you were someone worth saving.

All she was at that moment was part of a writhing sea of limbs, pulled into the tide of the heavy sound throbbing from the speakers. She became so violent in her moves that when she woke up in the morning every muscle was sore, and she was covered with cuts and bruises. She savored the pain.

People started to know who she was. They called her Angry Tinkerbell. She liked the name. She liked being part of the scene. She wore clothes that she bought in a second hand store, cheap, ugly clothes made out of polyester, a fabric she had never even touched before in her old life. It was so springy and slinky in her fingers and melted if touched to the glowing tip of a cigarette. She dressed in black polyester, tight pants and shirts, and her clunky black boots with big, ridge-like treads on the bottom. She wore make up now, too, and painted the orbits of her eyes a deep and shimmering charcoal. She didn't exactly look pretty, she knew. She looked disturbing and scary. She could be a young prostitute or drug addict. She could be anyone.

The other young people allowed her now to join their ranks on the smelly couches. Sometimes she stood in parking lots with them, passing around a bottle filled with something amber that tasted awful to her, like burning oak. The bottle looked expensive, with an antiquated looking label. Someone had stolen it, which made what was intolerable delicious.

And though she enjoyed herself very much, sometimes she had that strange feeling almost of déjà vu. That she was already an old woman somewhere, merely remembering this scene in future recollection.

She shook the feeling away, until she was back in the here and now in all of its richness and beauty. Young voices rang and laughed in the cool night air, hers among them. Through a whiskey haze she looked up at the moon, barely there, like a half dusted fingerprint.

In a crumbling building adjoining the club, there was studio space. Daphne rented one of the spaces so that she could begin painting again.

It was very unlike the studio she was used to in her mother's house. There were windows to let in the natural light, but this light was filtered through layers of grime. And this space had to be shared with two other people: a girl who made ghoulish sculptures from things like shredded insulation and glass eyeballs, and a man whom she had never seen, but left behind his paintings depicting different political assassinations in garish cartoon form.

She stretched and primed her canvas, but did nothing else for a while. The blank space was too intimidating. It seemed to be taunting her. She didn't even know what she wanted to paint, now that she was here.

So she fell to daydreaming, looking out the window down onto the street outside. It had been somewhat calm for the past couple of months. But now that warm weather was returning it seemed to be having some profound effect on people. They acted crazier, more defiant. There were a lot more fights in the streets, lots of shouting and breaking glass. And, more frightening, were the homeless people's standoffs with the soldiers who patrolled the streets. There were roving gangs of people, usually younger men, who would sometimes rush at and try to roll over a military vehicle. Once there was a Molotov cocktail thrown at an army truck as it drove by. Daphne had not seen it, but some of the kids at the club had. They said a soldier fired into the crowd and there was pandemonium. But the only one that was shot was an old man with a long white beard who couldn't run fast enough. They thought he was dead, but weren't sure. Daphne remembered the old man who had been kind to her the day the lynx was shot. But then she quickly tried to stop thinking about it.

Daphne knew she should be socially disobedient, should be marching in the street and protesting. Maybe throwing bombs herself. It would certainly make Ian proud and happy if she did that. He would probably love her tremendously more. But the truth was, she was too frightened. A coward, she knew. Not yet ready to make the leap. She liked to stay inside most of the time.

And if she was walking somewhere alone, she tried to make herself small and inconspicuous.

After a while, the paintings did come. The first one she painted took her two weeks to finish. It was a painting of her house on fire. It surprised her, the relish with which she painted the livid orange flames, the black collapsing frame like some sad prehistoric skeleton. The plumes of smoke that billowed into the night sky took on strange spectral forms. They looked almost like women, keening and moaning with arms outstretched, tendrils of hair floating up like submerged mermaids. All around, in the foreground, were black shadowy figures who merely stood watching. And waiting.

She was drawn into that one for hours, heart pounding, her breathing growing fast and shallow. After her painting sessions she felt enervated but happy, as though she had run five miles. She would come home and kiss Ian hungrily, pinning him onto the bed. It was the only time that she felt really good, intensely alive. She was able to love Ian without the misgivings and confusion that had begun to beset her more and more whenever she saw his unreadable face. She radiated love, and she needed him there to reflect what was inside her back again.

There came a night when they had a working assignment together. It was after midnight when Ian drove them in the van to pick up their client.

"This one is new," Ian told her. "I haven't been to this house before. But I've been to the general area. The name of the house is Wingate Place. There's no gate to get through. We just have to look for the placard and then drive right up the road."

Daphne was feeling tired. In the beginning, the work could be exhilarating. The whole concept felt so dangerous that it thrilled her. But now that she was getting used to it, it was becoming a little routine. The yelling and name-calling began to feel fake. And these men they serviced seemed not only sad, but embarrassing to be around.

"Why does a screwed-up business like this even exist?" she mused out loud. "I mean, I know some people have their fetishes and all, but...why are they all the same type?"

"I thought you of all people might know."

"How would I know?"

"Didn't your dad disappear when he was using the services of, what do you call it, The Black Box?"

"That wasn't the same. It wasn't the same thing at all. A trip to the Amazon is not the same as—"

"Come on. The Black Box isn't exactly your everyday posh travel agency."

"I know. I know. So they dropped them into the middle of the jungle with only a knife each. That I can get. But it wasn't like this."

"It is exactly like this."

"What? You can't say that—"

"I think a lot of these men hate themselves. And this is their way of facing it. The Black Box is no better or worse than RealLife or any of the other services these people are stupid or sad enough to pay people like us good money for."

"Well, I'm sorry that you have such a fixation on it all. Can we please drop it?"

He looked into the lights of the freeway, leaning back easily into his seat. "None of it matters. You're out now, you're above it all."

"I wouldn't say we are exactly above it all."

"Why not? We're free of that kind of bullshit."

"We're profiting off of it."

"So? What's wrong with that? We're providing a service and getting paid."

"And you have no problem with that?"

He looked at her pointedly. "No. I don't."

"So you could walk away from this at any time?"

"Yes. If I wanted to. I'm free. I live my life, and I don't compromise. That's the way life should be lived."

Yeah, she thought. Where else would we be getting money if we walked away? But instead, she asked, "Why don't you ever tell me anything about your family?"

"What does that have to do with anything?"

"Nothing. It's just that you know all about where I came from. And I know nothing about you. And it makes me feel like I'm at a disadvantage."

There was a long pause. Then he sighed and said, "The past is meaningless. It's irrelevant."

"You certainly think my past is relevant. You bring it up enough."

He did not answer. He had found the neighborhood and was looking for the right house.

At last their headlights washed over a placard on a low stone wall reading Wingate Place. They turned onto a long, winding road much like the others they had traveled. But this house, when they finally came upon it, was different. The brick house was, of course, large and impressive. There was a two-story entrance portico with Doric columns. There were long, single story wings off to each side. The place was stately, but the gardens looked untended and overgrown. The flagstone at the entrance was cracked and broken in places. There seemed to be no lights on inside, and it looked like it could be abandoned.

The front door was ajar, which they took as a sign to go in. Ian reached into his pocket and took two thin knit ski masks, ("The guy wants the whole experience.") and then they let themselves in.

It was dark, but they could still appreciate the grand entrance that opened up onto a large curving staircase. There were small gilt tables set beneath large, ornate mirrors on either side. And next to the staircase, what looked in the dark to be a human sized statue.

Daphne jumped as she unexpectedly glimpsed their

reflections as they passed the mirrors. They really did look frightening. They could be terrorists or executioners. She shuddered as they continued forward into the house.

Usually the client was waiting at the door as any good host would. This one appeared to be hiding.

As they came upon a hallway stretching to their right, there seemed to be a faint light coming from down at the end. They followed it to the source. It was flickering, trembling candlelight.

They entered a grand library. There was a man seated at a little Chippendale desk, dressed in jeans and a t-shirt. He was slumped over, his head down and resting on his arms. There were candles dripping and burning in a silver candelabra on one of the tables that flanked a brocade sofa with brass studs. There were several empty whiskey bottles on the ground next to the man, and a half filled glass next to his head on the desk.

They paused for a moment, taking this all in. Then Ian went forward, and it took him several tries to shake the man awake.

When he came to, he startled and yelped in fright. Astonishingly, he was a young man who looked to be in his twenties, handsome, with a thick head of blond hair that flopped into his eyes.

"You're coming with us. Get up." Ian growled.

The young man looked at him, gaping, for a moment. Daphne's heart raced in fear. Surely they had gotten the wrong person. An alarm bell would ring any moment. Her eyes raced around, trying to decide what to do next, where to run...

But the young man seemed to finally realize who they were. "Oh yeah, oh yeah," he slurred incoherently. "I got ya. I got ya." He stood up unsteadily and kicked his chair out of the way. He put his hands forward as though he wanted them to be cuffed.

"Just go!" Ian shouted at him, and the young man stumbled forward. But he didn't look afraid. He glanced up at Daphne through his floppy hair as he passed, and he merely looked annoyed and surly.

She gave him a shove, but he only gave a tight little smile.

He crossed the room and flipped on a light switch, suddenly flooding the room with light; Daphne squinted and blinked as her eyes adjusted.

The young man turned and stared at each of them, looking them up and down, assessingly. He had a heavy, furrowed brow and intense piercing eyes. Daphne found herself shyly looking away.

At last he walked over to blow out the candles. "So," he said. "This is it?"

Ian appeared stymied for a moment. Their clients were usually quiet and shamefaced. They had never had anyone like this before. "Yeah, this is it, motherfucker. You better move before I decide to cut you." But these words, though snarled, had a faint undercurrent of uncertainty.

The man walked over and drank from the whiskey glass on the little desk. "Aren't you going to tie me up? Or something?"

Ian grabbed him roughly and turned his body around, sloshing some of the amber liquid onto the floor. The man put down the glass and allowed Ian to bind his hands behind his back.

In the meantime, Daphne scanned the room around her. It was an impressive library, dark and leathery and masculine in a patrician type of way, with a deer head on one wall, a bearskin rug in front of the hearth. There were floor to ceiling walnut bookshelves full of volumes and volumes of gilt-edged leather books. But nothing was particularly different about it. Not until she noticed the painting.

It was a large painting of a beautiful woman. She looked like a runway model, very tall and thin, with long dark hair. She was dressed in a long, formfitting dress of what looked like interlocked golden disks, and she was lying in some woods in a patch of yellowish grass. The woman was bathed in what looked like blue siren lights of a police car. She was dead, her long, pale neck arched back with a deep red slash in it. The ruby blood pooled onto the blanched grass in a deep puddle. Her dark, elaborately made up eyes were open, her lips, red like the blood, parted in a kind of ecstasy.

Daphne could not stop starting at it. It was ugly, it was horrible, but its very luridness was what was drawing her in. She was hypnotized.

"You like?" laughed the young man.

"Is it...yours?" she asked uncertainly.

"I bought it, if that's what you mean."

"You like that kind of stuff? I think it's kind of sick."

He shrugged. "Investment. This artist has great earning potential. I was never really into art, until now. I mean, I've always been into money. I work in commodities. But I went to a seminar, once. About investing in art. And what's really hot right now is sex and death. That's where peoples minds are at, see? I studied the numbers. And then, I started going to museums, on my own." He smiled hugely, shaking his head, not seeming to notice or care that Ian was tightening the silk knot, and shoving him forward. "The more I saw, the more I started to get this fever. Sex and death. It gets your blood pumping, it sets you on edge. Right?"

Realizing he was looking at her, expecting an answer: "Right."

"It's primal. It's hot. My company is looking into launching a sex and death index fund."

He looked at her, eyebrows raised salaciously, and she didn't know if he was joking or not. She didn't know if she was being tricked. It was such an unpleasant feeling that she scrambled to get back in character, back in control. "Fuck you," she snorted. "Ian, why don't you mask him so we can go?"

"Wait." With his arms pinned behind his back, stumbling a bit into the furniture, he led them back into the entranceway from which they had come. With one elbow, he nudged a light switch, illuminating a dazzling chandelier above the staircase.

"Come check this out."

In the dark, she had made out what had looked like a

statue. Now, in the light, it was revealed to be a creepily realistic rendering of a sylphlike nude man, bound and gagged, covered with what looked like scratches and claw marks. He did not look dead, but his eyes were rolled upward as though in supplication.

"It's made of fiberglass. I picked this up on a trip to a show in Berlin. A great coup."

No one said anything. Daphne and Ian stood there dejectedly in their ski masks. The young man was smiling, pink faced with satisfaction.

"What, have I made you uncomfortable?" he asked.

Daphne felt a little sick to her stomach. She didn't like the man, didn't like the place, and felt she almost couldn't bear it another minute. She looked over at Ian, who had his arms folded and evaded his eyes.

She knew she had to do something, so she took the black silk blindfold from Ian's pocket and started winding it around the young man's head, covering up the eyes that now twinkled with belligerent amusement.

"Oh, so it's like this?" he asked sarcastically.

"Shut up!" Ian yelled, jolted back into the role he was supposed to be playing.

Once the man's eyes were bound, they led him out the front door to the van. Ian took the wheel, looking grim faced and embarrassed.

They drove in silence for a little while. All at once Daphne wished she could be somewhere, anywhere else. Though the young man looked to be nearly ten years older than they were, it felt as though they were a tense middle-aged couple driving with their misbehaving child in the backseat.

All was quiet until the young man spoke up again: "I'm finding this whole experience to be rather lacking."

"Why?" she asked wearily, resting her head on the window with her eyes closed.

"I don't know. It just doesn't feel authentic, does it? What you're doing to me. I guess I expected more. I guess I expected to be terrified. But I'm just not feeling anything. I can't feel it. It's sad, isn't it?" He laughed softly.

Ian was driving them to a new space they hadn't used before. He took them into the empty parking lot of an enormous sprawling shopping mall. He parked and they got out, holding their prisoner between them. Ian had a great loop of rope in one hand. There was an unmarked door that he opened with a key. It led through winding corridors and down some stairs to the ground floor of the empty parking garage.

Ian led the man to one of the concrete posts and pushed him against it, then proceeded to tie him to it with the rope. The place was cool and echoing and smelled of gasoline.

"You are a worthless piece of shit," Daphne began, her usual diatribe. "You don't deserve anything that you have. You're a fraud."

"You're probably right," the man answered, matter of factly.

She gaped at him, her mind blank. Ian took over.

"You hipster wannabe with your pseudo outrageous art. You think you're shocking to people. But you're not! You are so utterly mundane. You can't even comprehend how boring you really are."

"Yes, I can see how someone such as yourself would see me in that way. And what can I say? I'm no artist myself. I'm just an investor."

"So what?" Ian snorted.

"I'm not very deep. It's not the work that titillates me. It's the money."

"You're a chump."

"Chump or no. I'm the one with the power. I'm the one with the freedom."

"We are freer than you will ever be."

"You sure about that?"

"We aren't like you, we live off the grid," Daphne said as she kicked his shin, though not hard enough to bruise.

"Oh, honey. You are on the grid. You're tangled in it like a fly in a spider web."

"It isn't true!" Or was it? Her mind snagged on his words for an uncertain moment. But then she shook her confusion away and slapped him, hard, across the cheek.

Instead of getting angry, the young man sighed. "This is ridiculous, isn't it? People swear by your services. I was told by someone at this gathering of CEOs that this was a profound experience, that it would tear me down, but it would make me feel like a new man afterward. But I'm just not feeling it. It scares me, how much I just can't feel it. Ever. You know what I mean?"

They had no answer. Ian glowered at the ground. All was quiet but for the sound of traffic coming from the freeway, and the whispery scurrying of bats somewhere up in the steel beams.

Ian went away for a week to play some dates with his band on the road. Daphne was somewhat glad that he left. He had been getting on her nerves recently. He was either too quiet or he was jumpy and querulous. And she, herself, felt like she was always, alternately, either annoyed or weak with desire for him. She wanted to get away from Ian, but at the same time she felt terrified of losing him.

She lay in bed a lot, staring at the ceiling. The one thing that did bother her the most was the fact that he was all she had. It seemed like she had always been like this, having one confidante at a time. He had simply taken the place of Paige. Sometimes she wished she could go see Paige, just to talk or to help her in the office or have lunch. Something. Paige had been a friend. But surely she hated Daphne now. And with good reason. She could never show her face to her again.

If she had a girlfriend, she could get away from her mind for a while. Her mind was not a good place to be. There was too much to contemplate. Too many feelings knocking around her head, colliding like bumper cars.

And it didn't help things that she had begun seeing the man again, the one with the frog lips and round glasses. The last time was outside the club after a show. She saw him for just an instant, standing oddly still and alien-like among a crowd of rowdy youth, the streetlights flashing off his glasses and making them bright and blank. He did not come after her or say anything, but he gave her an unsettling feeling inside, like a vertical drop. A sense that she was falling from a great height.

In the past, whenever it felt like the whole world was against her, she could always feel her father's silent presence. Like he was laying a warm, strong hand on her shoulder. It gave her the same feeling she had as a small child, when he would talk to her about her day, or tell her those bedtime stories that he made up. He had always been warm, but grave. And he always treated her as an equal.

Now, the more she tried to conjure the feeling of his presence, the more elusive it became. She found that she could no longer remember exactly what he looked like. When she tried to remember those girlhood bedtimes, all she could visualize were a pair of disembodied eyes, loving but sorrowful, looming above her in the night.

Her memory of him used to be so sharp and definite. It seemed that having another man in her life had leached all the clarity and richness out of the private vision of her father that had nourished her for so long.

The thought of her father seeing her as she was now—morally compromised, a slut, a failure—was more than she could even contemplate. It seemed even when she tried to comprehend the thought of it, her brain would short circuit, slip its groove. Then there would be nothing left in her head at all. Only a sense of redness, a sensation of scalding, and the sound of blood rushing in her ears like steam.

～

When Ian returned, she was happy to see him. Once again, she was startled by his physical beauty. It flooded her senses, washing away any misgivings. And she had also missed his sharpness, his inquisitiveness. Whereas before he left, she had found it irritating. Now it made him seem so vivid and full of life and conviction. Perhaps, she thought, if she spent enough nights pressed against his body, some of that conviction and sense of selfhood would rub off on her.

But in the meantime, she would enjoy his physicality, that body, for itself.

He seemed happy to see her, too. He smiled and laughed a lot, and was full of stories about being on the road, the towns they had visited, and the clubs they had played in.

She had hardly left the apartment at all when he was gone, and it was nice to get out again, with him, going out to eat. Hanging around with the other young people at the club; she felt so happy that she could burst, leaning into his arms as they sat on the filthy couch, barely listening to what anyone was talking about, bathing in the warmth of his gaze whenever he looked down at her.

She was so happy, that for a while, she never felt depressed or uncertain. There was no more ruminating over whether she was a worthy, good person—or whether she was something else entirely. She felt light and free. She was so utterly fulfilled by everything she had, right in that moment.

Things were going very well, until one evening when Daphne was supposed to be working the snack bar, but came home early because she wasn't feeling well.

When she walked in, she found Ian watching a movie on his laptop in the bedroom. He was watching one of her mother's movies.

For reasons that she couldn't even comprehend, there was a sickening feeling in her stomach as though she had been punched. For a moment, she couldn't breath. When the breath did come again, intense anger flooded her nervous system.

"What are you watching?"

"Just...nothing. A movie."

From the easy tone of his voice, it was evident that he did not notice her emotional state. And so he looked over at her with a mystified expression when she cried out "Why are you doing that? How could you?"

"What do you mean? What's the problem? I've never seen any of her movies before. I've only ever seen her tabloid shots. You were in some of those, too. You were such a pretty little girl..." He smiled, trying to cajole.

"I don't want you watching that." Even as she said this, her eyes were scanning the screen, over his shoulder. It was one of her mother's first films. The thriller where she played the young wife of a Victorian era doctor who was actually a serial killer. In the scene, Ian was watching her mother was running down a stairway, long skirt raised, tripping over her buttoned boots. Eyes enormous and terrified. It was the performance that first got her noticed.

Daphne turned her face away as her mother ran through the foggy streets of London; she knew what would happen next. A dark figure in the alley, a stifled scream.

"This movie is such an overdramatic piece of crap anyway," she said, turning away.

"I was just curious."

"Well, don't be."

"Come on. Don't you even miss her at all?"

Daphne laughed bitterly. "No!"

"Come on. It's like, you always defend your father, but when it comes to her you—"

"I just don't feel particularly sorry for her, even if the whole world does!"

"Why?"

"I never saw her when I was growing up! She was never there! And even when she was there, she wasn't. She could never see me. When I was little, I was desperate for her to see me. To really notice me. She never did. After a while I gave up trying. I was better off for it."

When she was little, she used to watch her mother's movies over and over again. On the screen, her mother seemed more human and more accessible than she did when she was actually in the room with her. When she was home, in real life, she stayed in bed a lot with headaches. She cried a lot. And when she wasn't sad, she was a little too happy, in a manic, scary way. When Daphne tried to snuggle up to her, her mother seemed so high strung and tense, like she was made of wire. Like her voltage could give someone an electrical shock. Her breathing was shallow and forced. Her skin always smelled of those bruised flower petals, and that something metallic underneath...

It was these movies that Daphne turned to for comfort when she was feeling sad or lonely. Her movie mother was made of a gold and flickering light that bathed and warmed her as she sucked her thumb and fell asleep.

Ian turned the movie off, shrugged. "Well. It's your life."

"Please, don't even pay attention to this stuff. I'm begging you"

"I'm not searching it out. I just check the news sometimes. I want to know if they're looking for you. Because maybe I don't want them to take you away from me."

"Are they? Looking for me?" In her mind's eye, she saw the strange man again with the frog lips and the round glasses. He haunted her dreams.

"I haven't seen anything. It's weird. Nothing about you. Nothing about the nanny."

"Hmm." Again, there was that ache of emptiness that emanated from her chest when she thought of Cathy and the way she had let Daphne go. The sense of loss and betrayal always felt fresh. She had to remind herself that it was all inevitable, that Cathy had already warned her that she was going to leave. But that knowledge didn't blunt the pain.

"I thought you said the past was dead," she said to him after some time.

"Huh? I never said that," he said, frowning at her. He so seemed sincere that perhaps it was true. Had she imagined it?

"Well, I prefer to keep it dead."

"Okay. That's cool. Whatever." He closed his eyes. "I just think you should think things through. You know, from everyone's perspective..."

"You mean I should talk to my mother again?"

"I didn't say that..."

"Then what were you saying?"

But she didn't stay to hear what his answer would be, because she had already started walking out of the room.

For her sixteenth birthday, he took her to dinner at a good Italian restaurant, a dark place where they sat in a high walled booth with a single candle flame illuminating the space between them. Ian's face loomed in the darkness ghoulishly. It made her laugh. A lot of things were making her laugh recently, though they weren't funny. She had a permanent case of nervous giggles, she didn't know why. She didn't feel exactly mirthful. It was more like a convulsion she couldn't control.

"You think everything is funny."

"It's not that. I just..." But she couldn't get the rest out, laughter wretched from her tight throat like sobs.

She was touched, though, that he had taken her out, and even given her a present: a pendant shaped like a tiny silver dagger, a little drop of garnet blood at its tip. It looked like his wrist tattoo. Tenderly, he fastened the cool chain around her neck.

She was happy, but feeling also a bit queasy and light headed, as though she didn't quite inhabit her body. At home, much later as they were lying in bed, she told him, "I don't think

I want to work at RealLife anymore."

"Why?"

"I don't like those people. I don't like the whole...philosophy. It all feels really cheap and sort of demoralizing."

"To them?"

"To me."

He was quiet a long time. "You can do what you want."

"Okay."

This time, a longer pause. "But you know, I don't know if you'll find anything else. There aren't really any jobs. All the jobs are at places like RealLife and The Black Box, even though you don't want to believe it. People want these jobs. And you can't get them without connections."

"I'll find something."

"What makes you so sure?"

"I'm not sure. I just can't do this anymore. I'd rather starve."

"That's easy to say for someone like you."

"Someone like who?"

"Someone who's never starved! I mean, being born to the station that you were, I'm just not sure that you understand how money works."

"That's not true."

"Someone has always bailed you out."

"You think I'm that weak?"

"No offense. It's just the truth." He turned away from her. "I suppose you will look down on me for staying there."

"Of course not."

"I sometimes get this odd feeling that you always look down on me."

She sighed. She didn't know how things always changed so quickly between them, from good to bad. From laughing to fighting. Tears sprung to her eyes, but she would not let him see. She cried with no sound, no movement. Sometimes she wanted to walk away, but she couldn't. She loved him.

In her agitation and despair, she would hardly sleep at all

that night. She mostly stared up at the ceiling, and when she dozed she was startled back into alertness by sudden visions of the lynx that jolted her like an electric shock. In the jerky quick-motion of a silent film, he was running and bounding straight towards her, again and again. It made her flinch and gasp aloud.

6

Whenever Daphne asked him about his past, Ian had managed to put her off. He would tell her the past was irrelevant. Or he would smile coolly, shrug, and say he didn't remember a lot.

But Ian remembered it all, as much as he tried not to. The more he willed himself to forget, the more the memories would bleed into his dreams at night. And once again, he was fourteen years old, and he was with his father and his father's friends in the middle of the night. In the middle of the desert. Just a skinny, quiet, scared-eyed boy fiddling with his compass, trying to look like he knew what he was doing, as his father and the other men drunkenly hooted and zigzagged over the dry riverbed, hunting rattlesnakes. The full desert moon showed them in silhouette, like cavemen traversing a prehistoric land.

Ian stayed with his father on weekends when he was stationed at the military base. He never knew his father that well. A high ranking intelligence officer in the army, his father was a squat, sturdy man without much to say by way of small talk. He had been to war, but he would not tell his family where. The one thing Ian did know, by implication, was that his father thought that he was weak. Quiet. Effeminate. Given to listening to music and reading books, a waste of time, he always said. He would punch him in the arm with a wink, and say I'll make you into a real man if it kills me.

Summer evenings, his father would always take him out on these trips to hang out with his buddies, way out in the canyon. Their car would speed down dirt roads. It was such a desolate place, so far out there, mountains looming deep blue in the distance. It was all dust and tumbleweeds and nothingness. A man can do as he pleases out here, his father said with a satisfied smile.

When at last they got to his friend Len's house, the music would already be playing. Ted Nugent and Lynard Skynard. The meat would be grilling, they would drink beer after beer as the sun set spectacularly in the distance. Some of the guys were friends from the Army. Some were not. A couple looked like wild Hell's Angels. They would get good and drunk and talk about women and guns and hunting. Ian, after a while, would wander off on his own to catch lizards. It scared him, to be out so far from anything, with these drunk and unpredictable men. He had told his mother he didn't want to make the visits anymore. But she had given him a grim, purse-lipped smile and told him she had no choice. You only have to deal with him a couple days at a time. I spent my whole life with him.

Once it was dark outside, his father would bark at him to get his ass back, and they would pile into their cars and trucks and speed off, further into the desert. "Boy," his father would say to him, slurring his words, "I ain't gonna let you grow up to be no whiny ass liberal pussy. Imma teach you about snake huntin'. You're gonna learn a thing or two about living off the land, being a real man..." He went off on the same diatribe every time. Later, young Ian would settle down, look at the night sky with his large, watchful solemn eyes, wishing so badly that he was somewhere else, he could almost will his atoms to disassemble. He tried to will his body to fade away to vapor, to reappear far away. In his bedroom at home, in his mother's tidy little apartment in town...

But the snake hunting parties were something he had to

endure. He was given his own snake stick, a flashlight, and the compass. But all he did was stand there, too afraid to move, not knowing what was lurking on the ground near his feet. Some of the men wore chaps around their ankles, so nothing would bite them. Not Ian and his father. Ian shone his flashlight around and around near his feet. Sometimes the quivering beam caught the retreating white tail of a rabbit. Sometimes a lizard. Sometimes a tarantula.

And this was the part he still dreamed of the most now days: That he was alone in the dark with grown men growling and bellowing like animals in the dark, his paltry flashlight revealing something lurking, slithering, with flashing teeth...

When he woke from these nightmares, he would be breathless, heart pounding, not recognizing where he was in those first moments. Then he would find himself in his bed, the familiar outlines of the bedroom emerging. There was the girl, asleep next to him.

He was not sure how it was that he came to be with her. There had been others before her, of course. Many others. He could not even explain how she was different.

In the lonely hours of these insomniac dawns, he would watch her sleeping form. She was so young. And she had lived a life so sheltered, a life that he could not even imagine. Her stories of being raised in such wealth and privilege were repulsive to him...and yet had so much power over his imagination. He loved the girl, hated the father. Because it was her father and his kind who had ruined so many military men like his father, and so were responsible for young Ian's misery.

But there was something else there, too, that made him love her in spite of himself. A steely will and intelligence. And also, a purity of vision most people did not have. Maybe he really did love her.

Since he was sixteen and left home, he had always been on the move. He had grown up from that watchful eyed boy into a man. He was still skinny, but muscled with a wiry strength.

Though he had dropped out of school, he was well read, a self taught man. He had a quick, sharp mind, a scornful sarcastic tongue. He had found a niche for himself in the underground circles, playing in these bands, hanging out afterhours. Here, others respected him, even seemed to find him intimidating. They thought he was fearless. Wise. Sometime he even believed them. Maybe his father was wrong, and he was a real man. Did it matter either way? Yes, a voice deep in his head told him.

He lay in the dark, stroking the swell of Daphne's hip. He remembered more from the dream. The men had caught a rattler, at least five feet long, lashing furiously. They held it down and cut off the head, burying it in the sand because it could still bite. Once they had slit open the snake's belly, still writhing. It had been pregnant. The men scattered as the baby snakes came slithering out. They could bite, too. Young Ian had staggered back in horror, dropping his flashlight, vomiting in the dark.

He could still feel that fear, hear the jeering voices in his head as his fingers trailed over Daphne's sleeping form. He tried to reassure himself that only this was real, the girl, the quiet bedroom, here, now.

He was the older one, the stronger one.

In her beautiful innocence, she loved him. In her ignorance. Because surely he was not worthy of something so pure as her love.

He dug his fingers in a little deeper into her hip. She stirred, turned over, and wrapped her arms around him, laying her sleeping head on his chest. While he stayed ever vigilant, staring up at a long winding crack in the ceiling.

She sat in her favorite corner, sketchbook in her lap. She would spend long minutes watching Ian, her eyes intent and her lips parted. He was in bed, trying to read, trying to concentrate. But at the same time he felt the force of her gaze. It made him feel flustered, as though he were being stalked, and he put down the book and stared back at her. When he looked up, she looked down, sketching and scribbling away.

"Why do you always have to draw me when I'm not looking?"

"I want to remember you this way. Right now. In this moment."

At that particular moment, dust motes floated in a beam of sunlight. A television from the apartment next door rumbled faintly. A car backfired on the street below.

"Sounds ominous. You say that like I'm not always going to be here."

Daphne shrugged, glanced again up at him, her eyes tracing the line of muscle in his arm. She didn't seem to be really listening. He went back to his book.

"What are you reading, anyway?" she asked.

He held the book up, a black cover with red letters. Secrets of the Illuminati.

"Oh, come on!" she said.

"I'm not saying I believe in everything I read," he said with a smirk.

"So why do you read all those conspiracy books if you always tell me you don't believe them?"

"I'm just interested. I soak it all up like a sponge." He collected books about Bible prophecies, the Trilateral Commission, and various secret societies. Daphne teased him about it, and he acted like he didn't care. But afterward, he would always act a little cold toward her.

Daphne had been walking the streets that day, looking for help wanted signs. She still worked shifts at the club, but it didn't pay anything. She tried to work on her paintings, but she had trouble. When she tried to create, nothing would come. It was making her irritable.

"I don't know what's wrong with me. I'm blocked."

"Why?"

"I don't know. It's been since I started hating working at

RealLife. Especially since that guy with the creepy art collection. I think it did something to my head."

"It ought to inspire you."

She snorted. The subject was a sore point between them.

"I'm serious."

"I told you I hated that job."

"Well, as you can see, there's nothing else out there. Although I do have a lead for you. If you're interested."

"What?"

He smiled sheepishly and looked down "Well. It's a new agency called Living Angels. They want young, pretty girls like you."

"For what?"

"To pretend to be dead. Makeup, fake blood. It's a new thing, I don't know what it all means, but there are some people who like it when you pretend to be a dead girl, and the game is that they have to hide you. You play a corpse. I guess it's the thrill of danger of getting caught."

"No way."

"It's like dinner theatre. I'd do it if I were a girl."

"Well, I'm not." She flung down her drawing pad. "I'm sick of it all. I'll do one more assignment with you and that's it. But after that I don't know what else to do."

"We could always leave."

She looked at him carefully. "And go where?"

"Wherever we want. I have some buddies living in Detroit. They've taken over a whole neighborhood block. Bought these old stripped down houses for nothing. They grow their own food. They made these old cars into little greenhouses."

"I don't believe that. They're messing with you."

"It's true. They're pretty happy there."

"Well..." She stared into space, saying nothing for a while.

"We wouldn't have to go there," he said. "There are lots of places."

"Oh yeah?"

"Yeah." He turned to look at her, deadly serious. "There is no reason we have to stay here. This city is falling apart. It's unsustainable. Why should we stay here if there's nothing keeping us?"

"Well. I guess there isn't..." But she was surprised at how even the thought of leaving made her anxious. True, she was cut off from her mother. But she was still close. She was orbiting her like an invisible planet. Moving away entirely was something else altogether, It was so...final.

But she said nothing about this. Ian had a rapt look on his face, his eyes trained on nothing, a point in the distance that only he could see.

"We could start over someplace in the Midwest. New pioneers. We could go to Canada. We could go to the North Pole. I've always wanted to go to the North Pole since I was a kid."

She could see him, in her mind's eye, a lone stark figure against a barren tundra of white. Huge icebergs of lurid blue, floating in an icy sea. Ian, struggling alone in the arctic wind, planting a flag in the snow. It made her heart stop to imagine him in this way, so small and vulnerable. Maybe she really did love him.

"What do you think?" He asked, clutching her hand.

She didn't know what to say. It seemed in that moment their roles had reversed. She was the older, more jaded one. And he was the young dreamer.

"We could go to Israel and live on a kibbutz. We could go to Russia and sell batteries on the black market. All we have to do is decide..."

She thought, He might as well be talking about going to Mars. But it made her happy to see him happy.

"I have wanted to do this since I was a kid," he said. "I always have this feeling that if I can just find the perfect situation, I will just recognize it, and then my real life will begin. I've been waiting twenty years now for it to really begin..."

He let her hand go, looked away, then looked back at her nervously.

"What is it, Ian?"

"It's just...I've been doing nothing but running since I was fifteen. That was the last time I ever saw my father." He swallowed, looked away, then looked back. "I don't know if I told you, but he was an army intelligence officer. He'd just been acting more and more erratic since my mom left him. These outbursts and stuff. Then something happened, when he was stationed in the Middle East, when he had beaten up a woman. It took three men to pull him off. All this...stuff. He'd want to drive up into the desert mountains with me to shoot guns at glass bottles and rant about secret prisons and shit like that. Surveillance and reconnaissance satellites. He pointed up into the desert night, to show me the streaks and blips like dabbles of neon paint.

"When he talked about that stuff, he would start to slur and not make much sense. I'll show them all, he said, There's a lot more I got to say before this is all over and done. I don't know how much was real and what was not. I was there listening when he hung out with his army officer friends in the desert. They would get drunk late at night and start telling stories about killing militants at the Afghan border with rockets on mules and shit..."

Daphne didn't say a word. She just put a hand on his shoulder, which was trembling ever so slightly.

"Anyway, he was demoted from his position after he started to crack. Then later, as he got worse, discharged because of stress. An "adjustment order," they called it. Ha. The government took him away for weeks, for treatment. My mom and I weren't even allowed to know where he was. But I wasn't exactly that sad about it.

"But then, he came back. A civilian, for the first time in his adult life.

"He would not say anything about what had happened to

him, when he was away. He was all blank eyed. One hand was bandaged where an IV drip had been. There was a small scar on the top of his scalp, covered by a bandage. He had been sent home with all these amber RX bottles. When anyone asked what they were, he shrugged.

"His anger was gone. And he never did meet with his friends to get drunk and shoot in the desert again. He didn't seem interested in anything anymore.

"It kind of freaked me out. His silence was not the peaceful kind. Behind the flat, lined look of him, I could feel that my dad's old self still existed. Helpless, flailing, drowning. I couldn't stand to look at him, to even be near him." Ian blinked rapidly, his face turned to the wall.

"I'm sorry. That's awful. I wonder what they did to him?"

Ian snorted. "They used him as a human guinea pig is what they did."

"Who is 'they'?"

"The government. People like your father. That's why I thought you might know about this stuff more than me."

Daphne looked horrified; inside, her heart began to race with anger. It was true, it was all true. She felt righteous indignation for all the wrongs that were done by her people. It was all so much worse when it was affecting her beloved. It gave her a bloodlust to fight them back. Ian saw the pained look on her face and shook his head.

"Just, never mind that. Anyway. I had always been a quiet, sensitive kind of kid. I was happy just to hide in my room, reading books and strumming my guitar. But something about what had happened to my father had filled me with these emotions I couldn't even name. I became this angry kid, losing my temper, getting thrown out of class for talking back to the teachers. My anger seemed to fuel a growth spurt, and I grew to six feet two in the space of one summer. I started cutting myself with a razor blade and wearing white t-shirts smeared with the blood. I spiked my hair and wore dark eyeliner. And when I got my driver's license, that was it. I dropped out of school and took off in this old van and never went back."

"So that was it? You just took off and that was that?"

"Yeah. I don't know. Maybe it was out of sheer boredom." Or maybe, he thought, it was the sight of Ian's drowned-eyed father, sitting on a nylon lawn chair with his mouth open, that made Ian want to run. "It seemed like only noise and velocity could make me feel at ease. I never lived in one place for more than a couple of months. Never stayed in one band. And never stayed with the same girl."

He took her hand again, and looked into her eyes. "Until now." He had never looked at her like this before. Gone was the veil of cool irony. His face was flushed, his lips were quivering. She was astounded that he had opened up this way.

"Please, Daphne. Let's keep running together. Neither of us has to be alone anymore. Come with me."

She had never told anyone about the knife. It was a tiny switchblade with a mother-of-pearl handle that glowed a soft pink like a winter sky at dusk. It was cool and smooth and felt delicious the way it nestled in her hand, where no one could even see that she had it.

Mac, a guy she met at the club, had given it to her. "You need some protection," he said, "Everyone needs to be able to defend themselves." Mac was an older guy, mid-forty-ish with silver buzzed hair, but there was still something youthful and elfish about his face. He had pressed the knife into her hand out of nowhere one night, then stared into her eyes with a look of great significance.

"I don't need a knife, thanks," she said with a laugh, trying to pass it back.

He took it and showed her how to open it. It came alive with a spring and a click. All of the dim, dirty light of the place seemed condensed and transformed on the blade so that it gleamed back with a hard, steely glow. She was entranced, the music was pounding, it was two in the morning and she was half asleep. And yet everything was hyper-real. She could hear Mac's words perfectly over the noise as he held the blade to the hollow of his throat and said, "You are too soft for your own good. There may come a time when you have to cut a man. If I had a daughter, I'd have taught her long ago. But I don't have a daughter. So I'll teach you."

"But I don't need it. Nobody bothers me."

"You never know what's going to happen, girly. That's the problem. You have to use your imagination. There's infinite possibilities, every moment. You must consider all of them, and be prepared." He shifted and pressed the blade to one side of his neck. "Jugular. If anybody messes with you, pin him right there. Trust me, he won't move. Or," he motioned a short, savage slice. "He'll be geisering his life out right at your feet."

She did not like to picture such gory scenes. But she did like the knife. She liked the idea of it, so perfect and so small and so deadly, right there in her pocket if she chose to reach for it. She practiced when she was alone. In one quick fluid motion, she could have it out and sprung open, pinned to that pulsing pressure point, under which the rich flow of life throbbed through the vein.

She liked to walk home by herself in the early mornings. The streets and people were still gray and dirty, but the air seemed to glow with the promising yellowy wash of morning sun. The air felt cooler, and fresh in her lungs. She felt tall and expansive, strong. Passing her own reflection in windows, she barely recognized herself. All her life she had been the painted child, a hedge fund princess dressed in silk and pearls and flower petals. In tiny clicking heels that bound her feet so she could hardly walk.

Now, her blond hair was shaggy and rough. In her baggy pants and her combat boots, she strode through the streets with her hands deep in her pockets, fingering the knife, shoulders thrust forward, head at a cocky angle; ever since Ian had begun to show that he loved her, she had been deluged with confusing feelings. On the one hand, she was giddy with joy, and loved him too, with a desperation that swamped her body with pulsating desire. But she was also afraid. If she surrendered herself to this love, where would it get her? Where had it ever gotten her? She had loved her father, and her mother, and Cathy. All had in different ways deserted her in return. Vulnerability was a scary feeling. It was some consolation to at least look strong, and act strong, and to know that the knife, at least, was there if she ever needed it..

She had a chain wallet, which clanged merrily against her hip with each step. She felt like a mobster or a young girl-pirate. She thought about what Mac had said, about each moment's infinite possibilities. These possibilities seemed to jingle in her pockets like gold coins that she could spend as she wished. She felt rich, magnanimous, radiant with her own good fortune. There were possibilities to spare, but in those moments she was happy with things exactly as they were.

Daphne and Ian had a job assignment that night, the last she agreed to do. It was a client they had worked with before, a weepy middle-aged man with gold-rimmed glasses and a large signet ring on his pinky. Ian said he was an oil magnate. When they were through with him, he always liked for them to leave him in a drainage ditch on the edge of his own estate, blindfolded, with his hands left bound together so that he had to get out on his own.

Which they did, just the same as they had before. And as they left him behind, walking down a footpath through the sprawling trees, they could still hear him back there, grunting and sniffling as he tried to make his way over and up, like a turtle on its back.

"Poor thing," said Daphne lightly. Though she didn't feel much of anything. It all was becoming so routine.

"Poor nothing," said Ian. "It's nothing but a game. He's on his guarded property surrounded by an electric fence. What's going to happen to him?"

"It's sad he has to do this to feel anything."

"Well. It is kind of pathetic."

"I pity anyone who can't feel alive as I do."

It was a moonlit night. They could make out the form of a security guard up ahead, leaning against a tree, looking up at the stars. They flashed their ID cards at him, but he barely glanced over, giving them a slight nod.

"He out there in his usual place?" the guard asked in a softly gruff voice.

"Yep."

"I take it you're leaving then?"

"We're on our way back to the gate. We can find our own way out," Daphne told him.

"I'll keep an eye," he said, but he returned his gaze to the night sky.

She wanted to take her time. This was one of the loveliest places, out of all the estates they had worked at. Up ahead they came upon a Japanese style garden, complete with a waterfall and a Koi pond. They walked across a beautiful wooden moonbridge whose trellises were covered in wisteria.

"I love it here," she said, gazing at the moon reflected in the pond.

"It's okay."

"I think it's wonderful." One thing that she missed, since leaving home, was beauty. As invigorating as it was to live in the underbelly of the city, there was something to be said for cultivation and order. Something to be said of a pathway of smooth white stones, the soft glow of a hand carved granite lantern, the smell of evergreen.

"He has all of this," she said to herself, "and he can't enjoy it. He's paying us to tie him up and throw him in a ditch. Amazing."

"You can get used to anything. He probably doesn't see any of this anymore."

"Yeah, you're right." When she had lived in beauty, she was blind to it, too. It had even felt like a prison. But now that she had lost it, it was all clear to her. Now she could appreciate what she no longer had.

Ian was watching her profile as she stared into the lake. At last he said, "I've been looking into getting a car."

"Why? We don't really need one."

"We will if we decide to leave. It's not like we can take the RealLife van. I know a guy who has an old hatchback he wants to get off his hands. It's not much. But it has a new transmission. It seems to run okay."

He kept looking at her, to see her reaction. But there seemed to be none. She was as impassive as a stone Madonna.

He began to feel impatient. "What are you thinking about, anyway?"

"Oh. Nothing much." But there was just a hint of melancholy in her voice.

He took a step back and folded his arms, facing away from her. "You're thinking that you miss being rich, aren't you?"

"Don't be ridiculous."

"Well, what do you think about the car?"

"What about it?"

"What do you think about anything?"

"Well, there's a lot to talk about. Nothing has been decided yet."

"Because you always avoid the subject."

"I just don't see the rush to decide anything. I'm pretty happy right now, aren't you?"

He turned back, gave her a long, hard stare. She could feel his change of mood, feel his eyes burning into her like a laser. She could not look at him.

"Daphne, I can't even follow your constant change in emotions. Happy. Sad. Happy. Sad. Some consistency would be nice", He shook his head sadly. "But one thing I can tell. You really miss all this."

She sighed. "I can't help it. It wasn't all bad. Am I supposed to hate my old life just because it was beautiful?"

Ian shrugged. "I never experienced the good life. So I guess I'm not one to say anything." He tried to say it lightly, but it was hard not to have it sound like wounded self-pity. He gave a little laugh, trying to lighten his words, but it sounded bitter.

"I'm glad you told me about your dad," she said gently. "I'm just grateful you told me anything about your life. I want to know more about what you went through."

"There's nothing much to tell. I was middle class. I grew up on military bases. Then my parents split up and I lived in an apartment with my mom. It's not interesting. It's not romantic. It was just depressing in the blandest and most ordinary way..." He threw a stone into the pond, watched the ripples expand in the moonlight.

"Do you really think my father's company is involved with such awful things? It makes me wonder why you would even get together with me. You must think I'm awful. I feel kind of awful. I just want to renounce it all."

Ian touched the side of her face. "It's not your fault. I know you're different than the rest of them. We're here together now, and I don't want to talk about it anymore. I want to go away with you. If you want to renounce it, truly, then let's just go. Are you in?"

"I don't know." She was of two selves. She felt if she moved in any direction, she would split in half.

"Well. I do know that I'm not staying. I couldn't stay here any longer if I wanted to..." Inwardly, his own inconsistency gave him pause. Until recently, he had enjoyed working at RealLife, in his own cynical way. Until he saw it through Daphne's eyes, and then started hating it. Scowling, he shoved his hands in his pockets and walked away, toward the front gate, toward the van. Reluctantly, Daphne followed.

Daphne, too, felt like she had spent her whole life traveling. Just in a different way. Her life before had been full of so many flights on private jets, rides in the back of long, sleek black cars with fine German motors that purred like great cats. Trips to Aspen, trips to the Caymans. There were years when it felt like they never were home at all.

Her very first memory was of being two years old. People told her there was no way to remember anything before age three. But she could remember what it was to be two. She could remember what it was to be formless and sexless. She had had no identity or self image at all. She had been a being of pure, observing consciousness.

She remembered traveling with her parents to Paris Fashion Week. She remembered walking into their sumptuous hotel suite, all done up in glowing white; the only bits of color were the golden bottle of chilled champagne, the purple orchids in a vase, and the plate of pink macaroons.

A car had driven them to different places where they watched people walking around in strange and colorful clothes. Cameras followed the three of them, and they smiled and posed, her father's arm lightly around her mother's waist, Daphne pressed between them on her mother's hip. The noise and the color and the clicking cameras made her feel overwhelmed and dizzy, increasingly ill. She was happy to return to the hotel and splash in the indoor swimming pool, which was very long and broad and beautiful. Here, it was also blindingly white. White walls, high white ceilings, white cushioned chaise lounges.

Back in the room, her parents seemed happy enough, reading the paper and watching movies on the large television. They were pleasant and polite to each other, but Daphne got the feeling that something was wrong, that they were not happy underneath. There was a tension between the two of them, like a thin silver wire that only she could see, a thin, sharp line that hummed and vibrated and filled her with dread.

Daphne had dizzy spells in the room, too. Sudden swooning moments when the hushed whiteness of the room amplified itself until it hurt; her vision went hazy and she heard a noise of static in her ears. When the spell had passed and all was clear again, she would come to suddenly find both her parents leaning over, staring, their faces ashen with concern.

Her mother looked particularly ill at ease during this trip. Almost sickly. She sat on her bed, surrounded by the things she had bought, (garment bags, hatboxes, parcels wrapped in pastel paper) and she looked so small and fragile, like a wary, burrowing creature afraid of the light. She smiled at Daphne often, too often, and patted and smoothed her fretfully. Her tremor seemed to move through her manicured fingers into Daphne's young body.

When Daphne was tucked into her high, white bed of embroidered linens, she could hear her parents arguing from their bedroom. She could only work out bits and pieces of what they were saying, but she recalled her mother saying, "It was the wrong decision. Something has gone wrong. She's my child and I can feel it."

Her father spoke, fast and low and self-assured.

In response, her mother cried, "I don't care what we said our convictions are! How do we really know it was the best thing for her? We're interfering with nature and we'll go to hell for it if we were wrong..."

There was more of her father's murmuring, and then the clink and pour of drinks and then after a while, silence.

The next day her father had to go somewhere for a meeting and was gone when she woke up. Her mother dressed her warmly in a blue velvet dress coat and matching beret. They were going to go out walking together, and get some ice cream.

"How does that sound, Teacup?" Her mother asked. Her large blue eyes were beautiful in spite of the dark shadows underneath. They darted nervously, searching her little girl's face.

They went outside, walking the brick lane roads. She remembered the busy storefronts, the statues. A large group of pigeons that delighted her by suddenly alighting into the air in one fluid, silken motion, like the unfurling of a veil, lifting into the gray November sky.

They went into a gelato shop, an old fashioned looking place of dark wood and gold lettering. The great glass case held square bins of so many rainbow colors. So many choices. So many loud voices, and again that strange echoing sound in her head. Her mother lifted her up, and she began to feel the dizziness again as she chose, and was served, a large waffle cone topped with bright green pistachio gelato, served in the shape of a delicate flower.

Outside again. Tasting the cold green flower under the heavy gray sky. She held her mother's hand. Her mother stopped to gaze into a window. Inside was a beautiful dress. It was worn by a smooth domed, featureless dummy with its head arched delicately on an unnaturally long, thin neck.

The dummy wore a long black dress with black lace panels on the sides. It was full length, and spread out in great swaths around the dummy's feet. For some reason, the dummy was holding a great plumed, white bird on its cocked elbow. The bird looked taxidermied. It had amber glass eyes that looked much too real and frightened Daphne.

Superimposed over this display were the reflections of Daphne and her mother and the streets of Paris behind them. Her mother looked dazed, like a woman walking in her sleep, dreaming all of this. She barely seemed to be cognizant that she was clutching the hand of this little girl in blue velvet, her face like a pale little thumbprint.

The dizziness again: and then everything seemed to suddenly refract into scattered shards of sound and color. Daphne hardly knew where she was anymore. The gelato slipped from her tiny fingers and her legs went out from under her.

The next thing she knew, she was coming into a doctor's office. This room was bright white and immaculate like the hotel suite, but this room was very different. There were rows of brain scans on a lighted wall. The brains were coiled and delicate, ghostly. It was like looking at a wall of tanks full of ethereal sea creatures.

Daphne stared at the lighted images, entranced. Meanwhile, also in the room, were a doctor, a nurse, and her parents, huddled together in one corner. The doctor looked angry. He was speaking in French, rapidly, and gesturing wildly with his arms. The nurse tried to translate for her parents what the doctor was saying. But they all stopped and froze when they noticed that she was awake again and listening.

She watched them back, saying nothing at all. Her mother came to her, put a hand out to touch her but then pulled it back to cover her mouth, which was stretched into a smiling grimace, the way she looked when she was about to burst into tears.

But she wheeled around to all the rest of them and hissed, I've had enough. Enough of you people! You always think you know what's right!

As indelibly as these scenes were etched in her memory, whenever she brought the subject up with her parents, they said they didn't remember it.

"Do you remember the time I was sick in Paris, and I went to the doctor? The doctor with the pictures of brains on the wall?"

She first asked this when she was five, and her father, just back from another trip, red eyed and jet lagged, was sitting with her on his knee.

"I don't know what you mean, Teacup," he answered after a long pause.

"I was with Mommy, I got green ice cream. We were looking at a dress in a window when I got dizzy. You and Mommy took me to the doctor. He had the..."

"I think you're imagining it, honey. Sometimes when you're really young, you imagine things that didn't really happen. It's just your imagination is so big, sometimes it plays tricks on you. Even though it seems really real. Doesn't it?"

Daphne had been speechless. It had happened, of this she was sure. But now she was confused, because she always trusted her father, about everything.

She gaped at him, eyes large and already watering, not knowing exactly what to do.

At last she climbed down from his lap, and ran to her room, as fast as though she were being chased. Then she slammed the door.

It was the only time she could ever remember being angry at her father. Sometimes it made her angry, still.

She stood at her easel. White hot sunlight streamed down through the studio windows. The noise and thrash of the band that rehearsed downstairs barely infiltrated her brain. She was so intent on what she was doing that she paid no attention to what was going on around her.

She was painting a little girl with white blonde bobbed hair, dressed in a blue velvet coat, white stockings, and white calfskin shoes. She was stretched out on a gurney, unconscious. Her small face had the life blotted out of it. Her lids were shadowed so that they looked like the eyeholes of a skull. The lips were parted like an old fashioned doll's, showing a hint of tiny white milk teeth just in the front.

Tall figures loomed above her, watching, but the viewer could not see them directly. All that showed were their long, sloping shadows that were cast down over the sleeping girl and the white walls that surrounded her.

Floating, above the girl's head, were the beautiful and

ghostly brain scans. They hovered there like angels. Creatures there to protect the girl who could not protect herself.

Daphne worked all day and into dusk on the painting. It felt as though something else were compelling her to take up the brush, to fill in the outlines of these images. She worked in a sort of fevered trance. Every cell in her body was alive with electricity.

When it started to grow dark outside, she had to stop, even though she was not yet finished. She stood back and really looked for the first time at what she had done. She was not unpleased. For the first time, she was able to objectively look at her own work and say that it was good. She could not stop staring at the helpless little girl in the painting. She could not help but to be drawn in, to care. To wonder: what has happened to this child?

She vowed as she was standing there, looking into the face of the unconscious child, that one day she would find out the truth.

When Daphne went home that night, she felt completely drained. Exhausted. When Ian came home with takeout from the Tai place down the street, he had to wake her. She had fallen asleep, even though it was only eight o'clock.

But it was a good kind of exhausted, as though she had run a marathon. Working that day had made her feel right again, for the first time in a long time. And she was ready for more.

LEAH ERICKSON

184

7

Daphne had just ended her shift at the snack bar. It was late in the evening and she was in the club's filthy bathroom, leaning against the sink, eyes closed. She had another headache, the kind that made her see flashing lights in her vision, and was feeling sick from breathing too much second hand cigarette smoke. She splashed cold water on her face and dried it with her sleeve, looking wearily at her own reflection in the mirror.

Just then, the door slammed open, and a girl came tumbling into the room as though she had been pushed. But she was laughing. She stumbled into the overflowing trashcan, then into the bathroom stall where she took a long piss, still laughing, without shutting the door.

Daphne moved aside to give the girl the sink. She had a broad, plain face, round like a peasant girl's, her expression wide open and friendly. Despite her wholesome looks, her body was covered in tattoos and tribal jewelry. Her hair was buzzed short and bleached lemon yellow. Her eyes met Daphne's in the smudged mirror.

"Hey, I know you," she drawled. "You've got that boyfriend. The one that's always all..." she pantomimed someone standing ramrod straight, lips pursed, looking disdainful. "He always looks all judgy. It must be a drag."

"Well, it's not." Annoyed, she tried to walk past the girl.

"Television?"

"Excuse me?"

The girl fished out a gold pill case from her pocket, opened it and handed Daphne a small pink capsule. Daphne held it close to her face. It was, indeed, printed with a picture of a tiny, old fashioned television console.

"Take it!" the girl urged brightly. "It makes you feel like nothing's real and you're starring in a television show. I even get laugh tracks sometimes. It makes the tendons in your neck stiffen up, too, I don't know why. But. Yeah."

"No thanks." She handed it back, frowning. "I, uh, have to go..."

"Wait!" The girl gripped her shoulder. "I want to be friends with you. I've seen you around. I get this feeling you're always the smartest person in the room. Way smarter than your boyfriend, for sure."

"How do you know?" Daphne asked, amused.

"By your eyes. I can see those wheels turning. You're smart. But sad. You need some fun."

True enough, Daphne thought, but did not say so.

"I'm Liz," she drawled, getting close to her face, "And you are going to meet me out front of this place tomorrow. Noon." She shook Daphne's shoulder, playfully.

Daphne laughed, it was all so absurd, and she was so tired that she was feeling punch drunk. "Why? What are we doing tomorrow at noon?"

"You'll see."

"It's our own special game," Liz told her, the sun gleaming in her yellow fuzzy hair. "We're hunting drones."

The group around them, no one of which appeared to be over sixteen, started to laugh, seeing the startled face that Daphne made when they showed her the rifle. What am I doing here? she thought. The group was very gaudily clad. They wore metallic hoodies and had their faces painted with odd, asymmetrical patterns on their cheeks and brows. It's to throw off the facial recognition algorithms, Liz had said back at her apartment as she painted Daphne's face with the tickling brush. It was soothing and familiar, to feel another woman painting her face. Like Cathy used to in another, far away life.

Liz, her new friend, had brought her here to hang out. Though Daphne initially thought her insane, she came to find that Liz was actually a focused and ambitious girl, with a very cutting intelligence. She worked as a "cool hunter" for a corporation whose name she would not divulge. It was her job to spot trends on the street. She studied and catalogued young people's dress, their speech, their gestures, then reported her findings in write ups she produced for her bosses. Even though she was kooky and affable, she had a discerning eye and an unending stream of pronouncements. It made Daphne proud that Liz had studied and picked her of all people.

"It's all stone cold data," Liz explained as they spent an afternoon taking pictures of skateboarders. "I like my job. I'm like an evil genius. A spy. The inside of my head is worth huge money. And the suckers pay."

Daphne liked the contradictions in her new friend. She liked both the sharpness of her intellect, and her childlike enthusiasm.

And she knew how to have fun. Her friends were now Daphne's friends. Liz told her that later she could join her on her rounds to clothing and shoe stores to show off samples. And when Liz would interview kids on the street, Daphne could help, secretly recording them with a microphone hidden up her sleeve.

They had been drinking whiskey shots in the middle of the day, discussing these future plans; they had also both taken pills that were called manna rays. "They make you feel like you're under water. But in a good way," Liz slurred, "You're swimming, but fast. Like a torpedo going straight toward a target."

Daphne could see what she meant. There was a hushed quality to the outside world, but Daphne herself felt stealthy and sharp and lethal. "I don't want to be the torpedo," she said later, sitting on the curb watching the explosions of sun glinting on the chrome of hubcaps, the squashed soda cans that line the street where they are all sitting on the curb. It was all scintillating and beautiful. "I'm not the torpedo. I'm the target."

"You are both in one," says Liz, tipping her face up to the sky and smiling beatifically. "You are unstoppable. You are a beautiful genius. But you need to figure out what it is you want to do."

"I..." Daphne shut her eyes. "I just want to be heard. I don't want to be controlled anymore. I want to do something great all on my own. And I want to make money, just like you. "

Liz laughed. "You're smart, all right. You just need to learn how to hustle. You tell them what they want and they'll buy it. I'm an urban cowgirl myself." She leaned in confidentially, and winked. "Even though my blood runs as blue as yours."

"What do you mean by that?"

"I know who you are," Liz whispered. Then she laughed at Daphne's stricken expression. "Don't look at me like that. It's okay! I just keep an ear to the street, that's all."

Daphne gaped at her, feeling alarmed that Liz could know who she was. She was still sometimes afraid of being discovered and sent home. It was only recently that she had stopped spotting the frog-lipped man with the round glasses; she no longer glimpsed him watching her in the streets like a specter who disappeared the minute she stared back. He may have been gone, but the paranoia sometimes still reared its head.

In spite of these thoughts, the pill, the manna ray, began to seep a soothing indifference into her system. A smooth and slippery coolness. Everything would be okay. She recovered herself, smiled, and winked back at Liz rakishly. . All afternoon she had found herself taking on her new friend's habits. She'd adopted her wild, sudden laughter. She found herself imitating both her cool skepticism and her silly, goony sense of humor.

And now she was standing at the curb with this crowd of young people in their silver and face paint.

The tallest kid, a boy with large brown eyes peeking out from his peaked metallic head covering, was the one who handled the gun. Deer rifle, he said in a faint scratchy adolescent voice, when he caught Daphne staring.

"What exactly are we supposed to be doing?" Daphne asked, smiling gamely. Usually she was so cautious, always thinking before she acted. But the pills still coursed through her veins, making her feel invincible. She was speeding forward through great depths. She didn't need to know what was going to happen. She was compelled by a type of sonar. Everything felt intentional. She was in control. And yet she was flying free.

She thought of trying to explain that to her group of new friends. But they were all busy peering up into the sky.

"Hold on. Soon," said Liz. "Shh."

And there it was, if you listened hard enough, the faint putter putter from up ahead.

"Here they come!"

It was one of the drones that passed by overhead several times a day, so quiet and insignificant that you hardly noticed it or thought about it. This particular one was small, like a helicopter, flying at about bird height.

Suddenly, BAM! BAM, BAM! It dropped to the ground as suddenly as a shot goose. Little bits and parts were flying everywhere. It was so small! So like an eight-legged spider. It tugged at Daphne's heart a little bit because it reminded her of her old friend, Freddy, the robot swan. Suddenly, images of Freddy's little black camera-eyed face flashed unbidden into her mind, like a strobe light, flash, flash, flash, making her feel disoriented, making her head hurt. But she snapped out of it when Liz grabbed her and they were running down the street as fast as they could. After a bit they stopped to catch their breath in an alleyway.

Daphne could not stop laughing. She could barely get out her words.

"Oh my God! That was crazy. Who knew it was so easy to do that!"

Liz pulled out a cigarette from her pocket, lit it. The triangles and dots painted on her face made her look a bit scary and savage when she scowled as she was doing now.

"But Liz, what do you do it for?"

"We do it because it's fun. And it sends them the message that they aren't as powerful as they think."

Daphne remembered the night she had fled with Cathy in the soldier's jeep. The crowd of people throwing stuff, rushing like they were going to flip them over. It had frightened her so badly, not knowing why those people did these things. And now she had crossed over to the other side. She was them now. They had accepted her in spite of herself. Which was a good thing; her people hadn't come looking for her, anyway. It seemed they had just given up.

Even through the hurt of it, all she could do anymore was laugh. It was the best time she had ever had.

The pill she had taken didn't seem to be wearing off as the day went on. Even though she had taken a nap at home, she still felt unusual sensations when she went to the club that night. Y Shaped Coffin was playing. The place had always been dark and dingy, but that night she did not see the filth at all. The shadows of the place were deep and cool and mysterious, like sea coves. And all of the people seemed to glimmer with phosphorescence. A girl in a stocking cap swaying on her feet in the corner looked like a mermaid drifting in the tide. A group of dirty looking boys clinging to the edge of the stage reminded her of heaving barnacles. The dreadlocked boy working the panels of the mixing board was a beatific octopus, his arms everywhere at once. When he saw her watching he gave a nod. Daphne didn't do anything back. She was floating away in her own euphoria, too high to react.

She made her way to the stage. Ian was up there, but he didn't see her. He was playing his guitar. He was not hunched over his instrument like the others, but stood straight and tall. For just that moment she saw him as a stranger. Everyone else around him was so wasteful and sloppy looking, whereas he looked so intent and focused. She loved his large, squared off hands with the calluses on his fingers. She liked the veins threading up his forearms as he played.

Mine, she thought to herself as she drew closer and closer to him. I claim this boy for myself. She felt magnanimous with good fortune.

As they finished their set, she watched him as he made small talk with the band, gulped from his water bottle and lit a cigarette.

She came up behind him as he listened to something a short pixie-like girl was saying to him. Daphne put her arms around his sweaty ribcage, feeling the muscles under the skin contract with surprise at her touch.

"Oh, hey," he said as she put her mouth on his, cutting him off.

He drew back and smiled at her, took her hand and led her over to sit on the couch.

"We were just talking earlier. About the band. Steve's leaving. He's moving with his girlfriend to the east coast."

"Oh." She never knew Steve, the singer, very well. She had experienced him mostly on stage where he thrashed around anticly and scream-sang until his throat was raw. "Does that mean you're looking for someone else now?"

He shrugged. "I don't know. I don't think I'll be staying around much longer myself. The whole thing has kind of played itself out. I'm not feeling it anymore. The energy is kind of gone."

"It seemed like you had great energy tonight."

"Yeah. Well. You know what they say. All good things…"

He smiled at her significantly. She was drawn in again by his face. The lean foxy narrowness and that lovely contrast of his full lower lip. She stroked his cheek like a sculptor. She had a sudden image in her head of what this face would look like in thirty years. She could see him, wise and weathered looking. The tender skin would turn leathery, the eyebrows tuftier and threaded with gray…

"Hey, what's up?" he asked, frowning at her. "You look kind of weird. Are you on something?"

"I was with Liz today, and I made some new friends, and…" she began, but didn't know how to complete the sentence. She wanted to tell him how much fun she had had. Running through the streets with a gang of kids, not caring about anything for once. Just playing, as she never had when she was young. At last she said, "We took some pills. We shot down a drone."

He looked at her for a few beats, his eyes laser focused on her.

"What exactly did you take?"

"Something blue. Called a manna ray."

"You just take whatever this girl gives you?" Ian knew of Liz from afar, and did not care for her. "A party girl, a…a grifter like that?"

"It's fine. Everything's cool. Everything's the same as it usually is. Only more so."

"I don't like it when you take stuff."

"Why?"

"It makes you less you."

"But you take drugs."

He turned away and sighed. "That's different."

"How?"

"I'm nineteen years old."

"What difference does that make?"

"It makes a lot of difference. We're at completely different stages. You don't even know who you are yet. You're only sixteen. When I first met you, you were so pure."

"Pure? Give me a break."

"What I mean is, you saw life directly. You had an unadulterated view of things. That's what I liked about you. That's what I loved."

Daphne grew very still, trying to process this. "Is that what you thought I was like?"

"Come on. If you want to be an artist, you need to stay pure. Keep the portal open."

"Keep the portal open? What about your portal? You're always fucked up. So are your friends. Smoking weed and doing lines on our kitchen table. I find them there still spread out in the morning..."

"I'm not like you. I never got to be pure. I was born polluted."

He gave her a ghastly, mocking smile. Daphne shook her head in disgust and walked away.

Things began to change between her and Ian, wordlessly, like a change in light and season, a shift in the wind. One day they could be so close that they seemed to share the same heartbeat. The next, there would be a prickly silence between them, an impenetrable force field of mutual resentment.

One of these silences had overtaken them the night they went together to attend Daphne's first showing of her artwork. It was a group show, all of the artists' pieces thrown up on the walls of an abandoned clothing store. None of the store fixtures had been removed. Metal clothing racks still stood pushed together in one corner. Despite the last-minute feel of the whole thing, the place was packed wall-to-wall with people. All the "right" people.

Liz was the one who had gotten Daphne in. "How do even know about things like this?" Daphne asked when Liz sought her in the crowd and kissed her on the cheek.

"Oh, I keep my tentacles out," she muttered drily. "Ian?" She stood on tiptoe to kiss him, too, but he turned his face away. He was angry that Daphne spent so much time with her, drinking or taking candy-colored pills that gave Daphne such cool funhouse sensations that she babbled incoherently when she came home. He blamed Liz and the circle of friends that he felt were keeping Daphne from moving away with him.

"Mind if I steal your girl for a few minutes?" Liz asked. "I'll bring her right back, promise."

Liz looped her arm through Daphne's and steered her through the crowd to the drinks table. There she poured them each a plastic cup of white wine. Daphne sipped her drink eagerly, hoping it would settle her nerves. She used to have great disdain for alcohol. She had been to too many parties where grownups became drunk and acted idiotically. But somehow, drinking in groups of scruffy young people seemed so much more civilized, and she had learned to enjoy it.

Everyone who was older and important looking in the room seemed to know Liz. Daphne was impressed by the way she worked the room like a grande dame; her yellow hair was gelled down, and she wore a bizarre jersey dress printed with letters and numbers. It had very long sleeves that were bunched up at the wrists.

"You look great!" Liz said, looking Daphne up and down. (All she wore were her usual dark clothes and ragged boots.) "Isn't this all fabulous? You're going to get exposure!" She smiled, looking deeply into Daphne's eyes, a hand stroking her arm. There was something slightly odd and sedated looking in Liz's face. Drugs? Still, her eyes glimmered with heat, beaming right into Daphne, making her feel uncomfortable, So she broke eye contact, pretending to be suddenly interested in the art. "Remarkable pieces here," she said, eyeing the nearest painting. It was large and seemed to show a naked woman with crows flying out of her vagina.

LEAH ERICKSON

A second cup of wine, and the room began to hum and buzz in a more pleasurable way. Introductions were made and promptly forgotten. Photographs were snapped for which Daphne happily posed, feeling that old familiar feeling: the flash of cameras felt safe and warm and loving. She had begun to enjoy herself so much that it was a while before she realized she had forgotten Ian. She searched for and found him, hands in his pockets, pacing around restlessly.

"Hi!" she said, taking his arm.

"Hi yourself," he replied, his mouth a tense straight line.

"What's the matter? Are you happy for me?" she asked him.

"Of course," he answered.

"You don't look happy."

"I am." He glanced up at the wall in front of him, at what appeared to be a large blow up of a psychological test: the word "green" in red paint on one panel, the word "blue" rendered in orange on another. "I guess I'm just put off by the art world recently."

Daphne tried to seek out his eyes, but he would not look at her.

Suddenly, a hand gripped Daphne's shoulder, making her jump. It was Liz, eyes goggled with excitement. "Hey! You see that guy looking at your painting?"

Daphne craned her head to see where Liz pointed. Her painting that they had chosen was the self portrait of herself as a velvet-clad toddler in Paris, dead-faced on a gurney. Untitled.

Indeed, there was an unremarkable looking older man staring at the work intently. He had thinning blonde curls shot through with gray.

Liz's breath was hot in her ear. "Robert Mathers. Big time gallery owner. He likes you. He wants to set something up. Say yes! Say yes!"

Daphne, in spite of her confusion, felt a smile playing around the corners of her lips. Could this be real? Was he really interested in her?

"Yes," Daphne whispered definitely, more to herself than to anyone.

She turned back to see Ian's reaction, but it was too late. He had walked away and out of the building.

Later, at home, they fought.

"How can you be an artist if you constantly compromise yourself?" Ian shouted.

"Oh, please." Daphne didn't know how to carry on defending herself anymore. She didn't know if what he was saying was really true. So instead, she chose to be angry. "You think you know what it takes to be an artist? You think I'm doing everything wrong? Well, that guy with the gallery, Robert, was really interested. After you snuck out and left, Liz introduced me to him and we were talking. He likes what he sees. He's going to come up to the studio to see more."

Daphne had not wanted to tell Ian it because she had been ashamed of the way Robert had made her feel so weak-kneed. He was older, in his late forties. Grayish blond, with inflamed looking ruddy skin. Though his hair was thin he had amazing eyes. He had what she could only describe as presence. The way he had looked at her after he had studied her painting. He had looked at it a very long time, then looked at her. Then, he was smiling. It was the first time she had seen him smile, and it was startling as a lightning flash.. You really are very talented, aren't you? Do you even know it?

How those words had made her heart pound. Why was it that she always had to have somebody else see her so that she could see herself? The memory gave her a flush of pleasure all over again. But when she looked at Ian in the eyes, she had to look quickly away again. She didn't want him to guess what she was thinking.

Ian's lips pursed, and he looked at her coolly. "Maybe Robert just knows you are celebusprawn. Of course he'd want you in his gallery. Instant publicity."

"He doesn't know who I am. He doesn't know any of that!"

"Yes, he does."

She wheeled her face at him angrily. "How does he know?"

Ian shrugged, with a cold smile.

"You told him? Can I have no privacy at all in this town?"

"He didn't hear it from me. It's your good pal Liz spreading it all over the place, so don't even—"

"Yeah yeah yeah, okay! I get it." It hurt her to think that Liz was using her for her fame, that maybe that had been the attraction all along. "Well…" She didn't know what to say, she was so angry. "Why are you so obsessed with my parents?"

"It's nothing to me. I'm just warning you. To be aware. Some people might take advantage of you." He looked away, smiled slightly, then looked back. "And you know, for someone trying to go incognito, you sure seemed to enjoy having your picture taken at that show! When someone photographs you, you have this response, where…where you look up at the camera with this intimacy, like you're in love with it…"

"No, I don't! God! I'm so sick of you! And I'm so sick of this place!" She was dimly aware that she was yelling now, but she couldn't control herself..

"Then," he put a hand on her shoulder, "why do you refuse to leave it?"

"Not this conversation again! I won't discuss this now."

"Listen," he said softly. "I don't want to fight anymore. I don't want to pressure you. I've decided, after the band breaks up, that I am leaving. No matter what. You can come with me, or you can stay."

She looked at him, stunned. "You want to leave me?"

He drew her to him. She buried her face in his sweaty t-shirt.

"I don't want to leave you. You know I want you to come."

She felt the hardness of his chest beneath her cheek. Heard

the pump and whoosh of his heartbeat. It was so loud that it was drowning everything else out. She decided just to concentrate on that. Before she had met Ian, no one had ever physically touched her at all. It still amazed her that she could draw this close to another human. Never before had she realized how hungry she was for bodily contact. Would she ever be able to give it up now?

But he was still talking. "I realize you might have your reasons for staying. You're talented, you're doing good stuff, getting established. I get it. But I just can't stay around anymore. I'm ready for something new. I want to start over."

"I've already had enough newness," she croaked, her voice muffled. "I need to be still for a while and figure out who I even am."

"Well. I wish you would come with me. And it's up to you to decide. I won't pressure you anymore. That's it. That's all I have to say. I have a car. I'm driving east to stay with some people..."

"Fine! Go then!" She hadn't meant to yell. But she felt like she was jumping out of her skin. She turned away and covered her face with her hands. Not opening her eyes for fear that life would just keep hurtling on.

Robert walked around her studio space with his hands in his pockets, looking at her paintings. They were leaning against the walls in stacks. He would flip through the canvases, bring forth one, then another, then stand back from it, squinting as though looking off into the distance.

After a time, he asked, "So, this one. Is this your father?"

Of course, it's my father, she thought, don't pretend you don't know it.

It was one of the new ones. It was the father that she had pictured in her mind's eye all this time. It was him, dressed as he usually was in a well-cut Italian suit, black, double breasted. He looked as elegant as always, grey hair brushed back, platinum rimmed glasses gleaming. Except that he was in the jungle. He was squatting in a hut made of grass and sod, looking out guardedly. There were tribal markings in lapis blue painted under his eyes. He had a knife in his hand. In reality she knew he had taken his own knife on that final trip, that that was part of the deal. The Black Box dropped you into the Amazon with only a knife. She didn't know what kind of knife it was, so she painted her own pearl handled switchblade, the one that was in her pocket right now. Painting the knife in his hand made her feel strong and good, like she was actually giving him something for protection in the afterlife.

She tried to sound nonchalant. "Yeah. It's my dad."

He nodded, still looking dreamy and far away. "I'm sorry about what happened to him. Were you and he close?"

"I guess you could say that. He was away a lot when I was young. But when he was there, he was really there, you know? We used to discuss, just, everything. We always had great talks." The lavender bedroom, the fairy light with its reflected stars. That bedroom still seemed a place in herself that she could go to whenever she needed. When life was too fast and confusing.

One night the year she turned eight stuck in her mind. Her father had finished reading her a story. She had been very drowsy, in that twilit state between waking and sleeping.

"Dad? Did you ever think...that everything in the future... is already happening?" She looked at her dolls all lined on her shelf, at the underside of the canopy draped with lavender tulle, out the window at the cool starry night. She wasn't sure how to phrase this thought she'd had. "And everything in the past...is happening still..."

He laughed. "You're getting awfully metaphysical on me, hon.."

"Meta..."

"You're right Teacup. Time isn't linear. Life isn't linear. It's circular. On some level you understand that now. You may forget it, and then understand it again sometime in the future. When you are grown up."

A kiss, and then lights out.

"Daphne, are you crying?"

She started, quickly wiping her eyes. "No. I just…"

"It's okay, you know. You don't have to be embarrassed." He came over and put an arm across her shoulders. His hand was large and warm as it stroked her upper arm.

"I don't want anyone's pity," she said in a faint but haughty voice.

"You're still awfully young," he said, looking down at her with his brow furrowed, as though this was just coming clear to him. "You could be my daughter, you know."

"Just technically," she smiled.

He gave her a hearty pat on the back, like a chum. But she could feel his interest in her. More and more she was becoming aware of the way she could draw men to her. Even in her baggy, raggedy clothes. Men wanted to protect her, but that wasn't all. She could feel a tension, an interplay of heat. It was something she could will and control, she thought, with practice.

And Robert was attractive. It didn't bother her that he was older. She liked the lines etched on his face and the sadness that tugged down at the corners of his eyes. She wondered what he lad lived, what experiences he had had. What women he had been with.

As if zapped by an electric shock, he pulled his hand away and stepped back. He seemed to be hiding his face from her as he flipped through some more canvases.

"And this one?"

It was a portrait of her mother, her gorgeous young mother in a pale blue slip, all of her glossy and airbrushed to perfection, lying in a white room. White walls, a white floor. It gave her the illusion of floating in nothingness. She was surrounded by pills, tablets and spilled capsules that glowed in a profusion of lurid neon colors.

"That's my mom, I guess it's obvious..." she said, but stopped there. Her throat had grown tight.

Robert nodded. He was looking at her again. She couldn't meet his eye, so she looked down at his body. He always wore the same thing, faded black jeans and an old white button-down shirt, with the sleeves rolled up to show his forearms. He looked like someone who had once been muscular but was now going a little slack. A slightly aging body. But it was still a nice body all the same.

His attention was fixed on another painting. It was a portrait of the lynx. In this one the animal was a metallic gold, like a religious icon. Its eyes were emerald stones. She had also painted a golden halo of light above its head.

"It's interesting," Robert said. "Do you like animals?"

He said this with a fond, fatherly smile. She scowled.

"Well. Sure. I don't hate animals."

"Why did you choose to paint this particular one?"

"I know this will sound cheesy and New Agey. But...I used to kind of have visions. Of this lynx."

His eyebrows went up in astonishment. She couldn't tell if he was mocking her.

"I mean, I saw a real lynx right in the street, in a shopping plaza. He was confused, he must have come down from a mountain looking for food. He was running through the marketplace. I saw a man shoot it." That day, so long ago, a girl in a school uniform, skipping class,.playacting at life.

"I remember that spring," Robert said, face serious now. "All the animals were going crazy. It spooked me, at the time. There was something Biblical about it. I thought the end of times were near, to tell you the truth."

"Yeah. A lot of people thought that. A lot of people may be right." She looked at her lynx painting. It flowed in rich jewel tones, like a fresco. It wasn't bad. But the animal was no longer familiar in this version. It was untouchable. "After I saw the lynx killed, it started coming to me in dreams. Sometimes when I slept, but also sometimes when I was awake."

"It was talking to you," he said smiling. "How marvelous."

"I felt like he was coming to me to comfort me sometimes, and to warn me in other times. The last time I saw him was right before all the craziness really started, when I left home." Her mother's ruined fundraiser. When he had run through the smoke and the chaos and the ruined party decorations. He had not seemed like a dream at all. He had been so real.

"Does he come to you now?" Robert asked softly.

Daphne felt the sharp sting of tears rush to her eyes, but she was able to stifle it. "No. He hasn't been back. It's been more than a year. I don't think he will come back."

"I wonder why?"

"I think the problem is me. I was so innocent back then. I was open to magic, like a child. But then I changed." She thought of Ian's words, maybe he was right after all. "I compromised myself. In a lot of ways. I'm not pure anymore."

"Oh, come on! You're a child, still!"

She looked at him incredulously. "No. I know I'm not. And I can't go back to how I was. Even if I wanted to."

She started as Robert touched her on her cheek with the back of his hand. It was the very intimacy of the gesture that shocked her.

"You can always go back," he said. Up close she could see the gray threading through his shaggy hair, the frailness in the ligaments of his neck. Maybe he was older than she thought.

"Don't let them lie to you. You can always go back." He snapped back into his old, efficient self and picked up the notebook he always carried with him. Wrote some things down.

"And by the way," he called over his shoulder as he headed for the door. "I'm giving you the show. If you want it, that is. I'll call."

Sometimes she liked to walk by herself late at night. The streets looked different to her when everything was quiet. (But it was never completely quiet. When she listened carefully, there were always shouts in the background, the rumble of motors, often the sound of far away gunshot.)

It was the more dangerous streets she liked to walk, as a type of self-dare. In this way, she could train herself to become brave, a non-coward. Up near the shantytowns that had sprung up under the bridge, she walked alone. Where people were so desperate, they would steal the phone in your pocket, the shoes off your feet.

But she could slip through the street so quietly, she was convinced that she had become invisible. A night spirit. No one ever bothered her. She could stand so near to those people, living in their boxes and lean-tos, she could hear the sound of them breathing. They were just people, sleeping and dreaming like anyone else, momentarily in a state of silent peace. She, them, the night, all of them suspended for just that moment, like a scene in a snow globe, preserved in time.

His books were packed up in boxes, stacked in neat rows in the front foyer.

The first time Daphne walked into the door and saw them, she called to him, "What's with the boxes?"

Ian chuckled from the bedroom. "So. She actually noticed!"

"Why is your stuff packed up?"

"Because I'm leaving. I told you a million times…"

"Are you leaving, like, now?"

"No. Not exactly. But I know I am, so I'm just getting prepared."

There was a strained silence, then she asked, "Well, are you going to share any of your plans with me?"

She followed the sound of his voice to the bedroom, where

he was laying down smoking a cigarette and listening to music. Something techno, with an elliptical drum beat that sounded like a broken air conditioner.

He sighed. "I'm going to stay with some buddies of mine, the guys I told you about. The ones in Detroit. The ones that do the urban farming. That's what I'm going to do next. I'm going to study it. Organic soils and all that kind of stuff. I guess you made me really think about things. I don't want to work for RealLife anymore, either. I want to learn something real."

"Oh." She felt hurt by the coldness in his tone. And the sight of the stacked boxes had caught her by surprise. It sunk in, for the first time, that she might really be losing him. This gave her a panicky feeling. She felt as though the room were spinning for a moment. Even though they had been fighting more and more, long, draining fights with no end and no resolution, she had not visualized yet what it would be like to be without him.

She did not want to talk about the boxes anymore.

Instead, she straightened up and said, "Robert is giving me a show."

"Oh yeah?" he asked cordially, with as much cool interest as though she were a mere acquaintance, making small talk.

"Yeah. He likes the stuff that I have been doing. He likes the magical realism of it. He thinks I could go far one day. He even said I could be the artist of my generation!" This made her flush with pleasure, and at the same time, embarrassment.

"Oh, yeah?" He blew out a plume of smoke, then asked, in that same pleasant tone, "Is he fucking you yet?"

Daphne's mouth fell open. She was so stung, she could hardly breath.

When she was able to get her bearings back, she was flying high with anger. "What the hell is that supposed to mean? You think that's the only way I can get a show? By spreading my legs? I thought you said I had talent?"

Ian all at once crumbled, his face in his hands, the cigarette still trailing smoke between his rough knuckles. He breathed deeply, raggedly, then said, "I'm sorry."

"Damn well you're sorry, you...you...I don't even know what you are!"

"I'm sorry, I'm sorry, I'm sorry..."

"You can go to hell with your sorry." She had an eerie feeling that she had slipped into her old RealLife role. Except now it wasn't playacting. Her emotions were painfully real.

"I shouldn't have said it!" he now yelled. "I didn't mean it! I just don't want to lose you!"

"You have a strange way of showing it."

"Why won't you just come with me when I go?"

"But I'm going to have a show in the hottest gallery in town..."

"You can have a show anywhere! You're good at what you do! You can be a success anywhere!" He got up and came over to her, drawing her to him. "I believe in you. How can I make you understand that?"

"I do know. I know that," she said quietly, staring ahead.

"I think if you came with me, it would be good for you."

"Hah! Detroit? Good for me?" She shook her head, ruefully. "I keep telling you, I'll think about it."

"But when are you going to decide?"

"Soon. I will tell you soon."

She stood before the blank canvas, unsure of what would come. In the last month she had been having a streak where the images came to her easily, unbidden. Now it was much harder. It was like a force of will where she had to stare the blankness down, or reach a hand in and pull something alive, kicking and screaming, out of it.

She tried to paint Ian. She tried to paint him as he was at home on any ordinary day, shirtless, looking out the window pensively watching the passers-by. A candidly intimate scene that would capture how beautiful he looked, and how lost and sad he sometimes seemed in repose, when he didn't realize she was watching.

But she couldn't quite get it right. The body wasn't in quite the right posture. That wasn't the way he held his arms at all. And the face wasn't his. It was the eyes that were the problem. The eyes belonged to a stranger. Someone she didn't know. Someone she didn't like to look at.

"What's with you lately?" Liz asked as they were walking in the street one night after leaving a party.. There had been lots of booze and lots of pills and very loud music, but Daphne had not felt her heart in it all. "All night you looked like you were in a dream!"

"I guess I was," she said, looking up to search for the moon in the sky. At last she spotted the hint of it, behind a vapor of clouds. "I don't really know what to do next in my life. I guess I'm at sort of a crossroads, and I'm standing there with my mouth open, you know?"

"What are you trying to decide?"

"Oh. Whether to go with Ian to the Midwest, or whether to stay here on my own."

"Well. Which one appeals to you?"

She thought for a long time before she replied, "Neither."

"You don't want to go with him?"

"I love him. But...I sort of hate him, too."

"What do you love about him?"

"I don't even know anymore. His soul, I guess? But how far can you go on soul? We just don't get along."

"Well, there. That was easy. Don't go."

"But I'm scared!"

"Of what? Liz was wearing a floor length velvet skirt with a belt slung over the hips that looked like it was full of ammunition. Along with the ruffled blouse and the combat boots she looked like a strange hybrid of insurgent soldier and gypsy queen.

The thought came into Daphne's head, I'll miss Liz when I'm gone. But all she said was, "I'm just scared of everything, is all,"

"So. What do you think you will do?"

"Run away from it all, I guess." She had meant it as a joke. But the words now hung in the air. Maybe it wasn't a joke at all. Maybe she was serious. She looked straight ahead, lips parted, taken with this new possibility.

She couldn't say exactly what it was that made her decide to buy the bus ticket, but the gesture felt right to her. All I have to do is buy it. I don't have to use it if I decide not to.

It was a one-way ticket to New York. Only for her. Leaving in one week.

She had felt numb, in a daze, as she paid her cash money at the counter and received her printout. Neither happy nor sad. But the very action of it calmed her immensely. The mounting anxiety that had kept her mind spinning, that had kept her awake all night, finally abated. Keeping that ticket, secretly, hidden in a book, was like a security blanket for her. I can always go if I want to. She had always loved the energy of New York when her family stayed there on visits. That was where the action was. That was where to make her art. It was an idea that, since it had taken form, had gripped her in an unrelenting grasp.

Most of all, she wanted to go to a place where she could go incognito again, more carefully this time. Then she could truly be free. Make brand new art. She wouldn't have to feel the shame of her family connections. The moneyed privilege that had spawned her had been built on taking advantage of other, weaker people. Ian's father, Calvin's mother...and how many countless others? She would rise up, in this new place, against all that she knew was wrong.

Ian's eyes searched hers out over the next days, but they didn't talk very much. Sometimes he touched her on the arm, in a conciliatory way, but said nothing. He would never guess what she was thinking. But then, she had felt that way all of her life. She had always been full of secrets that no one around her could guess at. She had thought, when she had first loved Ian, that perhaps that would change. Maybe another person could know her, and still love her for it. But it hadn't come to pass.

Sometimes overwhelming sorrow would well up in her out of the blue, and she would look up at him helplessly, call to him, "Hey!"

"What?" he would answer.

They would look at each other for a few moments before she darted her face away as the tears started, mumbling, "Nothing, I guess."

When they made love at night, it was the best that it had ever been. Here they could communicate everything they couldn't say. But it always made her feel empty and sad afterward.

One of those times, when they had finished, the sweat cooling on her skin, she asked, "Do you really believe in me?"

She couldn't see him well, and his voice seemed to be floating in the dark, nowhere and everywhere at once. He said, "Of course I do. I believed in you before I even met you."

"What do you mean?"

"I always thought I'd meet a girl like you. I always dreamed I would meet someone pure. Someone special who could guide me, and I could guide her. I dreamed you up, and then there you were."

She blinked, confused. "That's not exactly what I meant when I asked if you believed in me."

Long pause. Then, sleepily, "What were you asking, then?"

She turned away from him, settled deeply into the pillow. "Doesn't matter." She sighed. "I just don't think I am who you thought I was. I think you made a mistake. The girl you were looking for is still a dream, in your head."

She waited for him to reply, but instead she eventually heard soft snoring. She turned and put her arm around his sleeping form, feeling sad. It felt like she was cradling a little boy. A child she was about to abandon.

The date of the bus departure approached, closer and closer. She went about her routine as usual, but sometimes would take out the ticket in a private moment, just to stare at it. She was starting to do this more and more, like when she was a little girl and she had found where her Christmas presents were hidden at the top of the closet. The clandestine thrill was the same. But I don't have to use it if I don't want to. As much as it excited her to think about it, it also filled her with regret and sadness.

At last, there came the night that she both dreaded and wished for. It was also the night that Ian was playing with his band for the last time.

"Are you sad about it?" she had asked him, "Even a little? You seem quiet."

"Well, I'm not quiet over that," he said, looking at her significantly. "I have other things on my mind."

"But you've played with those guys for two years."

"Two years, five years, ten years. What does it matter? When it's over, it's over."

She had kissed him goodbye, on the cheek, as he left at dusk to go set up. It was too much to imagine that this was the last time she would kiss him at all. So she put it out of her mind, and tried to concentrate on how it physically felt. The coolness of his skin, the rough feel of his stubble. The yeasty smell of his body, which even now filled her with a great yearning for him, even though he wasn't gone yet.

And then he was gone. His absence felt like a hole punched into the room, leaching out all of the oxygen. She couldn't breath. As quickly as she could, she began to pack a duffle bag with her few clothes, some brushes and paint. In their months here, she had never acquired any possessions other than these. Maybe she always knew she would not stay.

When she was done packing, she didn't know what else to do. There was still that panicky feeling, as though she would jump out of her own skin. She lay on the bed and stared at the cracks in the ceiling, tracing their paths until her mind went bright and blank.

Hours went by this way, until at last it was time to go. She picked up her bag and felt to make sure that she still had her pearl handled knife in one pocket, and a wad of cash in the other. Then she slunk out the door, quietly, as though she were afraid of being caught.

After a couple of blocks, the cool night air revitalized her spirits. Instead of feeling guilty about what she was doing, she was beginning to feel giddy. Giddy at her own daring. Giddy as though she were jumping out of an airplane into the unknown.

Maybe I am special, she thought. Maybe I am talented. Maybe wherever I go, I will attract the right circumstances. I did it before, and I'll do it again. I shouldn't be afraid, as long as I just move forward.

She hopped in the air a couple of times. Did a little spin. There was no one to see. Besides, she thought. I'm only sixteen. I'm still a child, or so I'm told. I'm allowed to play.

As if in response, there was a noise from one of the alleys in the block ahead of her. A scuttling of metal, the whisper of fleet padded feet. The shadow of a low, fast moving animal emerging into the street. Her heart jumped into her throat. A dog? Something worse? Occasionally a wild animal was still shot in the city streets, though it wasn't as common as it once was. Many of those animals had been eaten for food by the homeless.

Daphne braced herself to run. She could almost imagine the sharp teeth sinking into her shinbone, the flare of pain that would beat with her own pulse, and the blood.

But the animal wasn't rushing at her. It froze in its tracks, just looking. It was some moments until her fear receded as she saw that the animal was feline. Then she made out its familiar Kubla Kahn features and the delicate black markings on its golden fur. It was the lynx. Her lynx! And then, she knew she no longer needed to feel afraid, of anything. Her heart was pounding with happiness, not fear.

They stared at each other, but neither moved any closer. "My old friend," whispered Daphne, "I've missed you."

The lynx looked away from her, and lifted its head up, as though to show her its noble profile. She laughed aloud.

"I've been having some adventures," she said. "Some were good. Some were not so good. Were you watching over me the whole time? Do you already know about it all?"

Imperiously, the lynx yawned, showing its pink tongue, its ridged gullet at the back of its throat.

"And I'm about to leave on a new adventure. I don't know what's going to happen. But I need you. You're my guardian angel. My good luck charm," she made a few cautious steps forward. She put out a hand. "Remember the time you came to me in my bedroom, when I was so sad? You licked my hand. I knew everything would be okay. Can I just...touch you before I get on the bus? Please?"

This time, when she moved forward again, the lynx's whole body tensed up. Its eyes widened and its ears swiveled. Before she could call out an imploring word, it turned and ran away from her.

She felt a wrenching in her chest to see it go, but she did nothing. Oddly, even though she shut her eyes tightly to try to stop her tears, it felt like she could still see the afterimage of the lynx running across her retinas. She tried holding one eye shut at a time, and a twin image ran across each side of her vision. Until it dissolved all at once into broken, sparkly pixels and was gone.

She blinked, she felt strange, as though coming back up to the surface from some great depths.

Oh, well, she said to herself after some moments of trying to slow her heart and breathing. Maybe I'm crazy. Only crazy people have hallucinations.

She hitched her bag up higher on her shoulder and began walking again, in the direction of the bus station. No longer quite sure of herself. Moving like a girl in a dream.

She gave little notice to the sound of an engine behind her. She continued to walk down the sidewalk in a distracted haze. She didn't even hear the whisper of the tires as the vehicle slowed down beside her, keeping pace with her as she walked.

Finally, she became aware enough to look up. An unmarked government van, white, with no windows. It had stopped slightly ahead of her, engine still running, and two men in dark clothes were out and, in an instant, had their arms looped under hers on either side and were lifting her up as though she were light as air.

It was happening too quickly for her brain to process. She didn't scream, her throat was frozen shut with terror. Instead, she writhed around, trying to get to the pearl handled knife that was in her pocket. If she could just get to the knife, maybe she could stop this. She could almost feel it in her hand, smooth and sure...if she could only snag it with her finger, but it was jangling at the bottom of her pocket, and her arms were being pinned to her sides, and she was being forced into the van. She kicked, finally yelled, a deep, guttural growl of fury, a sound that she had never made before.

There was a third man sitting in the back of the van, not participating, just watching. With a lurch in her heart she recognized the man with the lantern jaw and the round glasses. The man with the thin, frog-like mouth who had known her that day on the street and said her name. The man she continued to spot in flashes at the edge of her vision. The man she remembered from somewhere in her past, and who haunted her dreams still. Now he was here, watching coolly as she kicked and struggled as the van doors slammed shut and they drove away.

"Hello, Daphne," he said. "I know you don't want to hear this, but your adventure has come to an end. Everything will be okay if you just don't fight us."

"Fuck you!" This came out in a whisper-scream, her face frozen in a rictus grin of stifled fury. But then she felt a syringe being plunged into her arm, and before she knew it, she felt very heavy, and everything was going white around the edges, and she was falling into unconsciousness.

8

A white bed in a white room; Daphne's eyes were bleary as she awoke and tried to ascertain where she was. She was in some kind of hospital bed, not strapped down, but she felt too heavy to move. There was a stint inserted into the top of her hand.

The whiteness of the room weirdly echoed the suite in Paris that was her first memory, giving her a disorienting feeling of déjà vu. But this room wasn't luxurious as the other one was. It was small, like a slot, with only enough room for the bed, a bedside table with a goose necked lamp, and a chair. A woman was sitting in the chair. She had a long brown braid that trailed over one shoulder. She looked young and kind and plain, wearing some sort of greenish medical garb. Her eyes were downcast like a stone angel's as she scribbled something into a notebook.

She did not know that Daphne was awake and watching her. When she finally did notice, she jumped a little, said, "Oh! There you are!"

"Where am I? Why is my arm so sore?" Her voice was scratchy. Her throat felt swollen and painful, as though there had been a tube shoved down it earlier.

The woman studied her face, her eyes darting in a triangle from eye to eye to mouth. Her brow was furrowed with concern.

"What?"

"Nothing," she said, closing the notebook with a sigh. "How are you doing?"

Daphne looked at her incredulously, said nothing.

The young woman nodded. "Yeah. I know, I know..."

"You know what?"

"I'm sorry. This may be a hard adjustment for you to make. I'd imagine you might be feeling that it's very unfair..."

"Why won't anyone tell me what is going on?"

"I can't tell you anything."

"Why not?"

"I'm just an intern." She leaned forward and mouthed silently, "I'm really sorry."

"Then help me get out."

"I can't do that."

"Why not?"

A remote, guarded expression dropped over the woman's face like a curtain. She looked down.

"Because your mother is waiting to see you."

It had not been that very long, but her mother looked like an utterly different person than she had less than a year ago. Daphne tried not to betray her shock.

The first notable change was the way she moved. There was such a hesitance in the way she entered the room, almost as though she had been forced in against her will. She took small, halting footsteps toward her daughter in the bed.

Her face was different. Where the skin had been smooth and taut and radiant, it was now gray toned and loose. Vertical lines etched her lips. The furrow between her brows, the first part of her face, she ever had "fixed", was back again, as stark as though someone had pressed the edge of a knife into damp clay.

Most startling of all were her eyes. It wasn't just the way

her upper lids sagged like a torn awning. It wasn't the purple shadows that ringed the eyes like perfect bruises. It was the look in her mother's eyes that shocked Daphne the most. It was a look she had never seen before. A rawness, desperation. Those eyes were too much to take in at once. It made Daphne feel afraid, that much naked love and fear aimed at her all at once. So she turned away from her mother's gaze, pretended insouciance.

"So. Mom. Did you go off your meds long enough to notice that I was missing for a little while? Did you, like, wake up and feel like you misplaced something? Like your favorite beaded slippers or that little Maltanese that you lost interest in?"

Her mother appeared to be in some kind of trance, unhearing. She was very close now, Daphne could smell that odd metallic smell that she had, a smell almost like scorched electronics. And the melancholy smell of bruised petals. That particular combination that was her mother's smell, that Daphne had known since she was a baby. It made her stop talking because she lost her train of thought. She closed her eyes and breathed in the terrible, wonderful smell.

And she concentrated on the feel of fingertips, softly stroking her cheek. The touch was so gentle, as though Daphne were a sleeping animal her mother was afraid would wake. Daphne gripped her hand and pressed it harder against her face for just a second, as though she were starving for her mother's touch. Then just as suddenly, she pushed it away again.

When she looked again, her mother's eyes were still open wide. Trembling and scalded looking.

"Don't look at me like that, God!"

"Do you have any idea," her mother said in a low, barely audible voice. A calm, dead voice that did not match the intensity of her expression. "Do you have any idea what it was like for me to miss you so much?"

"Well. You sure are looking a little rough around the edges. Sorry to say," She said this lightly, though she gripped the white bedcover in both hands, hard, her knuckles white.

Her mother shook her head. "I don't want to talk about that. I want to talk about you."

"What do you want to know?"

"You're my baby. I want to know everything. Are you okay? Were you happy? Were you scared? Did you want to come home all along?" Her voice wavered thinly.

Daphne looked back at her for some moments, trying to reconcile in her mind who this broken old woman was, and what relation she was to the beautiful, selfish mother that she remembered.

At last, she had to look away. "I don't want to talk about it right now."

"That's okay, honey. They told me that you might feel that way."

"Who is 'they'?"

Her mother said nothing. She came closer, stroked the top of Daphne's hair. "All gone," she whispered, as though in a dream. "All gone. Your beautiful long hair." She fingered the jagged edges of her blond hair that was now chin length. "I...I don't mean that you aren't still beautiful, though."

"My hair feels gritty," Daphne said, putting a hand to it. "And I feel something on my scalp. I don't know what it is. Something greasy. And my throat..."

"I'm going to take you home soon, Daphne. Don't mind all of that."

"What did they do with me when I was knocked out?"

"We're going to go home. To our new home. You have a new bedroom, I decorated it myself and tried to make it very special...though of course I will give you all the privacy you want, I promise I won't try to intrude. I won't push you, because they told me... Well. Y-you can spend time in your beautiful new bedroom, you should see it. It's done in gorgeous jewel tones. Turkish Bohemian, with the carpets and embroidered pillows, but we can redo it any way that you want..."

"I don't care about that. I want to know how you found me."

Her mother stopped talking about the new bedroom, her mouth frozen mid-sentence. She gaped at Daphne, again with that expression on her face that made her look like a lost, feral woman. There seemed to be a soft sound of clattering teeth, and tears were slowly moving down her cheeks.

"I swore to myself I wouldn't speak that way again," she murmured in a low voice. "That's where I went wrong before. Focusing on all that stupid shit. Haircuts and designer bags and bedroom makeovers. I despise myself sometimes. My soul is nothing but a balled up piece of tin foil."

"I'm not interested in your psychoanalysis. I want to know how you found me. Did you have spies or what?"

"Daphne," she said, shaking her head in disbelief, "You are only sixteen years old. Did you seriously think I was going to turn a blind eye? Just let you go disappear God knows where? You are a child. And I am your mother."

"So in other words, yes."

"YES!" her mother suddenly cried wildly. "YES, YES, YES, OK?"

"The cops?"

"It wasn't the cops who found you."

"Then who was it?"

She lowered her eyes and looked to the side. "Some of your father's people."

"My father's people? You know, you act as though you weren't even married to him. That he was some stranger instead of your husband. You always did. Poor guy. I guess I can understand why he disappeared."

"There's a lot you don't know about your father. He wasn't the easiest man to live with. Maybe sometimes I wanted to disappear, too."

"You did. You put chips and injections in your body and totally changed the way you were. If that's not disappearing, I don't know what is. Not to mention disappearing into a bottle of pills…"

"I've changed, Daphne. I've changed. If you would just give me another chance and stop judging me."

"Pffft."

"I'm done with all of it. I've had my procedures reversed. There is nothing artificial in me anymore. No chip to make me happy and sober. No genetics to make me young. No more filtering. I feel everything now as I'm supposed to feel it."

"And how does it all feel?"

"It feels like hell," she said, dead toned. But they both laughed.

"Why did you stop it all?" Daphne asked, serious again.

"I don't know. Penitence, I guess. I had come to a dead end in life. I didn't feel happy with a lot of my choices. And I wanted you to come back. I thought if I were a better person then maybe the universe would forgive me."

"I'm not in for that New Age crap."

"Do you forgive me?"

Daphne took a moment to look deep into her mother's eyes. The shaky desperation of her mother's love was too scary to contemplate. She feared being swallowed whole. So she looked away. In what way could she answer? She had no answer.

"I hate this room," she said at last, looking away. "I can't breath in here. And it smells like chemicals."

It was decided that Daphne would remain one more night in the facility. She had deduced that the place wasn't a hospital. There was no emergency room. There were no ambulances. From looking out her small window, she could see all those endless buildings with opaque windows and the parking lot full of armored cars, and she recognized it immediately. She was in the Clinic. Her mother's Clinic.

When her drip was removed and she was told that she

could at last leave her room, to walk up and down the hallway, she saw that it was made up like any other pediatric ward. There were borders of printed teddy bears at the tops of the walls. There were glass cases featuring children's drawings and clay creations. Inset in one wall was an aquarium of bright neon guppies. Daphne stood and looked in, watching their jerky movements.

"Don't tap on that glass, dear."

It was the nurse who had examined her and given her permission to walk. She had been following all along, three steps behind. Daphne glared at her, annoyed at being spied on.

She looked through a window into an arts and crafts room, full of low tables and tiny chairs. Some children sat painting with watercolors. They wore pale blue gowns like Daphne's and all had stints in their hands.

The nurse leaned to speak low into her ear. "There's one girl here that is the same age as you. Maybe you could go in? Tell her hello? Maybe the two of you can be friends."

Indeed, there was a girl older than the rest. Daphne's age or slightly younger. Her light brown hair was shaved on one side, and she had an ear full of silver piercings that went all the way up the cartilage. She was tall, sitting hunched in a little chair, mindlessly painting flaming streaks of orange and red and yellow with one arm. The other arm looked stiff and sore and was held close to her body.

"Come on, it would do you both good to have a friend."

The girl felt herself being watched and looked up. She and Daphne locked eyes for a long, shocked moment. There was no camaraderie, no welcome between them. Just a wariness, guardedness as each considered the other, and the girl looked away first, coming to some sort of private conclusion. She painted a long, low streak of murky purple into her picture, with a grave, focused finality.

Daphne kept walking down the hall, her nurse inches away, like a shadow.

"Why am I here? I'm not a child."

"In the eyes of the law, you are, miss."

"What is the name of this place?"

"It has no name. Only a function."

"It has three stories."

"Yes."

"What's downstairs?"

"The labs and such. Research."

"This floor?"

"Minors."

"The next floor?"

"That would be the elderly."

"We're all young or old here? Nothing in between?"

"Not that often. But sometimes. They go upstairs, too."

Daphne felt all at once tired.

"I want to go back to my room."

"Okay, Missy. Back we will go. The director mentioned wanting to check on you anyway. I expect he'll come to your room soon."

"I don't want to see the director. This is a horrible place."

"But the director wants to see you." She led Daphne back, gripping her arm gently with plump pink fingers. "Don't worry, hon. At least you get to leave. And that's what you want the most, right?"

It was late afternoon. Daphne had dozed off in her narrow white bed. Since arriving in this place, she had been very drowsy, often falling asleep at the oddest times. This time, it had been a grasping, shallow sleep. She had dreamed that she and Ian were trying to find each other in the dark, somewhere in the woods, full of moonlight and brambles. She could hear his voice calling to her, but she could not find him. This dreamy, nighttime atmosphere was interspersed with gradual dim awareness of her actual physical surroundings; while staggering breathless through the underbrush she was now and then transported back to the bright white room, where she lay achy and dry mouthed in her hospital bed.

At last she awoke for real. The sun was setting, throwing low beams of golden light through the window. There was a man in her room, his back turned to her, as he bent over smelling a vase of yellow roses that someone had brought in for her.

"What do you want?" she murmured, but her throat and her mouth were so parched that it came out as a rusty croak.

The man turned, and Daphne gasped in shock: It was him, the one with the round glasses and the frog-like mouth. His eyes were large, magnified by what had to be very strong lenses, and had an astonished look to them. The rest of his face showed no sign of emotion. That part remained as inscrutable as ever.

"Ah, yes," he said softly. "Ah, yes. I was hoping to catch you awake. But I know you're probably very tired. Considering."

She sat up higher in bed, stared at him boldly. She didn't want him to know that she feared him. "I know you," she said accusingly, though her voice still creaked. "I know who you are."

"Who?" He tilted his head to the side, like a preening bird.

"I saw you in the street that day. The day you saw me and said my name."

"Yes. I remember."

"And other places, too. You've been following me."

"Yes."

"And I know you from before that, even. I had seen you before then. I just don't know when."

He was taking her in with those large eyes that never seemed to blink. She felt almost sorry for him for being so odd looking: he had the mien of an outcast, a member of an alien species. But she quickly quashed those feelings and glared at him.

"Of course you have seen me before. I'm impressed that you were able to recognize me. I've known you all your life. I've been watching you since you were very small."

"What does that mean?"

"Studying you. We've not had a lot of face-to-face interaction. But of course you're very bright. Very intuitive. Excellent facial recognition."

"We've never met."

"Oh, but we have." He smiled at her fondly. "You couldn't have been more than two years old the first time I met you. You were such a serious little girl. Little Teacup. You had the white blonde hair, cut in bangs. And the chubbiest cheeks. You were bright even then. You had an excellent vocabulary. You were obsessed with birds! Sparrows. It was the cutest thing. The spa-wows. You looked like a very grave little old woman. You looked me in the eye, unsmiling, and asked, Do you know? Do you know where the spa-wow goes?"

"I don't remember any such thing."

He shrugged, not answering, still with a soft smile on his face. He took out a small light and shined it in each of her eyes, shined it in her ears. Quickly parted her hair and examined something on her scalp.

"Just an old scar, it's nothing," Daphne muttered, refusing to look at him. "I feel fine and I want to leave."

"And you will. I'm releasing you to your mother."

"I won't stay long. You can't stop me. I'll run away again."

"Yes, I'm sure that's true."

She felt frustrated. She wanted to fight with this man, but he had no edges to him. He was so fluid, like liquid mercury.

"Did my mom pay you people to follow me? No one has kidnapped my boyfriend, right? I hope you people will leave him alone, at least. Or I swear I will kill someone."

"We have no interest in your boyfriend."

"Why not?"

"Because I study you."

"That's bullshit."

"That's the truth. "

"You know nothing about me!" She laughed, a harsh raking

laugh that ended in a cough.

"I know everything about you." He sat down on the foot of her bed.

"No! I have my own life, inside and out. You can't even know what I experienced. It's all mine. All here." She pointed at her head, smiling.

"I know everything that goes on here," he said, excitedly. "And you were never lost to us. We knew where you were the whole time."

"That's a lie. You wish."

"But we did."

"Who is we?"

"Our company. Your father was a huge part in getting us started. He funded us. He believed in us. And he wanted the very best for you. And I've always meant to honor his wishes."

Daphne's heart began to pound harder, even though her brain hadn't comprehended anything yet.

"How would you know where I was?"

He didn't bat an eye. "There is a device in your body that allows us to track you. It's not uncommon, really. You are the child of an important man. There have always been concerns, of, as you say, kidnapping. Your father wanted to keep you safe."

"You mean I have a chip in me, like a pet?"

"Like I said, that isn't uncommon. Believe me."

She stared at him in horror, not knowing how to respond. "I...I guess I shouldn't be surprised, should I? You...you let me roam free? Just to mess with me for a while? Jesus, you people are sick..."

"There was no intent of cruelty."

"But wait, wait...my mother didn't know where I was. She couldn't have. Did you know how to find me and keep her in the dark? That makes no sense."

"Daphne. I believe you are in a new stage of development. One that requires me to be completely honest with you. I am speaking to you, equal to equal, because I respect you, and I'm not going to lie to you, and though it may be confusing at first, or seem unfair, I think you will understand..."

He was blinking now, rapidly. For the first time, he looked a bit flustered. He took off his wire-rimmed glasses and cleaned them on his shirt. The eyes that were huge and tremulous now looked small and weak. Vulnerable. She imagined that he was the type that had no friends in junior high; you just wanted intrinsically to look away from him. But this did not diminish her fury at what was going on.

"We let you live on your own...that is, I made the decision to let you live on your own, so that I could observe you..."

"What the—"

"Wait. Hear me out. I wanted to give you the freedom that you so wanted. Isn't that what you wanted?"

"Freedom..."

"I wanted to give you the illusion of freedom. I wanted to see what life choices you would make. I guess you could call it almost a simulated environment. I couldn't resist, though, the time I saw you in the street and said your name, I was moved so much by how alive you were. I just wanted to see you up close, just for a second."

She gaped at him, speechless.

"Well, let's just say you are a unique individual. With unique properties. You aren't like anyone else in the world."

"You sound like a guidance counselor in a cheesy movie," she chuckled grimly.

"No, I don't mean it in that way. You really are different. "

"Huh. That so?"

"I have the data to back it up!" He smiled suddenly, a smile of triumph that stretched across his face. His teeth were very small, and there seemed to be too many of them. At that moment, Daphne felt like it was all getting to be too much. Reality was stretching too far. She felt dizzy and slightly nauseous.

"I think you should go now," she whispered, "I don't want to talk anymore."

"Don't you see where I'm going with this? You're very bright. I know you are! I know you know what I'm going to say."

"Just go. Please."

"Your brain is what's very special. And it's all due to your father, and the innovations he helped pioneer."

"Don't talk about my father."

"Have you ever noticed the little scar you have on the crown of your head? Like a little inchworm?" He was starting to talk very softly, and reverently. "That's where they put it in. It's under your skull. On the surface of your brain. No bigger than an aspirin. It's always been with you. Since you were very small."

"Shut up!"

"You don't need to be afraid. It's always been there. It's a part of you. You have something that the other children, or at least their parents, could only wish for." He lightly touched the crown of her head. "It listens to your brain. It's always listening. Like a friend, or...or a mother. It's always there."

She did not answer.

"Like a guardian angel! It listens. And responds. It stimulates, gently, where you need to be stimulated."

"I don't know what you're talking about."

"You know of bioelectronics, right?"

"My father was pretty involved in it. I know about it vaguely," she looked into the distance. "My mother messed around with that stuff. She liked to try new things even though she didn't know what they were. It ruined her. For good, in my opinion."

"I'm much more concerned about you. You're different, you see. You started much younger. It's easier that way. When the brain hasn't developed yet." He shook his head. "Your mother. Now that's another matter. That's a work in progress. But you? You have been a complete success."

"But I am not like my mother."

"You are, and you aren't."

"I am one hundred percent me."

"You are better than one hundred percent. You are a hundred

and fifty percent."

"That's impossible!"

"You should see the data!"

"What does that mean?"

"We've been measuring your heart rate, your body temperature, your facial expressions. We knew when you were stressed. When you were happy. When you lied and when you told the truth. "

"But all of those things are mine!"

"We watched you fall in love for the first time." He smiled softly. "That was incredibly moving. It was a privilege to observe. "

"But..." She thought of Ian. Remembered his warmth, his smell. The way she could pick him out from the crowd by the way he walked with a very slight, lilting hop that brought joy to her heart. She didn't want them to know any of it. To share any of it. But already she could feel Ian, the experience of him, slipping away. Dissolving into data, endless ones and zeros. "You weren't there. It isn't yours."

"But I was there. Don't think I don't sympathize. I was rooting for you. I was happy for you! You can never imagine what it's like, to watch a girl becoming a woman. It was beautiful, to tell you the truth." He cupped his hands in front of him, gently. "The most intimate experience I've ever had with a subject—or, or with anyone. It was like holding a butterfly, so very lightly as not to hurt it."

"Go to hell."

"You did a lot of changing and growing. You should feel proud. I feel really proud of you, almost as though you were a daughter. And now, it's time to go home again."

"No way!"

"You were going to leave Ian eventually anyway! You were too good for him. Now you can take your new growth and knowledge, and come back home and do something great with it."

"I love him."

"You'll find a new boyfriend."

"I hate that word. Boyfriend."

"Well, whatever term you want to use. You can find someone your own age and experience level. Someone more suitable. Better."

"I'll never love anyone again."

He smiled again, that fond, gentle, absolutely maddening smile.

"You are extremely bright," he said. "You are extremely talented. We always wondered if you would be able to function in a real world setting. But you did, and then some. Your few bad habits along the way notwithstanding. But then, that's normal teenage development..."

Her head began to swim. She struggled to focus on something, anything, so she concentrated on the vase of yellow roses. They were just beginning to wilt. A single petal had come loose and dropped to the table. Somewhere, a fly was buzzing. She idly wondered how it had come to find itself trapped here, with its sealed windows and chill air-conditioned air. The sound of the fly grew louder and louder until it occupied her mind completely.

"You know, your father always wanted the best for you. Did you know that he always wanted to be an artist himself? He held a great esteem for artists. He felt that he himself lacked that gene for talent, and it always troubled him. So he wanted you to have it. And you do. "

"But my talent is my own."

"Of course it is. Isn't anyone with that kind of talent that way by grand design? The only difference was that you actually were designed. Not by the Almighty, ha ha. But by science. Science that your own father funded to pioneer."

She could feel her mouth falling open dumbly. She tried to think of some words to throw at him. Words sharp as spears that would hurt and cut him. Words that would make it all, everything, him, the room, the words she was hearing, all go away.

But no such words would come. Though her mind churned, she could only sit there, mute and helpless. Finally, her lips did move. She mouthed something quietly.

"Excuse me?" He leaned forward attentively.

"I said," she rasped, "Why do I always feel like everything I experienced, I've already experienced before?" She didn't know how to go on. This place and this feeling had a dreadful familiarity that she could not put her finger on.

"Well," he said patiently, "The brain stimulation you are receiving sometimes will make you experience déjà vu. It isn't real. It's almost like a…false memory." He shrugged. "It's ironic. In trying to catapult you into the future, we have also stranded you in the past, huh?" He smiled, patted her on the back. "It's OK."

"It's not O.K!" She yelled, pushing his hand away, wildly scooting her body away from him as though he were a huge hairy spider. "What the hell makes you think this is O.K? This is the opposite of O.K!" Her heart was speeding up as the full horror of it all spread itself through her nervous system like a plume of dark ink in water.

"I'm sorry. Many said that you should never be told the truth. I think differently. I respect you. I believe in you."

I believe in you. Ian had said those very words. Ian, now was growing fainter in her memory, though she still felt the same swoon of longing. She wanted him now to come and take her away from this place. To love her, to make her real again.

"I didn't want to leave you in the dark, Daphne. You are too smart for that. I know you can process this all, though it's hard now, in the beginning. I know it's a shock, but in time…"

"What other side effects does it give me?"

"What do you mean? What side effects have you experienced?" Now his face had an alert look. Of a scientist about to record yet more fascinating data.

"Can it make me have visions?"

"Visions? What do you mean. Like a religious vision?"

She looked down into her lap. "Animal visions. It started out as a real animal, a lynx, that I saw shot to death in the street. I sort of...bonded with it. Then it came to me in my bedroom. It licked my hand when I was sad."

"And did you keep seeing it? More than once?"

"Not every day. It seemed like it came to me as a sort of warning. When my life was about to change." She fought back tears, but they came anyway, silently rolling down her cheek.

He blinked at her, mouth slightly open, tongue poking between his teeth. "Did you have any other sensations when you saw the lynx? Smell? Taste? Any emotion?"

"Not really. I guess he always gave me a sense of relief. That things were going to be okay, because someone was watching out for me."

He nodded again, curtly. "I'd imagine that was a side effect. Overstimulation in the visual centers of your brain. Even when things are off by the tiniest bit, the implications can be huge."

"So, it was just a hallucination from what, this device that you put in me without my consent?"

"Yes, it was a visual hallucination. Nothing to be overly concerned about." He was kneeling down, looking closely into her eyes as though he could see right into her brain. "Yep. We can fix it. Most likely be from the device. And no, we didn't get consent from a two-year-old child. We got consent from your parents. It was they who made the decision,"

"My father, you mean," she said coldly.

"Yes. He wanted only the best for you."

Again, that feeling of unreality came over her. As if it were all a dream. And that no action she made truly mattered. It was this feeling, and the simmering rage and sorrow racking her body and mind, that caused her to rear back suddenly and punch the man in the side of his head.

It did not seem to hurt him very much. She couldn't hit very hard from her position on the bed. But his glasses went flying off and skittered across the floor. His face looked naked and blind and stunned as a baby about to cry. He hadn't been expecting it, and it took him some moments before he could compose himself enough to respond.

"You need rest," he said curtly. "You've had a shock. Only natural..."

"Get out! I hate you!"

Now he knelt to the floor, where he was searching for, and unable to find, his glasses. Daphne sprang from the bed. She felt a rush of power from the sense of being younger, faster, and more clear-sighted than him. She was able to spot the glasses right away, on the floor next to the wall. With one sock clad foot, she ground them into the floor, putting her whole body weight into the effort. There was a snapping and popping as they came apart.

"What are you doing?"

It was gratifying to at last hear him lose control of his voice. He was finally angry.

High on adrenalin, Daphne ran out the door into the hallway, going she knew not where. Down the hallway with its horrible teddy bears, past the fish tank, past the arts and crafts room. She focused on the red-lit exit sign at the end of the hallway. She ran for it, desperately, as though it held the promise of freedom itself.

There was an impression, in her peripheral consciousness, of an excitement, of yelling and frenzied movement. Then the buzz of an alarm. Footsteps. She was almost there, the sign glowing like a beacon. But the moment her hands pressed the metal bar of the door, something clicked, a lock fell into place, the door wouldn't budge, and from behind the frantic footsteps were louder, overtaking her. A voice cried out, and then hands were holding her back.

9

She fell asleep in the car even before they exited the security gate of the complex. The sedatives were still in her system. She dreamed that she was in the water, holding onto a tiny wooden raft. First, it felt as though she were going down a large slide or a tube, where she rushed forward at stomach curdling speed. Then she was out, riding rough waves and rapids. The raft was made of water soaked wood that splintered in her hands and threatened to come apart altogether. But she held on, until at last she was somewhere else. Somewhere where the water was calm. But she did not know where she was. It was so large, and vast, with no shore to be seen in any direction.

When she woke, she still had the sensation of swaying and rocking, but it was all in her mind. She was in the back of a large black car with her mother. The seats were wide and deep and made of very soft cushioned leather.

She had been lying against her mother, and her mother's arm was around her. The unaccustomed closeness shocked her for a moment. Her nose was swamped with her mother's very particular smell. And her hearing was taken over by the sound of her mother's heartbeat. It was strong and regular. (She had always pictured her mother's heart to be like a hummingbird's, tiny and weak and too rapidly beating.) The pulse and whoosh of the sound was too intimate to even bear. Daphne sat up and scooted back.

"Oh. Hi. You're awake," her mother said softly.

Here, in the natural light coming through the window, she could see her mother's new face, starkly. Her new old face. The skin looked so thin and fragile, like crumpled tissue. The lines that crossed from the corners of her nose to the ends of her lips were deeply grooved. Daphne almost wanted to trace the lines with her fingers, to see if they were really real, but she did not.

The ride was eerily silent and smooth and smooth, and Daphne felt cradled in a cocoon of luxury as they flew down the road in the glossy black car. She had not been in a nice car, an expensive car, in so long that the smoothness and quiet and comfort of it were strange things to behold.

"How are you feeling?" her mother asked. Even her voice had changed, subtly. It was rougher, a bit deeper, than she remembered it to be.

"I'm fine. Just tired," Daphne answered. She felt stiff all over. Her arm still hurt. But her throat was getting better. There was cotton batting and a bandage on the hand where the stent had gone in. Her fingers worried fretfully at the edges of the peeling bandage.

"Don't," her mother said, putting a hand gently but firmly over the bandage. "I mean, I think you should leave that on."

Daphne sighed. A part of her wanted to lay her head down again on her mother's chest, but she was unable. She sat up straight and looked at her mother from the corner of her eye. The hand, still with the huge, knuckle-brushing diamond on one finger. The diamond wedding band stacked underneath. Here, too, the skin was thin, the bones beneath clearly visible. As were the splotchy freckles of too many days in the sun.

And further down, on the underside of one wrist, Daphne could see the start of the thin white scar that was there. Just barely, beneath the silver cuff bracelet that she was wearing. Usually you could barely see it. But the sun was so bright and clear that it stood out more plainly than usual. It had always been there, as far back as Daphne could remember. But she had never given it much thought.

Now, Daphne put out one finger to touch it, very gently and wonderingly.

Her mother looked up with a quick startled glance. But though she flinched, she kept her hand steady, and did not move it away.

Instead, she took Daphne's hand in her own, and looked her in the eye in a beseeching way. Then turned away again, leaned her head back with eyes closed.

Daphne opened her eyes as she felt the car slow and ease into a turn; an electronic metal gate whooshed open before them. Then they slowly drove up a winding driveway, ascending a hill.

"It's your new home," her mother said, smiling nervously. "I hope you'll like it."

Daphne was too tired and overwhelmed to muster up much of a reaction at all when the house finally came into view. It was large, and pale gray, and though modern in architecture, there was something ancient looking about it. It made her think of a lonely Irish castle, perched up on its high hill. There were many levels, many staircases leading to stone patios that looked out at the gray blue ocean in the distance. It was a place where one could imagine a lone, witchy woman could stare out at the horizon, looking out for things lost to return again.

"We have a lot more security here. An updated system. We are guaranteed no intruders. I bet you can't even tell by looking at it, but it's true. So, if you're at all nervous or afraid, don't be. Though I can completely understand if you feel that way, considering...but there have been no more uprisings, no more arsons. The government showed a little more force and really tamped things down. It wasn't pretty, but at least things are peaceful again…"

Her mother had gone breathless and rambling. Daphne said nothing in reply as they were helped out by the driver at the front door.

"I sent the staff home for the day. I figured we could use the quiet and the privacy. Or at least, I could, ha ha."

The space inside was bright and airy. The view from the front foyer looked straight onto a remarkable spiral staircase that appeared to be made of blue glass. In back of it was a two story glass wall, also tinged the same ringing shade of blue.

"What do you think, Teacup?"

"I don't know. It makes me think of that hotel in Iceland. The one carved out of ice."

Her mother laughed, a faint tinkling noise that sounded crystalline and ice-like itself. "Do you want the whole tour?"

"Not now. I think I'd just like to go to my bedroom."

Up the stairs they went. ("They're made of some special kind of a polymer, they tell me…") Her mother led her down a hallway, and then opened a door on the left.

"I know it looks a little empty."

There was a queen size bed on a platform in the center of the room, with a beautiful cover in a type of iridescent ruby red silk. There were so many embroidered pillows that they covered half the bed.

Daphne walked into the room, looking all around. There was an enormous set of windows, with a sweeping ocean view. The light coming in was so bright, it overwhelmed. She searched for and found the pullies to shut the curtains, in the same silk as the bed cover.

"Don't you like the view?"

"Yeah. I just feel sensitive to bright light right now."

Her mother looked at her closely, worriedly.

"I have some pajamas for you, in the drawer. A robe is hanging in the bathroom."

She hadn't worn pajamas in so long, the concept seemed

bizarre. A custom of an old world. Then she remembered. "When they caught me, I had a bag."

"I wouldn't use a word like caught…"

"I had a bag filled with my things. What happened to it? The bag, the things I was wearing?" She longed for her boots. They had felt like a part of her. The rough, scarred leather, the soles with their deep, thick treads. Each one had weighed about five pounds. She longed to put them on and lace them up tight. If only she could, she would feel stronger and know what to do.

"I don't know about any of that. They never gave me anything."

"Nothing? I don't believe it!"

"There's no need to shout."

"I wasn't shouting." Daphne took a deep breath. Her knife was gone, too. Her pearl handled knife. The dawning awareness of just how much she had lost made her feel so naked and vulnerable. Despair threatened to crash down on her.

"Don't worry about it, hon. We will go shopping as soon as you're ready. All of those things can be replaced."

"No! They can't."

"Well, you have enough clothes to get by for now. Don't you like them?"

To come home, she had been given a simple t-shirt dress. It was buttercup yellow and very soft. On her feet she wore white canvas sneakers, new out of the box so they were blinding white. She had hardly noticed what she wore until this moment.

"I look like I'm going to spend the afternoon at the tennis club."

"It's fine just for now, though, isn't it?"

"It's not me."

"Is it really such a big deal?"

"Yes. Yes, it is." But in that moment Daphne realized that she was falling back to sounding like the recalcitrant teenager she once was, and it made her feel foolish. "Just…never mind. I just want to lie down."

"Would you like me to sit by the bed while you sleep?"

She gaped at her mother as though she were insane.

"Well, I don't know Daphne! I don't know what to expect or what to do! I'm playing it by ear, give me a break!"

She sighed. "I appreciate it, Mom. I really do. Things are going to be okay. Don't freak out. I'm just ready to be alone for a while…"

But her mother had held up her hand like a stop sign, shaking her head and backing toward the door.

"Oh come on, don't make me feel guilty for wanting to just catch my breath!"

But her mother had her head set in that stiff, upward tilt that she had when she had been hurt. "I'll be downstairs." She turned around one more time, with her hand on the doorknob. "Oh, one more thing. In that closet over there is a plastic bin. That's where I put the things of yours that were salvaged from the fire. There isn't much. And put the lid back on tight when you're done. That stuff has such a strong smell of smoke even now. I don't want it stinking up the rest of the house."

"Okay, okay."

And then she was gone.

Daphne collapsed on her new bed, on top of the covers, and lay there for a while. She found that her throat was hurting her. Not the scratchiness that she first had when she was in the hospital bed with a stint in her hand. This was an ache in the muscles of her throat, as though she had held tears back for a very long time.

Finally, she rose up and went to the closet. She opened its double doors. It was a walk in closet, with many custom shelves and drawers. Enough to hold hundreds of dresses, dozens of pairs of shoes. But it was empty. Empty except for a large, putty colored plastic bin with a lid on top, sitting on the floor.

Daphne lifted it up and carried it to her bed. When she opened it, there was indeed a strong smell of blackness and scorch, so strong it seemed to slap her in the face. She was brought back instantly to the night of the fire. She remembered the ghostly men crossing the lawn in the moonlight. Their shouts and laughter from far away. The sound of breaking glass. And her own pure animal terror, the instinct to run, run, run.

There was not much stored in the box. There was a stuffed bunny that was a favorite of hers when she was little. It had been a pale honey color with black glossy plastic eyes. Now it was dark, its acrylic fur singed. Only one of its dark eyes remained, and it was melted halfway down its face. She hugged it to herself. Marlo, she had called it when she was little. Marlo, named after the gardener's son, a wiry twelve-year-old boy who spoke Spanish and was kind to her, a lonely six-year-old girl with no one else to talk to.

Also in the box was a white satin pillow that she had always liked to lay on, now smoky and sordid. There was a crocheted blanket, pale blue, handmade for her by a grandmother that she had never met. Her mother's mother, who lived out in the Midwest. She had only seen one blurry snapshot of her, a large woman in a terrycloth top and shorts, shading her eyes against the sun as she sat with her feet in a turquoise motel pool, surrounded by a chain link fence.

Out of all the dresses that Daphne had once owned, only one had made it into the box. It was one that Cathy had made her. The one made of ecru satin, with an overlay of silk faille. When it had been new, it had been hand ripped in places, intentionally stained to look like it was old and ruined. The white beadwork had been made to look like it was torn and dropping off, bead by bead.

So now, pulling it out to examine it, Daphne thought that it was the one thing that looked unchanged; it had been constructed to look like it had been through time and catastrophe. Now it really had been. So it looked the same. It looked the way it had always been meant to look.

Except for the smell. The acrid smoke in the fabric stung her eyes as she buried her face in its folds. It was the smoke, she thought, that was making her cry. But then she couldn't stop. The tears came faster and heavier, and she was sobbing aloud with ratcheting heaves.

Cathy, she thought, how could you let me go? She thought of her friend's dark laughing eyes, her soft, plump arms that would hug and hold her tight when she was sad. Those strong fingers that had stroked her hair, and painstakingly sewn those beads one by one. She could see Cathy only in these fragments, but not all as one. She couldn't quite remember what she had actually looked like anymore.

But she remembered the way they had laughed together. The way that when Cathy looked at her, she had actually seen her. She made Daphne feel as though she actually mattered.

She remembered what Cathy had said that day, during that trip to the islands that had felt like paradise, now a lost dream. She had spoken of memory held in DNA. You're subversive. You're witchy. You are an artist, like me! And anyway, aren't you from English stock? When I look at you I see Druids, Stonehenge. Fog on the moors..."

Daphne closed her eyes and tried to will herself into being the strong and mysterious soul that Cathy had imagined her to be. But it was so difficult. If you only knew, Cathy. Even my DNA does not really belong to me.

Her mother wanted to have a picnic on the beach; she packed a basket with sandwiches, fruit, and sparkling water. Then they made their way across the lawn and down the set of wooden steps that led down to the strip of private shore that was part of their property.

The day was blustery and overcast, but still her mother wore a white wide brimmed hat to keep the sun off, as well as large sunglasses and a white shawl. Daphne was bareheaded and wore a sweatshirt and board shorts. She carried the basket of food, and found herself steadying her mother's arm as they made their way across the sand of the empty beach, toward the endless, slate gray sea.

They unrolled their blanket and settled themselves. "Maybe it's not perfect beach weather," her mother said, tipping up her face to the cloudy sky. "But I love it here, anyway. There's something that I like about the beach on a foggy day. Or a gray day. I've always loved the beach best in the winter."

Daphne was only half listening, looking out at the horizon line that was mostly invisible, the gray sky and gray sea blurring one into the other.

"I was lucky to get this property. I wanted to get away from the city a little more. Something about it here really suited me. I don't know what it was, exactly. I guess this is a beautiful place, but in an almost haunted kind of way. It looks like the kind of place you could go to try to forget."

Daphne wheeled around and looked at her. "That's a real thing of yours, isn't it? Forgetting?"

"I didn't mean it that way."

"Well, what way did you mean it, Mother? Were you hoping that's what we would do here together? Forget everything?"

"Of course not." Under the large black glasses, her thin, fair skin was reddening.

"I bet if we had it your way, we wouldn't even talk about anything that's happened in the last nine months."

"I was going to talk to you about it! They just told me to take it slow with you, that there was a lot for you to process and I shouldn't, you know, prod or poke..."

"They again. Is it the they that have been controlling your life since I can remember? The they that are responsible for this whole sorry business?"

"I will talk to you, if you would just calm down!"

"I am calm."

"Well. I will talk to you if...you stop judging me for even half a minute!" She gestured vaguely with her hands. "I know you're sixteen, and it's hard. But I'm trying to grow and learn too, you know. Even old women can still grow."

Daphne stopped and composed herself, breathed deeply and looked at her mother with exaggerated patience.

But her mother just looked down into her lap, breathing in short pants as though she were about to cry.

She raised her head, and looked into Daphne's face. "What is it that you would like to ask me?"

"Whose idea was it to have my brain... altered?"

"I don't know if I would put it that way."

"Well, what way would you put it?"

"We were doing what we thought was best for you."

Daphne snorted. "Well, I wish I'd had a say in the matter. At least when you had things done to you, you were old enough to consent."

"Daphne, I'm sorry. I've made a lot of mistakes in life. I'm trying to face that fact. When you were little and you had those seizures in Paris, I knew they were from the implant. I hated myself, I really did..."

"Couldn't you have tried to stand up to him?"

Something closed off in her mother's face. "Your father, you mean?"

"Yes! It was all his idea, right?"

"I don't know how to answer that..."

"You were weak. You allowed him to just...take you over. He ruined your life."

"That's not true."

"You had everything. You were a huge star. Everyone loved you. Why did you marry him and throw away everything and become this...corporate wife and inject things into your brain and...and implant things into your body, when you didn't even know what they were. Half that stuff wasn't even legal, I bet!"

"It's not your father's fault that I don't work in movies anymore."

"Oh, yes it is."

"It was a choice. I just didn't believe in that world anymore. I was done."

"You lie. It wasn't a choice. No one would film you anymore because you couldn't act anymore."

"Daphne! Just stop it! Just stop it right now. You've never walked in my shoes. You don't understand my life. So don't judge me. You have no right!"

"I can judge you all I want, for what you did to me. I hate you for it. And I hate him even more."

"You can hate me, fine. But please don't hate your father."

"You were both completely selfish! You ruined me!"

Her mother hid her face in her hands and rocked, moaning softly, "You don't understand."

"Understand what?"

"Just how it is that we are so different. My childhood was such a different experience from yours. I would have killed to have parents who cared about me the way we did about you. I came from white trash."

"Boo hoo."

"You were so spoiled that you don't even know it. I didn't have a father. He left us when I was eight. My mother was the neighborhood drunk, always fighting with her boyfriends in the front yard in the dead of night until the cops came. And those boyfriends. Some of them...tried to touch me. Did touch me. And my mother did nothing to help. I was just a girl."

"I know these things, I know it was rough..."

"But you don't really understand it! I left home and moved to the city when I was just your age. I worked my ass off waiting tables and going to casting calls. It was love and beauty that I was desperate for. I knew there was the good life out there. Full of beautiful enlightened people. And I wanted in."

"And you got your big break and shot to stardom, and everyone loved you."

"It's true. I got all the attention that I thought I wanted. But the fans loved me for no reason. It feels really empty for so many people to love you that unconditionally. It made me feel so hollow. It messed with my head. No one loved me when I was a child. And then there was this great tidal wave of love and approval, and it made me feel so dirty. I can't explain it. It made me hate myself more than ever. Even though it was everything I had dreamed of."

The ocean breeze tugged at the brim of her hat as she spoke, so she gave up fighting to hold it onto her head and took it off. Daphne was surprised to see that even her hair had gone thinner. And the roots were growing in their natural color, an ashy light brown run through heavily with strands of gray. She has finally let herself go. The words ran through Daphne's mind unbidden. The thought filled her with both pity and admiration.

The basket sat between them on the blanket, untouched. For some time there was nothing but the roar of the surf and the cries of the gulls.

"And then, you met my dad," Daphne prompted.

"Yes. I met him when I was pushing thirty. I wasn't in a good place. I was very confused. Working a lot. I had just been through a string of bad relationships and I was drinking and partying too much. Living in hotels in strange cities. The people I had met were neither beautiful nor enlightened, I'm sorry to say. Sometimes I would lie on the floor in those hotel rooms and listen to the fans calling my name from outside. It frightened me to death sometimes, the sound of those fans. Like the mob wanted to tear me apart."

"They loved you."

"Honey, like I said, I was confused." She smiled hazily. "But I did love your father, the best I knew how. There were…moments. Where we connected. And he was a very deep man. But very sensitive, like I was. And the world sometimes depressed him. He always wanted to make it better."

"Make what better?"

"The world. Himself. Me. He really believed in biotech. He wanted to help create something that could really help people.

But then things got bigger and bigger. The money and the power, it just...he had conflicts within himself. And they were never resolved."

"Did he make you do those things to yourself?"

"No! Of course not. He would never make me do anything I was uncomfortable with. I wanted to do it. I was so sad, I wanted the chance to be better. Stronger. Happier. Younger. It felt like a second try at life, to become pure again. And you know what else? I wanted to help him! I really wanted to be a success for him."

Daphne leaned back on the blanket, hands crossed behind her head with her eyes closed. "But what about me?"

"Well..."

"What. About. Me?"

"I was getting to that! I just wanted you to know the background!"

"Oh, I know the background."

"I'm saying, I thought the procedures were a good thing. For a while. I had already had things done to myself, and I thought they helped. When they wanted to have work done on you, I was reluctant."

"You could have said no if you wanted to."

"But it's not that I didn't want to. And your father loved you so much. And he wanted you to have everything that was missing in himself."

"Like?"

"Well, he wanted you to be smart. And to be healthy."

"Dad was those things."

"Most of all, he wanted you to be an artist. It was what he most respected in life. Artistic talent. And it was the one thing he didn't have."

"Couldn't he alter his own brain then? Mess with his own genes?"

"He thought it was too late for him. He seemed to think his destiny was set in stone. But you? In his eyes you could be anything. And you were everything he dreamed of. He was so proud. And I am so proud."

Her mother leaned over and awkwardly stroked the side of her face. But Daphne had gone still and cold.

"I don't think...you can understand exactly how it feels," Daphne murmured.

"In a way, I do know how it feels."

"No, you don't. You had it done willingly. But I had no idea. I thought I was all natural. I thought I was all me."

"But you are you."

"But I'm not."

"You're so smart and talented. I was amazed, and I mean amazed, to see how far your work has come along."

"You saw my paintings?"

Her mother bit her lip and turned away.

"Yeah. I guess you would have seen them, wouldn't you." She shook her head as though to clear it. "I thought my work came from me. But now I find out I was just designed that way."

"It's still your work."

"I thought my visions were my own. But they're just some kind of algorithms. Preplanned. And I hate it." Tears were springing to her eyes.

"Oh, Teacup," her mother said, "It's not too late for any option. I had my implants removed. I had the injections stopped. If you want to stop..."

But the words she called out were lost on the wind, because Daphne was now up and running toward the sea. The surf broke and bubbled around her ankles, and her mother's calls were faint, like a gull's, in the background. Forward into the water she ran, feet sinking into soft sand, until the ocean engulfed her whole body, and there was nothing in her world but crashing gray and the taste of salt.

~

LEAH ERICKSON

246

The mirror, for a time, became Daphne's only companion. For hours she could sit on the upholstered stool of her dressing table, gazing into her own reflection. For many months she hadn't looked into a mirror at all, and she'd found that she'd forgotten exactly what she looked like. Now, with solitude and time on her hands, two things she had gone without for a very long time, she was able to contemplate her own image.

It was like looking at someone she used to know, but who had changed subtly, either in real life or through a trick of her own memory. It was an odd sensation, like meeting a sister she had never had. The eyes were the same startling pale hue, but their expression had changed. No longer was her gaze bold and unflinching. It was a little bit sadder, a little more vulnerable. The face was longer and leaner, the baby fat worn away. There was a permanent furrow between her brows that hadn't been there before.

Is this the face that Ian loved? She wondered. She tried to imagine him in her strange new bedroom. Tried to see him behind her in the mirror, smiling, happy to see her, coming up to put his hands on her shoulders, or stroke her hair that was growing in longer now, almost to her shoulders, and darker than it used to be. No longer flaxen, but a deeper color like wet sand.

Would Cathy be happy to see her, if she were here in this room now? No one had mentioned her name at all since Daphne had come to this house. But if Cathy did return, would she take Daphne in her arms and beg forgiveness for letting her go that night during the riot? Maybe she really had meant to take Daphne with her on the bus. Maybe she would be shocked and proud and amazed to see how Daphne had grown so tall. To see that she was a young woman now. And Daphne had so much to tell her. She realized now that the whole time living on her own, she had been saving up stories to tell Cathy one day. The whole time, living in the industrial room, working for RealLife, making paintings in her studio, she had been imagining Cathy watching her, a silent audience. Watching and applauding and rooting for her. But she hadn't really been there, not at all.

It seemed as if the room was filling with silent ghostly presences, though she never looked away from her own reflection in the mirror. She imagined her father was there, sitting on her bed, waiting for her to get under the covers so he could tell her a story. It made her happy to imagine him there with her, but then again, now she didn't know if he had ever really loved her for herself, like a normal father would love a natural, red blooded, genetic accident of a girl. Was his a hopeless, unconditional love? Or was he in love observing his own creation, looking into her eyes to search out the flickering of synapses, flashing in the concert of a symphony that he himself had arranged and conducted?

She gazed into her own eyes, searching out the answers to these questions. But the girl in the mirror only looked back at her, mysterious and impenetrable. She continued to stare herself down as the ghosts in the room with her grew stronger and warmer before starting to fade again, and then disappearing, until it was only her. It had, all along, been only her.

Never before had Daphne been so aware of space. The empty space around her in the huge house that could have sheltered an entire city block. All for just herself and her mother. The place was so quiet. Mother and daughter had said very few words to each other since Daphne had returned. Most of the time she did not even know where her mother was. She could walk and walk and walk, down staircases and across endless white-carpeted floors, across walkways of Italian marble, and still not find her. They were like two small planets orbiting an enormous unseen sun.

One day, she found her mother sitting outdoors in the beautiful walled garden on the south side of the house. The garden was cloistered by tall, streamlined stone arches. There were olive trees, rose bushes, and a burbling stone fountain in the center.

Her mother did not hear her approach. She was alone, staring down into the fountain as though in a trance. In her new, older form she looked almost like a conjuring witch.

"Mom?"

She looked up, startled. "Oh. Hello, hon. Have you been down here before? This is my favorite part of the house." She looked down into the water again, fondly. "I've always loved walled gardens. So medieval." She looked up, frowning. "It makes me think of mythology, too. Cupid and Psyche. Psyche entered Cupid's walled garden, and bang! She was hopelessly seduced!" Her face wore a veil of remembered enthusiasm. "Remember when I told you stories from the Metamorphoses when you were little?"

Daphne stared at her. "That's weird. I thought it was Dad who told me those stories."

"No. That was me. I never went to college, and I never considered myself exactly educated, but I always loved the Greek and Roman myths. That's where I got your name. Daphne the Titan. Daughter of Uranus and Gaia. Daphne of the mysterious moon!" She smiled and shrugged. "Well...I guess I just always like the name."

Daphne was disturbed to think that her memories of her father telling these stories was wrong, because they seemed so clear. It seemed like something he would have done. Was it really her mother? She couldn't fathom it.

She stared at her mother for some moments. It was still so hard to get used to seeing her because she seemed so much smaller than herself. So much older than herself. So much more human than she ever remembered,

"Mom? Can I ask you something?"

"Of course."

"Why did you finally have your procedures reversed? I thought you said you were happy with them."

Her mother smiled at her. There was still great beauty in her face, the same beauty that had peered out of countless movie and television screens. Back when she had been the next great thing, the girl with all the glory and talent. But now, the lines around her eyes, the slackening jaw line, the age spots that speckled the tops of her cheekbones...all of it added a depth to that beauty that had not been there before. It was as though Daphne could see where the rivers of time had invisibly marked themselves in the terrain of her visage. The sun seemed to light her up from within, making her translucent. She looked more real, and more lovely, than Daphne ever remembered.

"Well," she said, looking into the fountain with an expression of humorous irony. "I guess I was ready to let go of a segment of my life that I had tried to hold onto for too long. I was working on getting sober for years, and then...when you were gone all that time, and I was alone so much, it really gave me a lot of time to think. I realized how long it had been since I had really felt anything. I didn't want to be numb anymore. If I had to live without you, I figured I should respect the pain by at least feeling it. It was hard. Sometimes I thought the pain would kill me. But it didn't. I missed you terribly and I sat in the middle of that pain and just felt it. One by one, I stopped the drugs. I stopped the injections. Then, when I was ready, I removed the chip. I was terrified to do it, because I thought there would be nothing there anymore when they were through with me. But I was wrong. For the first time, I became an old woman. I sat down in a chair and looked out at the sea. I dreamed of my daughter and loved her with all my heart."

Before her mother even finished her words, Daphne had her arms around her, burrowing her face into the crook of her neck, wracked with silent sobs. She had never imagined she could feel this way. That the only thing she had wanted all along was her mother's love. And now that she had it, she felt starving and desperate and ravenous. All the sorrow of going without it all those years hit her in a great surge that almost knocked her to her knees. But she held onto her mother, who, though she was small and fragile, held Daphne up with the wiry strength of a young maple.

10

Six years had passed since her reunification with her mother, and Daphne found herself, at the age of twenty-two, walking through the airport and crying. Crying not in sadness, but in anger and indignation. Her eyes were blazing, and she wiped the tears away with the back of her hand impatiently as she walked with a quick pace, unseeing the hustle and bustle of people around her.

She had just been fired from her job, with no warning at all. She was an artist. Under the new Public Art Ordinance, public art was a requirement for all major construction projects. Daphne had been commissioned to create art for the airport. As young as she was, not even out of college, she was considered to be a major new talent.

She was known for her nature-base work, most of it large and abstract. Fig leaves, tree rings. Spider webs. All of these were rendered hugely in limestone, plaster, mirrors and glass.

Six years ago, when she had had her implant removed, she worried that she would be unable to work again. Her own father, god-like, had designed her mind himself. He had breathed life into the secret world of her neurons. What would happen if she took away the one part of her father that was left? It would be like losing him all over again. She struggled with the question, but decided to go through with the procedure anyway. When she was in the hospital bed, feeling herself being pulled under by the anesthesia, she said silently in her head, I'm sorry, Dad.

Indeed, she did feel enervated and blank for a long while during her recovery. There were long bouts of dizziness and brain fog. Her mother took care of her, making her soup and sitting quietly by her bed while she rested. When Daphne gained her equilibrium back, she took her on long walks on the beach.

"What if I've made a terrible mistake?" She asked her mother. "I don't know who I am anymore."

"But you will know yourself", her mother answered. "You'll discover your true self all over again. I promise."

After a long, frustrating while, her drive to make art did come back, little by little. She began to spend days at a time in her new studio, producing a type of work that was different from what she had ever done before. She felt compelled to make work that was physically huge in scale, and much more organic than it used to be. She shocked even herself. She couldn't believe that it had come from her.

Daphne grew calmer, and stronger, and more confident as the years went on. When the time came, she did move alone to New York after all: to attend art school.

And by her senior year, she was noticed by the world, for better or for worse. Both for her talent and her family name.

"I'm fascinated by repeat patterns, the things that connect us all. Plant and animal." This was her quote, printed in a glossy magazine. She had also been invited to pose for a fashion spread, as she was considered to be young, slim and strikingly featured, if not conventionally beautiful. "Like a Nordic queen!" the photographer said, delighted with her high cheekbones and long golden hair. They dressed her in bright butterfly wings, painted her lips a wet fuchsia. Posed her on a tree stump under the sun-spangled leaves, her skirt hiked to reveal her slender thighs. Flora and Fauna, the article was titled. And in the corner of one of the pages was a small black and white photo of

Daphne as she really was, working in the studio, hair tied in a rag, covered in plaster dust.

It gave her such an odd feeling to see herself looking so hotly gaudy in the fashion magazine, dressed and painted that way. It reminded her, again, of her days with Cathy. And whenever she thought of Cathy, there was still that slight, hollow ache in the pit of her stomach. But as she was getting older, the feeling was growing a bit fainter every year.

Anyway, it was all nonsense. Just promotion in the name of art.

There was grant money, lots of it. There were dinner parties in mansions, just like the ones her parents threw when she was a little girl. But this time, no one wanted to discuss her parents at all. There were so many older, wealthy men who were captivated by her air of mystery and wanted to date her. It all moved very quickly. Daphne wasn't used to the attention and the validation. She had always been the quiet one, standing in the corner with her arms crossed, mutely protesting the superficiality of it all. But now things were changing. She was changing.

What can you do? You have to learn to play the game, her father used to say to her wryly, winking, as he put on his cuff links before he went out to parties at night.

But now when Daphne concentrated on the memory, it shifted. Her father morphed into her mother, young and beautiful in a shimmering bronze gown, putting in her emerald earrings in front of the mirror. She looked back over one shoulder at Daphne with a knowing smile and said Just remember, never let people imagine you into something you're not,

Since the implant was removed, her memories were so much more clear and true, her sense of self less refracted. And it made her both happy and sad at once to realize how much of each parent she carried inside of her, all the time.

But when it came to her art, there was no ambiguity. No conflict. In the studio was where she could always be only Daphne.

She worked very hard on the new airport pieces. She was energized by her work, it flowed through her fingertips. It was kept completely secret until it was finished. And then she couldn't wait to show it to the board and the public.

The opening was celebrated with a lavish party. Daphne was beaming in a dark blue kimono dress. She wore a large uncut ruby on a chain at her throat, a gift from the son of a state Supreme Court justice. The ruby was rough and warm to the touch, like a living thing.

Her mother was there, too, standing off to the side and smiling serenely; the photographers did not bother her anymore, now that she had grown older. She was able to enjoy her daughter's opening in peaceful anonymity because now it was only Daphne's photograph that they wanted. Champagne was poured, congratulations were rampant, and Daphne was rosy cheeked with pleasure, in spite of her self-consciousness.

Even Mister Holmes knew of her triumph; he had had flowers delivered to Daphne the day before, a rather oddly funereal arrangement of white lilies, with a card that read in a shaky, palsied script: Dearest Teacup, I am so proud of you, as your father surely would have been. Always stand up for your truth, no matter what. Your friend, Nelson Holmes. The note both puzzled and touched her, and made her smile.

But then, three weeks after her celebration, members of the committee called her in for a meeting at the airport office.

"There is a problem," a patrician looking blond woman said. "There are complaints about some of the new pieces."

The most prominent of these included a huge, magnified image of Daphne's left eye. Also, there was her fingerprint, four feet high, superimposed on a mirror.

The public didn't like them, it was explained. Actually, they were disturbed by them. There had been a marked increase in petty crime since the pieces were installed. There was fighting among passengers, graffiti in the bathroom, and worse. Whereas the city had been calm for a long time, now the disruptions seem to be back again.

"But... I don't understand. How is my work to blame for any of this?"

"Well, I don't think it is causing it per se..." An airport official, a middle aged man in a suit, looked down at his feet, then back up at Daphne, "My guess is that the pieces are stirring up feelings of paranoia that were already there. Retinal scans, digitized fingerprints. You know? Biometric monitoring!" He laughed nervously, but Daphne felt a chill go down her spine. "Everything's found, everything's archived nowadays. And people just want to be anonymous. It's all too close to the bone. It makes people lash out. It's all unconscious. It's not your fault. But you have to admit, that eyeball..."

"But these pieces aren't about that! They are supposed to be about what connects us as human beings!"

"But they are seeing Big Brother, you know what I mean? They would have responded better, I think, to something such as your gingko leaves, your seashells. Pretty things. You know, nature."

"But the work is me! Am I not nature, too? And you? And you?"

The art director, a tall man with inky black hair combed straight back, interrupted her with a smooth, melodious voice. "Well, I guess you can say the art world is like an ecosystem. The artist, the work, the given space...they're all interactive. It's all encompassing. I'm sorry, Daphne. That's nature."

Daphne was fired unceremoniously, her contract broken. She was stunned speechless. At last she was able to stutter, "Let me get this straight. You're firing me because my work is too powerful? Because I'm scaring people?" The men did not answer. She laughed a bitter laugh. "I don't believe this!" Then she stalked out the door.

Her head was spinning as she rushed through the airport. What am I going to do? My career is over before it began. I just want to give up...

But then unbidden, in her mind, she heard a soothing voice say, The world may seem very confusing now. It's a building up. A rising tide. The hive mind building upon itself. It's OK. Things are just changing into something else. Patterns will become apparent. Connections that you can't see now. But don't worry. You will.

She was passing through the great domed food court, pondering this, when she heard a rustle of excitement, scampering and shouting, and she turned her head.

An animal on the loose again. She was able to catch just a glimpse, a flash as it sped past the Sbarro's. People retracted, scattered, and there were screams.

A coyote, skinny and rough furred, but fluid and graceful and oh so fast. It didn't know which way to run. It seemed confused by the noise and the lights and the large plate glass windows. She could swear it had paused for one moment and looked right into her eyes, appealing. Eyes pale blue and penetrating like a husky's.

It was real. She didn't have electronics in her system anymore, nothing that could cause a short circuit of a hallucination. It's real! She thought exultantly. The past, present and future seemed translucent and superimposed on each other. And all at once she was aware of her own youth, her strong beating heart, her clear lungs, the light in her veins. She felt there was something to be reclaimed. Something noble and good. All of this went through her mind in a flash as the animal sped by her, and she smiled in wonder. I think this one will be okay. This one will live.

Just as suddenly, there was a single loud gunshot. In the stunned silence that followed, Daphne felt a mute explosion inside her body. A current of energy that carried her away in its flow and sent her running forward toward the animal. No more no more no more! This time I will be brave. This time I will save him!

～

The gunman was not a man at all, but a boy of seventeen. A boy who did not like killing, so he told himself that killing the animals that flooded the city in the springtime was not a personal act, that he was just performing the work of nature.

He was startled to see the girl in the white dress, coming straight toward him. Her blond braids were pinned to the top of her head and there were flowers woven in. At first he didn't even know if she was real, she might be a dream. The feeling was ancient, bigger than himself. The girl called to mind stories of mythology that he loved. He had read myths in school, and loved them. Stories of gods and goddesses, shape shifters, animal messengers. There was always drama, retribution. He had been reading Ovid's Metamorphoses when the officers took him out of school and told him he would learn to shoot a gun. He wondered if he would ever go to school again. He hoped so. But he was tired, he was lonely. Tired of wandering the streets and parking garages and public buildings with his gun, only to sleep in the corner on a bare mattress with all the other sad boys with guns. It wasn't the life he wanted. Frankly, he was thinking of strapping a bomb to himself. He'd walk to his old school and blow it all up, everything, himself, too.

But now the girl was running toward him, and she was shouting something. But what was it? Her eyes trained right on his, fierce and unwavering. It was the first time anyone had looked him in the eye in a very long time. It felt unsettling, but good. It gave him hope. He lowered his gun to the ground. The animal, unharmed, went on its way out of sight. And here she came now. If she was a goddess, then her message was for him alone.